# Fields of Blue Flax

Sue Lawrence

**FREIGHT BOOKS**

First published 2015

Freight Books
49-53 Virginia Street
Glasgow, G1 1TS
www.freightbooks.co.uk

ISBN 978-1-910449-10-3
eISBN 978-1-910449-11-0

Typeset by Freight
Printed and bound by Bell and Bain, Glasgow

the publisher acknowledges investment from
**Creative Scotland** toward the publication of this book

Sue Lawrence was born in Dundee but lived and went to school in Edinburgh, before returning to Dundee to study French at university. She then trained as a journalist with DC Thomson.

Having taken time off her career when, with her pilot husband, they lived in many different places – and her three children were small – she took up writing again after winning BBC Masterchef in 1991. She was cookery columnist for *the Sunday Times* then *Scotland on Sunday* and also wrote for several magazines and appeared regularly on TV and radio.

She won a Glenfiddich Food and Drink Award in 2003 and two Guild of Food Writers Awards, in 1998 and 2001. She was President of the Guild of Food Writers from 2004 – 2008.

She is author of 14 cook books, including Sue Lawrence's *Book of Baking, Scots Cooking* and *A Cook's Tour of Scotland.*

*For my family, with love*

# Prologue

She strode over the bed of wet greenery towards the glade, pausing to bend down and rub a leaf between her fingers. Wrinkling her nose at the distinct smell of wild garlic, she straightened up and made for the gap between the trees. There, she stopped to look around. All was still and calm; not even the chirrup of birds disturbed the air. Perhaps they too were hiding in the spring mist.

She glanced at the blanket of white ramson flowers all around, their beauty belying their pungent aroma. Though their leaves strongly resembled lily of the valley, the vital difference between the two was life and death, one deadlier than arsenic.

Then she heard him approach, his footsteps soft on the damp vegetation. He checked he was alone then came to stand before her. Smiling, he looked at her, then extended his hand in front of him, showing the way. Together they walked, her skirt swishing against the wet shrubs, towards the cottage. He took the key from his pocket and looked at her again, his head tilted to one side. She nodded as he pushed open the door and they both stepped inside.

As he pulled the door shut, another figure emerged from the wood into the clearing. Tall, lean and dressed in black, he picked his way nimbly over the moist weeds and clambered over the gnarled roots of the hazel trees. He took out a large handkerchief to mask a sneeze then pushed the cloth back, deep into his pocket. Standing still, he merged with the dark, knotted trunks all around. He cupped his hand round his ear, listening. But the only sound was the rustle of leaves on the trees, their lofty branches swaying in the breeze.

A couple of hours later, the door creaked open. She looked out, then darted back inside, leaving the door ajar. A curtain was tugged open in the front room then she stepped once more onto the doorstep. As she closed the door quietly behind her, her expression changed. Once sombre, her eyes were now keen and a smile played on her lips. She hurried away from the cottage as if with a new sense of purpose.

# Chapter 1
2014

'That a new ring, Mags?'

'This? No, it was Granny's.'

Christine snatched at her cousin's hand and stared at the garnet and gold ring. 'So how come you've got it?'

Mags pulled the ring off her finger. 'Here, you can have it if you want.'

'Don't be daft, I was just asking why you've got it.'

'Mum can't get it on her finger any more, her arthritis is playing up.'

'Poor Auntie Peggy,' said Christine, still staring at the ring in Mags's palm.

'It'll go eventually to one of our girls, don't worry, Chris.' Mags grinned and put it back on.

Christine bristled. 'Of course it will, sorry, that makes me seem grabbing.'

'It's not exactly a family heirloom, garnets aren't worth that much, but I really like it.' Mags smiled as she held it up to the light.

'Talking of family, I've got a favour to ask.' Christine took a sip of her cappuccino. 'You know I've been wanting to do this for ages, but I just thought, while Dad and your mum are still with us, we ought to ask them stuff about the family history.'

'Why?' Mags scooped the foam from the top of her mug and sucked it from the spoon.

'I thought it might be interesting. If we knew a bit more about their parents, our grandparents, we could go into

Register House and research even further back.'

'You been teaching family trees at school, Chris?'

Christine grinned. 'You know me too well. Yes. So what do you reckon?'

'Sounds as dull as dishwater to me but I can always chum you. As long as there's plenty stops for coffee and chat.'

'Of course there will.'

'Have you got the death certificate?' asked Christine.

Aunt Peggy nodded and heaved herself up from her armchair. Once upright she looked down at her knees, as if willing them to work. She fumbled for the spectacles dangling round her neck on a chain and shuffled towards the table.

She peered down. 'Here it is, sweetheart.' Her hand, dappled with liver spots, rested on a large brown envelope. On the front, scrawled in black marker pen in large capital letters was, "Duncan – Death".

'It's in here. I've got Grandpa's too but you just want Granny Duncan's, do you?'

'Yes. Thanks, Auntie Peggy.'

Christine had taken her father, Charlie, to see his sister in her house in Leith so she could ask them both about the family. The death certificate Auntie Peggy had just handed over was that of Christine's great-grandmother, known as Granny Duncan.

'I don't know why you're interested in the Duncans, Christine,' said Auntie Peggy, settling herself back into the pile of cushions in her armchair. 'I don't think there's anything other than mundane about them all. As far as I know, they're all from Dundee and...'

'No, Peggy, some of them were from a farming place to

the north, can you not remember?' Charlie interrupted.

'Well, Mum had a McLauchlin cousin who lived in Kirriemuir but we know her other relatives were all from Dundee. The Duncan family shop goes back to the late nineteenth century, they were all involved in that, remember?' Auntie Peggy looked at her niece. 'The Duncans have been Dundonians for generations, I'm absolutely sure of it.'

'Thanks, that'll make it easy for me when I start looking them up.' Christine eased the envelope into her handbag. 'So, can you remember your Duncan grandparents?'

'Oh yes,' said Auntie Peggy, her weathered face wrinkling into a smile. 'Grandpa Duncan was a gentle, kind man. I used to love sitting on his lap when I was little – he always smelled of pipe tobacco, he was forever puffing away on it.' She laughed. 'Can you imagine nowadays, a child being allowed to inhale pipe smoke like that?'

Christine smiled and turned to her father, sitting beside her on the well-worn sofa, his scrawny frame hunched into the curves of the cushions. He seemed lost in thought and she momentarily felt a pang of sadness as she gazed at the strong jaw and rheumy eyes; his lack of interaction and forgetfulness was becoming a worry, she really ought to take him to the GP for those dementia tests.

'But Granny Duncan, she was the opposite. We were scared of her as wee ones.' Peggy continued. 'I seem to remember she never hugged us, yet Grandpa was always one for a cuddle, strange really.'

'Well, if there's anything else you can tell me, it's useful to have as much information as possible before I go to Register House,' said Christine. 'I've persuaded Mags to join me.'

'Well, good luck with that, sweetheart. She'll be more interested in the coffee breaks than the research. Your cousin's never been one to dwell on the past, she's more of a now girl, isn't she?'

Charlie opened his mouth then shut it again. He scratched his chin, frowned, and turned to his sister. 'Peggy, can you not remember something about a family secret. It came to me just now while Christine was talking, but I can't quite remember.'

'I think I'd have remembered if there was anything vaguely juicy about anyone in our family. No, you're imagining things, Charlie.'

'There was something hidden, definitely,' Charlie pronounced. 'And secrets are bad, no doubt about it.'

He turned away and gazed out of the window.

'Nonsense,' Peggy tutted, pouring tea from the shiny brown teapot in front of her. She turned to her niece. 'Now, tell me about Jack and Anna, Christine. How are their studies going? And their love lives? Will I be needing to dust off my wedding hat anytime soon?'

Christine shook her head and laughed.

'Not yet, Auntie Peggy, definitely not yet.'

Christine folded her coat over the back of her chair and turned to her cousin. 'Right, here's how we proceed.'

'Okay, ready to be bossed,' Mags said, taking a couple of sweets from her pocket and offering one to Christine, who politely declined. They were in Register House, at the east end of Princes Street in Edinburgh, to investigate the history of the Duncan family.

Christine brought out the large envelope, removed the fragile document and spread it out carefully on the desk.

'Here's the death certificate. Your mum gave it to me.'

Mags unwrapped her toffee and popped it into her mouth.

Christine put on her glasses and peered at the parchment. 'So, Elizabeth Duncan died on 26th January 1952, aged ninety-four, at 33 Park Avenue, Dundee, of myocardial degeneration.'

'Pretty old for someone who'd had what Mum always says was a hard life.'

'Exactly. I'd have thought seventy was a good age in those days.'

Mags pointed to the certificate. 'And it says her father, David Barrie, was a ploughman and her mother was called Margaret Harris.'

Christine pulled the document away. 'Watch your sticky fingers. This is all we've got to go on,' she muttered.

'Oh, God. Chill!' Mags flung her jacket on top of her basket on the floor and sat back in her chair. 'So what do we do now?'

'We go backwards to find Granny Duncan's wedding certificate, birth certificate and so on. Can't be that difficult, everyone else here seems to be managing by themselves.' Christine pointed at the people all around them, sitting in front of computer screens.

Christine started to take notes from the information on the certificate. 'You know Dad's losing it, so he can't remember that much now, but Auntie Peggy's memory is still brilliant, we'll need to keep asking her things. I mean, all we've got is this.' She pointed at the faded certificate in front of her.

'Yeah, Mum's memory's pretty awesome, considering her age. It's just her body that's not so good. Her knees are giving her such grief but she refuses to do anything about it, says it's all just part of getting old.' Mags shook her head. 'Bless her. Oh, I popped into your dad's earlier and he mentioned that family secret again. Remember you said he'd insisted there was something but Mum said it was all rubbish?'

'Yes. Could he remember what it was?'

'Nope. But he said you know all about it and I need to speak to you.'

Christine looked up from the screen. 'Why on earth he thinks that, I don't know. Oh and I've got a photo from Auntie Peggy as well. Here, have a look.'

They both studied the black-and-white photo, taken in a park. In the foreground was a large, old-fashioned pram with a baby stretching up at one end.

'Dad looks like a meerkat straining his neck up to see out better!' Christine laughed. 'Must be 1925, he looks about nine months old.'

'God, how scary does our great-granny look!' said Mags.

The pram handle was held by a stern woman dressed in a dark suit and hat, with a fox-fur collar at her neck. Her eyes were downcast and her expression was uneasy, perhaps worrying that the baby might topple out of the pram, or simply irritated that her photograph was being taken. By her side and with hand firmly grasped, stood a little girl wearing a dress with a petticoat hanging down at one side. She was the only one looking directly at the camera.

'Look at Mum, that tatty petticoat makes her look like an urchin from the poorhouse!' Mags chuckled, then mouthed "sorry" at the man opposite who was scowling at them. 'Bit like a library in here, isn't it!' she whispered. 'Let's go for a coffee.'

'We've only got till five and there's loads to investigate. It's only half past ten, let's wait till eleven.'

'No way, I'm in serious need of caffeine.' Mags pushed back her chair and looked around for the exit to the café.

Christine sighed and stood up to follow her along the corridor. 'So what else has Auntie Peggy told you about her? I only got the scary bit.'

'Well, Mum said she never smiled, ever. That she had amazing brown eyes, really dark, almost black. And that she had been a servant in some big house in Dundee. That's about it.' Mags held the door open for Christine. 'Does Uncle Charlie not remember anything about her?'

'He said she was the opposite of his other granny who was all warm and cuddly. Cappuccino or Americano?'

'Don't suppose they run to double espresso? I'll go for Americano, but I'll get these, Chris. You grab a table.'

Christine drew out a chair at a table by the window and looked out at the rain streaming down the pane. She pulled her thick blonde hair back into a ponytail and tied a band round it. Lifting up the menu card, she started to fan herself. 'Not exactly tropical outside is it, why on earth am I so hot?'

'Age, Chris.' Mags sat down. 'Bloody menopause, yet another inconvenience of being a woman!' Mags leant in towards her cousin as she took a gulp from her mug. 'Talking of hot, have you seen that young guy serving?'

Christine put down the menu and glanced up at the servery. 'He's about the same age as our kids!'

Mags shrugged then peered over the rim of her mug at her cousin. 'Have you got new eye make-up on? Your eyes look even bluer today.'

'Yes, a new eyeliner, navy blue. Anna gave it to me.'

They were first cousins and close friends, yet the two women were night and day. Christine had piercing blue eyes and a mane of thick, straight blonde hair. Though she was two years younger than her cousin, she appeared older, a reflection perhaps of the sensible, staid clothes she always dressed in. Whenever her daughter tried to get her into more trendy clothes, she insisted that standing in front of a class of eight-year-olds every day was not conducive to glamour. Knee-length skirts, thick black tights and sensible shoes were her daily uniform.

Mags, on the other hand, was beautiful in a relaxed, bohemian way. One of Christine's male friends had told her that men found her cousin sexy, though Mags seemed unaware of it. Her auburn hair invariably tumbled out of a loose bun and her hippy style of dress – boho skirts and bright, embroidered tops – made her appear a throwback to the sixties.

'Is Gerry going to that dental conference next month, Chris? Doug's talking about going so it makes sense if they drive down together.' Mags twiddled with the chunky green beads round her neck.

'He never mentioned it. Where is it?'

'Birmingham, just before Easter I think.'

'I'll ask Gerry tonight about it. He's been getting home so late recently. Gone are the days when a dentist only worked nine till five. Is Doug the same?'

Mags nodded. 'Certainly is. I sometimes wonder if he's got a mistress. I mean, patients can't be in the practice till seven, can they?'

Christine took a paper tissue from a packet in her bag and wiped at the coffee Mags had spilt on the tray. 'No, they can't, but you know they often go out together for a quick pint after work.'

'I know, I'm joking. Doug would never do that. Besides, why would he want a mistress when he gets to go to bed with me every night!' Mags laughed. 'Anyway, we don't eat till after eight. If he's late, it just gives me more time to get stuck into the wine.'

Christine finished her latte and put it on the tray. 'Ready to go back in? The next thing we need to do is check out Elizabeth Duncan's marriage certificate – well, she'd have been Elizabeth Barrie – and that'll tell us more about her parents, our great-great-grandparents, and where she was born and so on. Did your mum know when she got married?'

'She said it was probably 1887 or 1888, but she wasn't sure, though she knew Great Auntie Annie was born in 1889.'

'Great, that helps.' Christine stood up and lifted her bag. 'Coming?'

'Yeah.' Mags picked up her basket. 'Remind me why you're so fascinated about this great-granny of ours?'

'Well, I wanted to investigate the family in general, but after Dad mentioned that secret about her it just caught my imagination, I suppose. He said she'd had a really tough life.'

'Imagine if she'd spent her entire life harbouring some great secret,' said Mags. 'Could explain why she always looked so bloody miserable.'

'Not all secrets are bad,' Christine mumbled, following her cousin back to the research rooms.

Ten minutes later, Mags whooped and elbowed Christine at the next computer. Christine looked around to check no one had heard the shriek and smiled at an elderly couple who were both grinning over at them.

Mags was jabbing her finger at the screen. 'Look, I've found Granny Duncan's wedding certificate.'

Christine put her forefinger to her lips. 'Don't speak so loudly!'

Mags spoke in an exaggerated whisper. 'This is way more interesting than I'd have thought. Fab seeing it right here in front of us.' She pointed to the name Elizabeth Barrie.

Christine began to read, 'Marriage of George Duncan, jute mill worker, aged thirty-four, to Elizabeth Barrie, domestic servant, aged twenty-eight, on 25th December 1888.'

Mags chortled. 'Look at their addresses, they both lived at 7 Ellen Street. God, even in those days, living in sin, amazing!'

'Surely not.' Christine frowned.

'Mum always used to say, "There's nothing new under the sun, Margaret, nothing new!"' She pointed to the date. 'Hang on, was that normal, getting married on Christmas Day?'

'Probably. Christmas wasn't such a big deal in those days in Scotland.' Christine continued to pore over the details of the certificate. 'Look.' Christine pointed to the right side of the screen. 'This'll give us something to go on, their parents' names. His are Donald Duncan, farmer, deceased and mother Susan Muir. Her father's David Barrie, ploughman, deceased and her mother Margaret Barrie, née Harris.'

'We know both fathers died before 1888, so we can get their death and wedding certificates and go backwards from there.' Christine grinned. 'Right then, you go for death, I'll go for wedding.'

'Cheers! I get all the fun.' Mags said, swigging from her water bottle.

'Can we print out this wedding certificate? It'd be handy to have, don't you think? I'd like to show Mum anyway. Will I print one for Uncle Charlie as well?'

'Okay, it might jog his failing memory.' Christine leant back in her chair. 'I wonder what weddings were like in Dundee in the 1880s.'

# Chapter Two
1888

'No' sae tight, Jane!' Elizabeth scowled at her sister who was tying a bow at the back of her waistband.

'Are you wantin' a full bow wi' big loops or a wee yin wi' lang tails?'

'Dinnae mind, just make it looser, will you?' She placed two hands over her stomach and exhaled slowly. She peered over her shoulder to supervise the bow. 'That'll dae fine Jane, though actually it's maybe a bit skew-whiff. Can you try again?' She ran her hands lightly over her hair. 'Why's my hair sae curly, it willnae settle doon right.'

'It's fine, Elizabeth. You're lucky to hae oor Ma's curls.'

Elizabeth pursed her lips and raised her chin towards the ceiling until Jane had finished retying the bow. 'Are you sure Mrs Donaldson disnae mind you takin' time off tae help me get ready?'

'No, I'll only be awa' an hour or two,' said Jane, moving round to face her sister and pinching her cheeks between thumbs and forefingers.

'Ow! What're you daein'?'

'Just makin' your cheeks look rosy, like the country girl you really are.' Jane smiled then ducked her head away before she got a slap.

Elizabeth laughed then walked to the chair to pick up her coat. She turned round to check everything was tidy. It was gloomy inside, but not as bleak as outside; you'd think it was night-time, not the middle of the day, the December fog was so thick. She glanced at the cooking range, so clean it sparkled in the candlelight. She'd decided to black lead it last night and now it was gleaming; at least it looked like she had made a bit of an effort. The bed in the recess was covered with a new bedspread and two plaid cushions – gifts from her mistress, Mrs Donaldson – so with a bit of imagination you might think it was a sofa instead of a bed. She fastened the top two buttons of her coat then kicked at the bulge of the chamber pot at the foot of the bedspread to make the material hang down straight. It didn't exactly look like the drawing room at the big house, but it was a lot more wholesome than most of her neighbours' flats in Ellen Street.

She frowned at the bare table. If she could buy even a small bunch of flowers for the church, she'd put them in a beaker once they returned, to make the room look nice. It would never be like the big house with tall vases of flowers in every room, but it would help. She shook her head. She couldn't afford such luxuries and besides, Jane would clype and tell her mother who would rant about it being an unnecessary indulgence, spending precious money on flowers.

But Margaret Barrie had made it very clear she would not be joining them today, so perhaps Elizabeth would just go ahead and buy a tiny posy on her way to the church. She went to the mantelpiece, reached up to shift the tea caddy to one side and lifted down a small blackened tin hidden behind it. She prised off the lid and removed a small coin which she wrapped in the handkerchief she took from her coat pocket.

Jane turned round, a hairgrip between her teeth. Her lank hair was now pulled back into a tight bun. 'Whit time does it start?'

'Half past two.'

George had left after his porridge for his job at the jute mill and was due to meet Elizabeth at the church at two. Since it was Christmas Day he could finish early and the minister was booked for half past the hour. His cousin Mary-Anne was coming from Nelson Street after she'd finished work at the mill. After the short service, they would all come back to Ellen Street for the usual Christmas Day broth then cloutie dumpling. It would be a small gathering, but it was all just a formality, a necessary ceremony; she and George had been together in this flat for some time anyway.

She pulled the collar of her dark coat up around her neck and turned to Jane. 'Thanks for helpin' get it a' ready. Try an' get off early from the big house if you can. There'll be plenty dumpling leftover for you to hae wi' a cup of tea.'

'Aye.' Jane grinned. 'Or maybe I'll tak' a dram wi' my new brother-in-law.'

'Aye, an' maybe you willnae!' Her sister shooed her towards the door, laughing. 'Mind and behave yerself, ye gallus lassie!'

Elizabeth blew out the candle by the bed and lifted the heavy key from the hook on the wall, locked the door and headed down the dingy tenement steps.

# Chapter Three
2014

Christine set the table with her usual precision. Each fork and knife was lined up alongside the charger plate, the spoon placed along the top and the glass set at the top right corner. She smiled as she recalled teaching the kids how to set the table when they were younger. Jack had been intrigued with the connotations of the word charger, asking if it had something to do with battles and horses. Anna had looked at her mother, puzzled, when she had told her the glass had to be placed at two o'clock.

'She means at the two o'clock position of a clock,' said Jack, ever helpful.

'What if there's two glasses?' Anna continued, always one to question facts.

'Two o'clock and one o'clock,' Christine had said, trying not to sound like the teacher she was.

'That's silly,' Anna had muttered before abandoning the lesson and heading for her doll's house.

Jack had just smiled then followed his younger sister out. He had always hated confrontation and had become a peace-maker at an early age, whereas Anna tended to thrive on conflict.

It was a pity they couldn't be here tonight for Gerry's birthday dinner but neither of them could get away midweek, especially now they were in the middle of exams. They were due up soon for Easter, by which time Christine hoped she'd feel less frazzled. Her class of eight-year-olds were a nightmare; why hadn't she opted for the little ones this year?

The phone rang and as she crossed the room, she glanced at the table. The tulips looked good, the colour matching the dark burgundy napkins. Burgundy – dammit, she'd forgotten to get out the red wine and Mags always drank red at dinner, whether she was eating meat or fish.

'Hello?'

It was her cousin, wondering whether she should bring a cake stand. As usual, she was baking the birthday cake.

'Yes, please,' said Christine. 'I still haven't got around to replacing the one that was smashed at Anna's eighteenth.'

'No probs. Half seven okay?'

'Yes. Oh, and I promised Gerry we'd not go on too much about Register House and the genealogy thing. Think he's fed up hearing about our family history.'

'Doug won't be interested either. We can talk about something else.'

'Okay,' said Christine. 'Definitely not teeth though.'

Christine poured herself a glass of water at the kitchen sink, and caught a glimpse of her reflection in the window. She was looking more and more like her mother these days and she knew why: it was those lines across her forehead and round her eyes. Her mum had only been seventy when she died but her face had been as wrinkled as a prune for years.

Christine pressed her fingertips to her cheeks and frowned, thinking of Mags and her clear skin. She had hardly any lines, which was so unfair considering what a lush she was.

Before she could forget again, she pulled two bottles of red out of the wine rack. As she rifled around in the cutlery drawer, looking for the corkscrew, she thought back to the previous week and their second visit to Register House.

Mags had been looking for marriage certificates for the parents of both Elizabeth Barrie and George Duncan, while Christine concentrated on the extended Duncan family. She leant in towards the screen and clicked on the magnifying icon.

'Mags, look at this.'

'What?'

'Here's Elizabeth Barrie's daughter. You remember Great-auntie Annie, Grandpa Duncan's sister?'

'Yes, she was a real sweetheart, lived in that tiny tenement flat with a kitchen no bigger than a cupboard. Is that her birth certificate?'

'Yes, but look at the date. Anne Duncan, born at 7 Ellen Street, Dundee, on 26th February 1889.'

'Yeah, Mum thought she was born in 1889.'

'But don't you remember when the wedding was? 25th December 1888. Elizabeth Barrie was seven months pregnant when she married.'

Christine pointed her pen at the date and continued. 'I know it's no big deal now but surely then it was a bit scandalous. Seems a bit late to leave it, I mean she must have known she was pregnant well before then?'

Mags tucked her hair behind her ears. 'Trish Hay – remember I told you she's working at The Balmoral now – well, she did her mum's family tree with her sister and almost everyone they found was either illegitimate, which they have to mark on the birth certificate, or born only a few months after the wedding. There were some illiterates too, as they have to mark a cross.'

Christine leant back on her chair. 'The thing is though, why did Elizabeth Barrie leave it so long to get married. I mean, the bump must have shown, surely?'

'Suppose so. Hey, maybe our family's far more interesting than we thought.'

After a couple more hours of searching, they had found the marriage certificates of both Elizabeth's parents, the Barries, and her husband's, the Duncans. The Duncans all hailed from Dundee, the Barries from Tannadice.

'Mags, why don't I carry on looking for births, marriages and deaths for the Barries and you can look at the 1881 census. Might shed some light on what she did before she got married.'

'Okay, boss.'

After what had seemed an interminable trawl through many Barries, Mags gasped. 'At last, found her! Well, it must be her. There are no other Elizabeth Barries born in Tannadice but resident in Dundee. She's a domestic servant in a big house. See, here's her name at the end of a long list of children… God, six of them! And there's a governess and a nurse too.'

'When was that census? 1881? It says she's twenty-four, which doesn't tie in with being twenty-eight at her wedding in 1888 though, does it?'

'True, but maybe she lied about her age to get a job as a maid?' Mags drew her pen down the screen. 'The family owning the house is called Donaldson. See, David Donaldson was head of house, a linen manufacturer. They lived in Perth Road. That's the main one coming into Dundee from Perth.'

Christine turned from the screen to look at Mags. 'Linen was a big business in the city, as well as jute. I can remember those houses on Perth Road, they're big Victorian piles.

They must have great views over the Tay.'

Mags peered at the screen. 'Look at the last name on the list for this household. It's difficult to read but looks like Jane Barrie? Aged twenty-one. Both girls born in Tannadice it says, so it was probably her sister, she must have worked with her.'

'It says she was a table maid.' Christine rubbed her hands together. 'See, it's quite exciting, isn't it. Let's print out that page.'

Christine opened the oven door. Why was the chicken looking so brown already, when it had only been in for an hour? She pulled out a drawer, ripped off some tinfoil and tucked it loosely around the top of the bird, frowning. Perhaps, on reflection, she shouldn't have done that French recipe for chicken roasted with forty cloves of garlic. But she'd had it at Sabine's house and it was delicious.

She was already anticipating both Gerry and Doug moaning that reeking of garlic while peering into someone's mouth was unprofessional. Dammit, why was she such a rubbish cook. Mags could whip up luscious food without even trying, though you usually had to wait for hours till the meal was actually on the table.

She heard a key in the lock and went to greet Gerry.

'Hi, Chris,' he said, shaking his umbrella at the door.

'You're soaking the carpet, Gerry!' Christine scowled. 'Here, let me take it.' She grabbed the umbrella and rushed through to the kitchen.

'Nice to see you too, Chris,' Gerry said, shrugging as he followed his wife. He entered the kitchen and sniffed the air. 'Wow, garlic! You trying to put tomorrow's patients off?' He chuckled and went towards his wife, pulling her into a hug.

Christine drew herself away. 'Sorry, Gerry, there's too much to do.' She took out a large wooden salad bowl and started tipping in bags of rocket and watercress.

'Anything I can help with?'

'Open the red, please. I couldn't find the corkscrew.' Christine turned to see her husband pulling the cutlery drawer out fully and lifting the corkscrew from the back. She bit her lip as she looked at him, his dark beard now flecked with grey. She had hoped he'd shave it off when he stopped being a student, but all these years later, perhaps as an attempt to cling to his youth, the facial hair remained. He looked up and beamed at her and she felt a pang of guilt that she was being so nippy.

'Sorry, I know it's your birthday, but my day's been a nightmare. That new boy kicked off big time, and you know how stressful I find entertaining.'

'It's fine, it's only Mags and Doug. They wouldn't care if you gave them beans on toast.' Gerry smiled then went to the fridge. 'Would a drink help you relax?'

'No, I'm fine. I'll wait till we open the champagne, but you help yourself.'

'Might just do that,' said Gerry, stretching in for a beer.

At quarter to eight, Christine removed the chicken from the oven with a sigh of martyrdom and shouted through to the living room, 'If they don't come soon, it's going to be ruined.'

'They're only a few minutes late. You know what Mags is like about timekeeping.'

Christine stood at the door, scowling.

'Relax, everything's done. Come and sit beside me, give

me a kiss.' He patted the place beside him on the sofa.

Christine headed for the table. 'I'm just going to light the candles.'

The doorbell rang and Gerry put down his beer and went to open the door. Mags stepped into the hall and tipped her head back to flick down the hood of her raincoat, her glossy hair, loose for the occasion, tumbling over her shoulders. In her hands was a large white box with a flamboyant gold ribbon on top.

'Here you go, birthday boy!' She nodded down at the box then smiled at Gerry and reached forward to give him a kiss on both cheeks. 'I'd better put it somewhere cool, you can see it later.'

Christine leant her head out of the kitchen to see Doug stroll in, swinging a plastic bag, surely the only man who could look cool carrying a Tesco carrier bag. He shut the door behind him, brushed some drops of rain off the shoulders of his leather jacket then shook his friend's hand and patted him on the back. 'Happy birthday, mate. How does it feel to be fifty-five?'

'Old! Come in, I'll get the drinks.'

The four of them stood in the sitting room and raised their champagne glasses to toast Gerry. He smiled, and looked round at the small group.

Christine took a sip of her drink and fiddled with the gold chain round her neck. She was staring at Mag's hand as she raised her glass. There was no disguising the fact she was stressed. It was nearly the end of term, when the kids were always hyper and she really hated entertaining. Gerry blew her a kiss which she acknowledged with a forced smile.

Mags took a gulp of champagne, laughing as the bubbles went up her nose. She was dressed in a floaty black skirt and cropped purple cardigan, unbuttoned at the top. Gerry's gaze was drawn towards her plunging neckline but he quickly looked away lest Christine saw him looking at her cousin's cleavage. But Christine didn't notice, distracted as she was by the ring on Mags's finger.

He turned to Doug who raised his glass. For a man who had been fawned over by all the nurses and fellow students at the dental hospital, Doug had lost some of his good looks. Though his eyes were still striking – dark, like shiny brown currants, Mags had once said – his face was now ruddy and he was starting to develop a belly. That must be down to all those cakes his wife bakes.

Mags picked up a photo from the mantelpiece. 'Chris, this is a cool pic of the kids. Love it!'

'Thought I gave you that one. I found it in a box in the attic when I was looking for photos for Anna's eighteenth. I'll get you a copy.' Christine leant over to see it close up. 'It makes me smile every time I see it. Look at Jack's little face.'

Mags shook her head and laughed. 'He's obviously been told to put his arms round his sister and his cousin and he's not too happy about it, is he!'

'I know, it's a hoot.'

'He looks like he's been wading through mud, what's that on his face?'

'Well, remember that was the stage he wanted to be a soldier, so Gerry had daubed him in face paint and he was wearing all brown and green, as camouflage.'

'So was that his seventh birthday?'

'Eighth, I think. Anna looks like she does in that primary

one photo with her hair in bunches. Remember she insisted on having them even though her hair was so short and curly?'

'And what about Lottie and those bloody pigtails!'

'I think that was why Anna was so keen on bunches, she wanted long hair like her big cousin's.' Christine laughed. 'Right, let's sit down.'

During the starter, Christine kept apologising about the fact she'd had no time to produce anything homemade.

'Who cares,' said Mags. 'It's really nice. And you've been at work all day.'

Christine scuttled off to the kitchen and Mags followed. Soon they emerged with four plates, reeking of garlic.

'Hopefully it doesn't taste as strong as it smells,' Christine sighed.

'It smells fab,' said Mags, topping up both her own and Christine's wine. 'Bon appétit!'

'So, what news of the kids?' asked Doug, poking the skin off a garlic clove.

'Both good thanks, though typical students, we hardly hear from them,' Gerry said. 'Jack's got some exam today and Anna finishes on Friday, so…'

'Jack's exam's tomorrow, Gerry,' Christine interrupted.

'Oh, right. Anyway, they'll both be up for Easter. Good Friday is it?'

'Yes, they're driving up together. Jack's leaving Durham after breakfast and picking up Anna in Newcastle. How about Lottie? Still enjoying her piano teaching?'

Lottie had a degree in music but had struggled to find a job after university.

'Yeah,' said Doug. 'It's not what she'd wanted to do, but needs must. Though what her pupils must think when they go to her flat for lessons... It's a shambles.'

'It's not that bad, Doug, and mostly she goes to their houses anyway.' Mags turned to Christine. 'This is delicious, the garlic's almost sweet, not as strong as you thought it would be. Gorgeous!'

The conversation turned to dentistry, both men bemoaning the fact things were not as they used to be. Mags gave an exaggerated yawn then turned to Christine and asked, 'So how was class today, Miss?'

Christine had just started to tell her about the project her class were doing on farm implements when Gerry put his hand up to his mouth and yawned. Silence ensued while they all scraped their plates clean then Gerry went to the kitchen to fetch more wine. He began filling up the glasses.

'How's the cake business going, Mags?'

Mags took a gulp. 'Well, if I'm honest, a bit slow, but I've not got the website up and running yet so it's still only word of mouth.'

'Tell them how much that chancer quoted you to build a website, darling.' Doug held out his glass to Gerry.

'God, yeah, four thousand pounds. And he knows I run my own business. So Lottie's setting it up for me instead, with her friend Ben – you know, the really tall guy who did IT? I'll pay them as little as I can get away with. No choice really.'

'Your cakes are delicious, darling,' said Doug. 'Once more people know, you'll be rushed off your feet!'

'Talking of cakes, is it time?' Mags winked at Christine and they headed for the kitchen before re-emerging with the cake. On top was a set of dentures made of marzipan and a large candle in the shape of a figure dressed in white with a stethoscope round his neck.

'Sorry Gerry, I know you guys don't use stethoscopes, but it was all I could get!' Mags placed the cake stand in front of Gerry and Christine lit the candle.

Gerry guffawed then sat back on his chair, shaking his head. 'You're a genius, Mags. How on earth did you get that?'

'Oh, I have my sources,' Mags smiled, as Gerry blew the candle out.

'Talking of sources,' said Doug, stretching back in his chair, swirling his wine around in his glass. 'I'm feeling strong enough, I've had enough booze. Tell us boring dentists all about the exciting time you've had researching the Duncan Family Scandal!' He rubbed his smooth chin between his thumb and forefinger as he looked from Mags to Christine, eyes twinkling.

'You really want to hear?' said Christine.

'Too right, girls. Gerry and I talk of little else over our pints these days.' He grinned and raised an eyebrow.

Mags cut large slabs of cake while Christine started to tell the men how far they'd got in their research.

# Chapter Four
1881

Elizabeth blew out the last candle in the dining room and carried the pile of pudding plates downstairs to the scullery.

'Here Jane, the last lot o' dishes.'

Her sister looked round from a large stone sink of soapy water and sighed. 'Why do yon folk need so many courses? Surely a plate o' soup, some mince then a wee puddin'd dae fine?'

Elizabeth smiled and shook her head.

'The mistress fair wanted to impress those jute barons tonight.'

Jane continued her scrubbing. 'Aye, well, they've no' been up since five in the morning like us.' She yawned. 'Whit was yon main course again?'

Elizabeth went into the pantry and brought out the ashet of meat. She removed the muslin cloth, pulled off a piece of meat and fed it to her sister whose hands were still deep in water.

'Braised leg o' mutton. Though she had some daft fancy French name for it. But the thing is, it's meant to cook for aboot four hours wi' vegetables an a' sorts to mak' it tender, but she was in such a state after wee Mary's accident, she started it too late.'

'Is the wee one all right now?' Jane mumbled, her mouth full.

'Fine, just took a tumble doon a couple o' stairs.'

Jane was still chewing the meat. 'Aye, it's tasty, but a bit tough,' Jane said. 'I'd rather hae a mutton pie.'

'An' the mistress still willnae trust me wi' a big joint o' meat, even though I did a' that stuff at the Patullos' when cook Jessie was off ill for months.'

Jane nodded at the cloths hanging above the range. 'Gie's a hand wi' the drying, would you?'

Elizabeth pulled down a cloth from the pulley and reached for a plate. Her sister plunged one hand down so it was elbow deep in soapy water and pulled out the plug. 'I've just got tae shine up the copper pans then that's me finished,' Jane said, wiping her forehead with the back of her hand. She took the wet cloth from over her shoulder and handed it to her sister. 'Hang this up for me, will you. Wish I was a giant like you.'

'Tall for my age, not a giant.' Elizabeth took the cloth and tossed it over the pulley.

'Mind when you were ten and someone thought you were married and aboot eighteen?'

'Aye, bein' tall's handy sometimes. You can get away with all sorts!' Elizabeth grinned.

The sisters worked in silence for a while, eager to get their work finished quickly. 'Right,' said Elizabeth eventually. 'You'll be wantin' a wee taste o' puddin' before bed?' She went into the pantry and brought out a large round dish with a half-eaten pudding.

'That looks good, whit's it called?' Jane wiped both hands down her apron then untied it and hung it on a hook by the sink.

Elizabeth went to get a large spoon from the kitchen drawer. 'Golden Puddin', meant to just have marmalade through the mixture but I put a puddle o' it underneath so when it was turned onto the dish it looked like a golden crown. The master said it was the best puddin' he's ever had.'

Jane took the spoon and devoured a large bite. 'Aye it's good, Elizabeth, no' too sweet. But if he thinks that's the best puddin' he's had, then the master's obviously no' had oor Ma's dumpling!'

Elizabeth yawned widely and nodded. 'Aye, you're right there.' She looked around the kitchen. 'Grand, everything's clean and tidy now. Awa' upstairs wi' you. It's bed time.'

# Chapter Five
## 2014

Christine told Mags later that the phone call that changed her life forever did not come at a convenient time. The moment she had to drop everything, drive a hundred miles and be away from home for a week was at a time she was not ready to face the world.

She had just finished cleaning the house and was exhausted. There were plastic Sainsbury's bags all over the kitchen floor. The supermarket van had just delivered but she couldn't face putting the things away yet so had put on the kettle to make coffee. *Woman's Hour* was blaring from the radio on the window ledge.

Christine looked out to the garden, her pride and joy. She was contemplating whether to plant some more pansies in the corner when she noticed a dead starling lying in the middle of the lawn, feathers still fluttering. A large crow was perched on the tree above, looking down menacingly. Why do some birds kill each other if not for food; was it just for fun? She made a mental note to go out after she'd had her coffee, remove the prone body from the lawn and bury it.

She was filling the cafetière with water when the phone rang.

It was Anna. 'Mum, there's been an accident.'

The words every parent dreads.

'What?' Christine held onto the sink and felt her entire body tighten.

'Jack and I have had a bit of an accident on the A1. He's been taken to Newcastle hospital and...'

'Very funny. So where are you now?'

'Mum.' Anna's voice faltered. 'This isn't a joke, he's been taken to hospital.'

'Is he okay? Are you okay?'

'I'm fine.' Christine heard her daughter take a deep breath. 'And I think, I hope, Jack'll be fine, they just need to check everything.'

'What do you mean, you think he'll be okay? What's that noise, Anna?' She could hear someone speaking in the background.

'It's Andy, the policeman. I'm in a police car, Mum. Jack's been air-ambulanced to the hospital.'

Christine felt sick. She staggered over to the table and dropped into a chair. Her two children had already been on the phone earlier, teasing her, saying they were nearly in Cornwall. 'Very funny,' she had said, laughing. 'Just turn the car round and get up to Edinburgh as soon as possible.'

There was no laughter now.

'Got to hang up, Mum. Andy says we're nearly there. I'll phone you or Dad when I know more.'

Anna had hung up before Christine had had time to tell her she loved her. She couldn't quite grasp what Anna had just told her. It was impossible. Things like this don't happen to us, she thought. Accidents happen to other people.

She stared at the phone then punched in Gerry's number. He'd had some patients first thing then he was off to North Berwick and was due home at lunchtime. But his phone was engaged so she hung up and sat looking down at her hands, twisting her wedding ring round and round. A couple of seconds later, the phone rang.

It was Gerry.

'Chris, did Anna get through to you?'

'Yes.'

'I've just heard, I'm on my way to the hospital. I'll be there in about an hour, I'm already on the A1.'

'Gerry, I don't know what…'

'Jump in the car, I'll meet you there. Just put Newcastle Royal Victoria Infirmary into your sat nav.'

'What could've happened, Gerry?'

'No idea, just get going. And drive carefully.'

There was a click at the end of the line. She pictured Gerry tapping his handsfree device, putting on his glasses then concentrating on driving his Mercedes south as fast as possible. Christine ran upstairs to grab her bag from the bedroom. She threw in her phone charger and hurried into the bathroom, flinging in her moisturiser and toothbrush. She raced downstairs, taking the steps two by two.

Then she remembered the shopping. She rushed into the kitchen and picked up the supermarket bags from the floor. She rammed them all into the fridge and headed for the door.

Christine pulled the front door shut and raced to her car. This was not how she'd anticipated Good Friday would turn out.

The journey seemed interminable. Christine focused on taking deep breaths, trying to concentrate on her driving as she squinted into the bright spring sunshine, cursing the fact that her sunglasses weren't in her handbag. The roads were busy; other cars were taking forever in the overtaking lanes. Why were they driving so slowly? Then as she passed Berwick, she looked at her petrol gauge.

Dammit, why today of all days did she need petrol?

Christine swerved into the next petrol station and filled

up the tank. As she hurried into the shop, she took out her phone from the depths of her bag and saw that she had two missed calls from Gerry. Quickly, she called him back, pausing next to a stand of cheap sunglasses.

'How are they?'

'The news isn't great. Anna's got to go for x-rays and Jack's having a CT scan so I'm staying with Anna for now. We can see Jack later.'

'What happened?'

'A car rammed them at speed, while they were stationary.'

'Oh no, my babies…'

'Just get down here, Chris.'

He hung up, and Christine felt her eyes well up. She picked up a pair of sunglasses and headed for the till.

'Number?' asked the greasy-haired girl.

'Just the one pair,' Christine whispered.

'No, which pump?'

'Oh.' Christine looked through the glass at her car. 'Two.'

'And you want those too?' The girls pointed at the glasses.

'Er, yes, please.' Christine stared at them as if for the first time.

'You know they're kids' glasses, it's all we've got.'

'Fine, how much altogether?'

Back in her car Chris tried to put the glasses on. They were far too small. She threw them on the passenger seat, flipped down her sun visor and started the engine.

Before she drove off, she reached for Lottie's piano CD – ideal for keeping her calm. As she put the car into gear, she suddenly remembered that Mags was meant to be visiting that morning with a Simnel cake. She'd no time to phone, Mags would want every detail. Christine tapped out a quick text: 'Not home. Kids had accident, off to Newcastle.

More later. X', and drove off.

A couple of minutes later there was a ping on her phone. She slowed down and peered at the screen. 'WHAT? Phone me!' Christine put her phone on mute, flung it into her bag and pressed her foot down on the pedal.

Christine burst into the hospital's A&E department, frantically looking for Gerry. Scanning all the people sitting there, she saw an elderly couple holding hands. There was a teenager pressing a bloodied bandage to his temple. There were a couple of toddlers, dummies in their mouths, sitting on the floor beside a woman in a baseball cap. And there was a man in a suit, rather too shiny to be well made. He looked straight down to the floor through parted knees and beside him sat a girl, about ten, resting her head against his shoulder. No one looked up as Christine sprinted to the desk.

'I'm looking for my family, they've been in an accident. My husband said he'd be here but I can't see him.' She steadied herself against the desk.

'No problem, what's the name?'

'Christine.'

The man raised his eyebrows.

'Sorry. Wallace. Christine Wallace.'

The man tapped on his keyboard then looked up. 'Your daughter Anna's still in x-ray but should be back soon in the ward at the end of that corridor there. But there's a man – your husband, I presume? – in the day room just round the corner from here.' He pointed his finger round to the left. 'He's with a policeman. Just knock and go in, Mrs Wallace.'

As soon as she opened the door to the day room, Gerry

rushed over and hugged her tightly. His beard tickled her skin and she sprang back, noticing as she did so how pale her husband was.

'Chris, this is Sergeant Price.'

Christine shook his hand as Gerry said, 'Have a seat, we need to give some details.'

'Where are they?' Christine was abrupt. 'I want to see them. Please.'

'If you'd like to sit down, Mrs Wallace. I was just telling your husband…'

'Why can't we see them? The man said Anna's in x-ray. Where's Jack?' Christine clutched her bag tight to her chest and stared at the men.

'I've only seen Anna and she'll be fine, they're doing x-rays to check no bones've been broken, but we've not heard any more about Jack yet. There was talk of him going to intensive care.'

'Well, can't we ask someone? A doctor? A nurse?' Christine was aware she was shouting, but couldn't hold herself back. 'I need to find out what's happening. I need to know they're okay.'

There was a soft tap on the door. A slim woman with bobbed black hair, dressed in dark trousers and a white shirt, hurried in. She had dark shadows under her eyes.

'I'm Doctor Ali, from ITU. You must be Mr and Mrs Wallace. Please sit down.'

'How are they?' Christine whispered.

'You can see your daughter, I've just been to check on her. She's fine, just a bit shaken up. She's being wheeled back from x-ray right now. We'll need to keep her in overnight, just a precaution, but she's in the ward at the end of this corridor for now.'

'And what about Jack?' asked Gerry.

Dr Ali's beeper sounded, but she ignored it and continued, 'We're waiting for the results of his CT scan. He's in an induced coma so we need to check a few more things then you can come up to us in intensive care to see him. Third floor.' She glanced down at the beeper at her waist. 'Give us half an hour?' she said, and rushed from the room.

'But what's wrong with him?' Christine shouted, as the door slammed shut.

Sergeant Price broke the silence. 'They don't like to commit till they know more. Why don't you see your daughter just now then you can go up and see your son later.'

Christine nodded.

'If you don't mind, Mr Wallace, maybe you and I could finish here for just now. I'll give you my contact details and the duty sergeant's too. It's a bank holiday weekend so we're on skeleton staff but there'll be someone there any time you need to speak.'

Gerry and Christine sat motionless, listening.

'My colleague's got the bags, phones and all the things that were in the car. We'll have to keep those for a bit.'

'Why?'

'Nothing to worry about, Mrs Wallace, just need to check a few things.'

'I suppose that's to check they weren't on the phone when it happened?' asked Gerry.

'Of course they weren't,' said Christine. 'They're sensible drivers, and they'd never speed. Who was driving?'

'Jack,' said Gerry.

'Well, it doesn't matter who it was, they're both good drivers.' Christine stood up. 'I'm going to see Anna.' She glared at her bag where her phone was ringing. 'Are you allowed to use phones in here, Sergeant?'

'Here's okay, but not in intensive care.'

'Okay,' she said as she headed for the door, delving into her bag and switching off her phone.

Christine strode along the corridor and into the ward at the end. She scanned the patients in the beds until she saw Anna's familiar shock of blonde curls at the far end. She rushed to the bed and threw her arms round her daughter.

'Sweetheart, are you okay? Let me see you.' Christine took a deep, shuddering breath as she looked at her daughter; she had two black eyes and her face was swollen and covered in livid purple bruises. 'Oh, my poor baby.'

Anna burst into tears as her mother pulled her gently into an embrace. 'Mum, not so tight, I'm sore all over.' She pulled down her hospital gown to reveal red and purple marks all over her chest.

'What are those?'

'Seatbelt burn marks, but it's okay, I'm fine. What's the news on Jack? I keep asking, but they aren't telling me anything.'

Christine took her daughter's arm and stroked her hand. 'We've to go and see the doctor in half an hour. I don't know any more. What happened?'

'I can't remember much, but I managed to get out of the car from my door. Jack had to be cut out, his side was all mangled up. It was horrible, Mum.' Anna started to cry again and Christine circled her arms round her and patted her back as if soothing her baby twenty years earlier.

She looked up to see Gerry appear in the doorway. He hurried over to his wife and daughter. He grasped his daughter's hand and tears trickled down his cheeks.

# Chapter Six
## 1876

'Mrs Donaldson,' Elizabeth said, bobbing a curtsey at the door, 'can I speak to you for a moment, please?'

The lady of the house sat gazing out of her drawing room window. 'Of course, Elizabeth.' She beckoned with an imperious finger. 'But draw nearer so that you might see the seals over there.'

She pointed outside to the sand banks dotted with grey seals. The view from the drawing room was the best in the house. Elizabeth often stood entranced by it when she was supposed to be cleaning the room. She gazed over the lush garden of flowers and well-tended shrubs. She had asked the gardener the names of her favourites: the purply-red flowering currants, the cerise camelias and, in the middle of the lawn, a beautiful milky-blossomed magnolia tree. Beyond this the River Tay stretched below, over to the rolling hills of Fife. This view was never the same. Today the water was shimmering through a pale summery haze.

'Look,' said Mrs Donaldson. 'I have been counting. I think there are some thirty seals on that bank there.'

Elizabeth peered out at the estuary. 'I've never seen as many, Madam. Is it because the weather's sae – so – warm?'

'Perhaps it is. What a life that must be, lolling around on those sand banks, bathing in the warm sunshine. Imagine how wonderful that would be, Elizabeth.'

Aye, you'd fair like that, you and your afternoon naps and pampering a' day long, thought Elizabeth.

'I try to imagine how our magnificent new railway bridge

might affect the view of those poor people who live within the city. At least here on the outskirts it will not alter our vista towards the Kingdom of Fife.' She raised an elegant hand towards the east. 'They have built most of the girders already. I fancy it will be a fine sight when we see trains on it. Mr Donaldson tells me that the rail ferries to Broughty Ferry will cease within two years and then we will see the very first train steaming over the bridge.'

'It's a miracle, Madam.' Elizabeth looked out at the high girders. 'I have never been on a train.'

'No, no, of course not,' said Mrs Donaldson, straining her neck to see further. 'Dundee shall be the talk of dining tables across the country; it is to be the longest railway bridge in the whole world. There is even talk that Her Majesty the Queen will attend the grand opening.' She sighed. 'Although I personally believe she will not come. How many more years can she continue to mourn her husband?' Mrs Donaldson looked up at Elizabeth. 'But you had something to say to me?'

'Yes, Madam,' she said, clasping her hands together in front of her. 'You remember I said I knew someone who was ready to join me in service?'

'Ah yes,' her mistress mumbled, stifling a yawn. It was nearly time for her afternoon nap. 'Well?'

'I was wondering if she might be considered for the post here when Mollie Andrews leaves to get married? It's my sister Jane.'

'Ah, now why did I have the impression you had neither brother nor sister? Well, perhaps she could come to see us one day soon and we can decide if she is suitable.'

'Thank you, Madam.'

Mrs Donaldson stood up and smoothed down her

grey taffeta gown. Elizabeth could not help but look at her waistline where the tiny black buttons were straining. Surely she couldn't be expecting again, the wee one was still a baby.

Her mistress looked at the vase of tall flowers on the little table beside her and bent over, leaning towards the ivory petals. She inhaled deeply. 'Exquisite. What an aroma. I've asked the gardeners to cultivate more of those scented roses; beautiful, are they not?'

Elizabeth nodded.

'Not dissimilar in colour to the magnolia you like so much.'

Elizabeth smiled and waited for her mistress to return to the topic.

'So, back to your sister. Perhaps you could take on the superior role of house maid and if we deem your sister suitable, she could become scullery and laundry maid, helping Cook with menial tasks in the kitchen? We might need you to continue as table maid, depending on how I find your sister in terms both of appearance and speech.' She stopped fingering the rose petals and stood up straight. 'But that might leave you more time to help Cook with the food preparation. She tells me you are skilled in the kitchen?'

'Thank you, Madam.'

'Good. This household is about to become even busier. We are hoping to employ a governess soon.'

'That will be good for the children, Madam.'

As Elizabeth turned to go out, the sound of a piano could be heard. She tilted her head and listened to the rhythmic melody. 'Is that Miss Traves playing the piano, Madam?'

'Yes, it is. Roberta is having her first lesson today so I

asked the teacher to play some pieces to her to start with, to try to encourage a love of music. Though I doubt that, aged eight, she will manage anything as splendid as this Mendelssohn.'

'Chopin.'

'I beg your pardon, Elizabeth?'

'Sorry, Madam, I am mistaken. You are right, of course, but it sounded like Chopin to me.'

'Might I ask how you know about piano composers? Surely you do not play yourself?' She drew herself up tall.

'No, Madam, but my mother did.' Elizabeth curtsied and left the room.

The following week, in the same room, Mrs Donaldson sat at her bay window seat, gazing out at the rain-drenched gardens as Elizabeth ushered in a small, slight girl.

'Mind what I said aboot speaking proper,' she muttered, then turned towards the window and inclined her head. 'Madam, this is my sister Jane.'

Jane bobbed an exaggerated curtsey and smiled. Mrs Donaldson looked the girl up and down, taking in her lank, straight brown hair and her freckles. She looked rather plain beside her statuesque sister, but was not entirely unpleasing to the eye. She would probably do at table, eventually, though that hair would need to be seen to.

'Elizabeth, if you can leave us for a short time, I should like to conduct my interview with Jane alone. Please wait outside.'

After some questions about her experience, Mrs Donaldson stood up and said, 'Well, Jane, you can go and find your sister outside in the hall. I will let you know of my decision soon.'

And as she opened the door, there again was the sound of the piano, this time not the mellifluous notes of the teacher playing, but Roberta, practising a scale badly, with a heavy hand.

'Elizabeth tells me your mother played?'

'Played, Madam?'

'The piano, child.'

Jane frowned. 'Oh I dinnae... Sorry, I do not think so, Madam.' And she bobbed once more and shut the door behind her.

# Chapter Seven
## 2014

Mags turned the key in the lock and tilted her head to one side. She could hear the piano. Thank God, he was home.

'Doug!' she shouted, running to the dining room. 'You'll never guess what's happened.'

He turned round, broad shoulders hunched over the keys, both hands raised, hovering. 'What?'

'Jack and Anna have been in an accident. Chris texted me but I can't get through to her. I've tried Gerry but his phone's off.'

Doug stared at her and leant back on the piano stool. His face had turned deathly white. 'Are they okay?' he whispered.

'I don't know. All Chris said was the kids had had an accident and she and Gerry were going down to Newcastle immediately. You try Gerry!'

Doug darted past her and into the kitchen where his phone lay on the table. 'There's a new message!' He tapped at his phone, his jaw clenched. 'It's not Gerry, just work.'

'Phone Gerry!' Mags dumped her basket on the table and fished inside for her phone. 'I'm going to try Chris again.'

But Christine's phone was switched off. 'I wonder if Lottie's heard from Anna?' said Mags, lifting the phone back to her ear.

'Lottie, darling, have you heard from Anna?' As Mags explained what had happened, she moved to the fridge and pulled out a bottle of wine. 'Can you pop round after your

lesson's finished? Okay, see you soon as you can, darling.'
Mags hung up and reached for a wine glass on the drying
rack.

'What are you doing?' said Doug. 'We might have to
drive to Newcastle. Put the kettle on instead!'

'Put the bloody kettle on yourself, I need a drink.'

'I'm going to find out the names of the hospitals in
Newcastle and phone round, find out where they are.' He
opened his laptop and typed 'A&E Newcastle' into Google.

An hour later, Lottie rushed into the kitchen. 'Any news?'

Mags put down her glass and hugged her daughter.

'Gerry's just phoned Dad, but there's not much more.
They were on their way to intensive care. Said they'd text.'
She motioned towards the wine bottle. 'Want a glass?'

'God, Mum, it's only four o'clock. I'll make myself a
green tea.'

Doug hugged his daughter tightly then went to fill the
kettle. 'They're at the Royal Victoria hospital in Newcastle.
I think we should get down there right now but Mum says
Auntie Chris won't want us.'

'I didn't say she won't want us, but she'll be so stressed,
it's best with someone like her to wait. Besides, Gerry
said there's nothing we can do, not until they know what's
happening.'

'Well, I think we should just drive down anyway. That
way, if anything happens, if they need us, we'll be there.'
Doug rubbed his hands through his hair. 'I can't stand
being stuck up here like this, just waiting.'

Mags glowered at him then turned to her daughter,
'Darling, don't you agree with me? We should wait,
shouldn't we?'

'I don't know, don't make me take sides as usual.'

Mags took her hand. 'Sorry, darling, we're just undecided. Gerry said Chris is too distraught to speak to us, and we don't want to tip her over by pitching up. You know what she's like, Lotts.' She sighed. 'But we don't know how the kids really are. What exactly did Gerry say?'

'He couldn't say anything except Anna was black and blue. He had no idea how Jack was.' Doug bit his lip and turned away from his wife and daughter, his eyes glistening.

'Let's go,' said Lottie. 'Dad's right. If anything happens to them... Just for moral support?'

Mags stood up. 'Okay, I'll pack an overnight bag.'

Doug went to the back door and pulled the snib along at the top.

'Mum, why don't we take some food too, some of your flapjacks or brownies?'

'Good idea.' Mags bustled over to the other side of the kitchen and lifted a cake tin down from the shelf. She glanced at Doug and Lottie's backs then at the bottle on the table. She upended it into her glass, tipped her head back and slugged the wine down.

# Chapter Eight
1874

Elizabeth Barrie adjusted her bonnet and rang the bell at the back of the big house. The door creaked open and a plump woman wearing all black with a white apron and small lace cap greeted her.

'The mistress is waiting for you,' she said. 'Whit d'you ken aboot the job?'

'It's a maid-of-all-work, but maybe helping in the kitchen? I heard Mrs Donaldson likes to sometimes dae some cooking for herself?'

'It's the "mistress" tae you. An' I wouldnae exactly call it cookin'. She has these queer recipes wi' fancy French names but Cook refuses to mak' anythin' she cannae pronounce.' The woman, who looked in her late twenties, had a scowl on her face. As Elizabeth followed her into the house she noticed that she was not, in fact, fat. She realised this must be Meg, whose job she was hoping to take over when she left to have her baby.

'Excuse me,' Elizabeth whispered, as they traversed the wide expanse of polished black and white tiles in the hall, 'are you Meg?'

'Aye,' she said, still surly.

'Meg, is there anything I need to ken before I see the mistress?'

Meg studied Elizabeth's face and said, 'She'll be fine wi' the way you look. Just mak' sure you speak proper.'

She knocked on the door and announced, 'Elizabeth Barrie, Madam,' and shuffled backwards out of the door.

An elegant lady in a striped gown of violet silk, her auburn hair tied in a neat bun at the nape of her neck, stood up from a seat by the wide bay window.

'Come in, Elizabeth, let me see you.'

Elizabeth stepped towards her and stood up to her full height.

'My, you're a tall girl. How old are you? Seventeen?'

'Yes, Madam.'

She peered into her face. 'What extraordinary eyes you have. The colour of molasses.' She sat down and gestured to her companion to sit too.

Elizabeth perched nervously on the edge of the chair.

'And when was your birthday?' Mrs Donaldson asked, dipping her pen into the ink pot at her desk.

'February 29th.'

'Ah, no wonder you look so young, you only have birthdays every four years!' She looked pleased with her little joke; Elizabeth was unsure whether to smile. 'Now, tell me a little about your work at the Patullos'.'

'Yes, Madam.' She cleared her throat. 'I was a table maid for Mr and Mrs Patullo for three years and…'

'You began employment at the age of fourteen?'

'Yes, Madam, but only light duties, helping in the laundry and the dairy, sometimes serving at table. Then last year Cook was ill and off work for a wee while so I helped the mistress in the kitchen. I learnt a lot.' Mrs Donaldson paused to take a note of this and Elizabeth cast a sidelong glance through the bay window. All she could see was grey.

'I see. And was this cook the Mrs Jessica Malcolm who has referred you here?'

'Aye – I mean yes, Madam. Cook was awful kind to me but she thought I would do better to move to the city so, since she knew Meg, she asked if there might be a position here.'

Elizabeth looked once more out the window. She realised the grey must be water.

'Excuse me for asking, Madam, but is that the sea?'

'Yes. Well, it's really an estuary, the widest part of the River Tay before it spills out into the North Sea. Have you never seen the sea?'

'No, Madam. I thought it was blue.'

'Grey on a day like today. Blue when the sky is blue. Presumably you have never visited Dundee before?'

'No, never.'

'The view from this room is the most wonderful aspect of this house.' Mrs Donaldson swept her arm gracefully towards the window as if taking a bow. 'Most days we can see all the way over to Fife, unless there is a low mist. You know what they say about living with a good view, Elizabeth?'

'No, Madam.'

'Those who live with a view live longer.' She dipped her pen once more into the ink well. 'And before you began employment at the Patullos' in Strathmartine, where were you?'

'Tannadice.'

'Tannadice? I believe my husband has passed through there, visiting his farmers. Are there flax fields there?'

'Fields and fields of blue flax the length and breadth o' Angus,' Elizabeth said, smiling.

'As I thought. Your family are there?'

'Aye.' Elizabeth's voice faltered. 'Sorry, yes, Madam.'

Mrs Donaldson put down her pen and studied Elizabeth's face once more, taking in those striking dark eyes. 'I think that, given the references I have from Mrs Patullo about how diligent you are, we might be able to accommodate you here. Should we decide you are to serve at table however, your diction must be improved.'

Elizabeth swallowed. She had no idea what diction was.

'And one final thing. We are blessed with five children and though we employ a nurse, it is important to me that you like children. The little one is only three.'

'Mrs Patullo has seven bairns and there's always plenty noise, they run aboot all over the farmhouse.'

'Our children do not run about and they are never noisy, Elizabeth,' she said, standing up, the heavy silk of her dress rustling. 'Now, I will have Meg show you the room you will be sharing with Nurse Myles.' She rang the bell and turned round once more to gaze out over the water.

# Chapter Nine
## 2014

Christine and Gerry walked into the relatives' room in intensive care in silence. The walls in the windowless room were bare except for a notice above the sink about hand washing and hygiene. Four chairs were arranged around a coffee table, which had nothing on it apart from a box of tissues. Christine sat down, staring at the one white tissue poking out from the top; inert, it looked like a sail on a flat calm sea. She chewed at her nails, thinking there was nothing calm about the way she felt.

Gerry sat down next to her. 'How long did the doctor say she'd be?'

Christine looked at her watch. 'Half an hour, but that was over an hour ago, so it must be soon.'

'He's going to be fine, you know,' Gerry said.

'We don't know, Gerry, we just don't know.' Christine grabbed the tissue and blew her nose.

'Do you think they'll let Anna up here later?'

'I don't know. I'm not sure that's a good idea.' Christine balled up the tissue and flung it at the bin. She slumped back into her chair. 'What did Doug say?'

'Just that they'd be down in a flash if we needed them.'

'But you didn't tell them to drive down, did you?'

'No, calm down. I said to wait until we had more news. I'll phone him again after the doctor's been. You still not ready to phone Mags?'

She shook her head. 'Not sure I'll be able to hold it together on the phone.'

'Okay, I'll do the phoning. What about Charlie?'

'Help, no. The least of our worries is telling Dad. We can let him know later, once everything's fine. Don't want to bother him yet.' She looked at her watch again. 'I can't stand the waiting.'

Gerry took her hand in both of his and held it tight. 'I know, but it'll all be fine, you'll see.'

The door burst open and Doctor Ali strode in, looking grave. 'Sorry to have kept you waiting again.' She was followed by a tall man with a closely shaven head. 'This is Staff Nurse Yates.'

'What's happening?' Christine cried out. 'Why can't we see him?'

Doctor Ali sat down opposite them. 'When Jack came in to us he was in a pretty bad way; I'm told he had to be cut out of the car. The air ambulance team intubated him and he's been in an induced coma ever since.'

Her beeper went off but she ignored it.

'I wanted to do a CT scan to check for head injuries which would be consistent with the large gash and swelling on his forehead. We found there was diffuse axonal injury but only mild, which is surprising given the nature of the impact that must have caused the laceration on his forehead.'

Gerry coughed and lifted his hand. Christine glared at him.

'Doctor Ali, I'm sorry to interrupt, but this might be important. Anna was telling me earlier that Jack sustained an injury last night at rugby training. She said he had a big gash on his head and she was worried he might need stitches. He said it was nothing though, and that he wasn't concussed or anything. He didn't tell us on the phone last night as Christine would've just worried.'

Dr Ali nodded. 'Well, that makes sense. Had his injury occurred during the RTA, his head injuries would have been more severe.'

'RTA?'

'Road traffic accident, Mrs Wallace.' She looked at her watch. 'Well, that's encouraging news. And his seatbelt burns imply that his seatbelt was functioning. Perhaps the jolt brought on repeat concussion and opened up the wound.'

'Doctor Ali,' whispered Christine, 'he'll be all right, won't he?'

'The signs aren't as bad as we thought now. We were worried mainly about his head injury, which doesn't seem to be as serious as we'd feared. There's no internal bleeding. We're looking into injuries to his pelvis, which we think has been fractured or broken. Do you want to see him before we take him off the ventilator?'

'Yes!' Christine gasped. 'Please.'

'Okay, but bear in mind that we don't know how he'll be once he comes out of sedation. Follow us through, please.' The doctor nodded to the nurse to open the door.

The moment she looked through the wide glass window of the room ahead, Christine recognised the unconscious body of her son. She saw his hand, a cannula taped to the back, his long slim fingers dangling limp over the white sheet. She took a deep breath and followed Dr Ali into the room where a young nurse, who looked no older than a girl, stood by the ventilator.

Christine bit her lip as she looked down at her son. Jack's forehead was bloodied and bruised, his closed eyes swollen, yet he looked peaceful and serene. Christine took his hand and felt herself start to shake as she tried to suppress sobs.

'Love you, darling.'

Gerry, at the other side of the bed, stared at him and touched his wrist. 'You're going to be fine, son,' he whispered and glanced at his wife whose shoulders shuddered as she silently wept.

Doctor Ali spoke quietly. 'If you want to wait in the relatives' room, we'll call you back once he's off the ventilator.' She looked at her watch then at the nurse. 'A couple of hours – about eight o'clock?'

The young nurse nodded. 'We'll come and get you when he's ready.'

Christine took her seat once again in front of the box of tissues.

'Shall I go and see Anna?' Gerry stood at the door. 'And I'll get a sandwich or something for us on the way back?'

'Yes, check on Anna. I need to stay here, but see if she's allowed up to join us?' She turned and glared at him as he scratched his beard. 'How can you think about food, Gerry?'

'Chris, we need to eat.'

'Well, I don't need to if I don't want to!' She spat the words out then realised how childish she sounded. 'Sorry.' She reached for his hand. 'Just try to get Anna up here. Maybe they'll give her a wheelchair?'

'I'll see what I can do.'

Christine watched him pull the door gently behind him then took out her phone and switched it on. There was no reception, which, on reflection, was just as well; she had no wish to speak to anyone.

She closed her eyes, stretched out her legs and leant her head against the back of the chair. As she thought of her boy, lying unmoving, with tubes everywhere, the tears started to flow. She stretched forward and ripped out one tissue after another as she began to heave with uncontrollable sobs.

# Chapter Ten
1873

Elizabeth opened the heavy wooden gate and made her way around the side of the field. The flax was in flower and she gazed at the shimmer of blue under the weak summer sun. They were such a beautiful colour, the shade of blue matching the cloudless summer sky. Mr Patullo was at the far end of the field with one of his farmhands; she walked towards them with her basket.

As she approached, the farmer put down the tools he was using to repair the fence and smiled. 'Ah, I was just wondering when you would arrive with our piece. What do you have for us today, young Elizabeth?'

'Cook said to tell you it's beef frae yesterday's dinner, sir – she's potted it. And there's a loaf o' her wheaten bread, a pat of fresh butter and a hunk o' cheese frae the dairy.' She took out a bulging cloth and untied the knot at the top, concentrating on her task with a frown.

'Gie's a smile, Elizabeth Barrie,' said the farmhand.

'Let her be, Fred,' said Mr Patullo. 'She's not one of your common village girls.'

He looked at Elizabeth, tall and straight in her long, heavy serge skirt. She was trying to suppress a smile. 'Thank you, Elizabeth. My, you seem to become taller every day.'

She nodded and knelt down to lay out the food on a cloth, then took out a flagon of ale and two mugs and poured. 'Shall I wait over there for you to finish, sir?'

'Yes, that will be fine, Elizabeth. I know you would rather look at the cattle than converse with us.'

Elizabeth grinned and tripped away towards the next field where the black cattle stood. Leaning on the gate, she gazed at the great lumbering beasts. She had always admired the broad deep backs and sleek coats of these beautiful Angus Blacks. Though she only tasted the beef when Cook gave her leftovers from the family's dinner, she loved the flavour. Cook had been teaching her how to make good soups and it had surprised Elizabeth to hear Cook's advice about adding a cow heel. She marvelled at how a heel from one of those great beasts could give such a strong flavour to a simple pot of soup.

She had been learning to make other soups too. And though the leek and tattie soup at supper the night before had been tasty enough, her favourite was the ramson soup they had made earlier in the spring. She and Cook had picked the wild garlic in the woods up the hill. It reminded her of home and she loved the strong oniony flavour that lingered even after she had scraped her plate of soup clean.

She looked back at the men. Mr Patullo was getting to his feet. She gathered up her skirts, rushed back over to them and began clearing the remnants away.

'Thank you, Elizabeth,' said Mr Patullo. 'Will you tell Mrs Patullo I shall be home presently? We have only one more fence to repair.'

'Yes, sir.'

'See you later, Elizabeth,' said Fred, winking.

'It's Miss Barrie to you. Mr Patullo cuffed his farmhand around the head. 'Now get yourself off the ground and back up the field to your work.'

Elizabeth put her hand to her mouth to suppress a giggle and headed round the field and up the grassy hill. Once she reached the farmhouse, she stopped and looked around.

Fields of blue flax stretched across the rolling land for as far as she could see. Surely even the sea could not be this blue, she thought, picking up her basket and running towards the hens clucking at the back door.

# Chapter Eleven
## 2014

Gerry ripped the wrapper off a triangular cardboard pack and took a large bite from a beef sandwich.

'I got you a tuna salad, but there's an egg mayo too?' he said, his mouth full.

Christine sipped her coffee and picked up a packet. Without looking to see what it was, she slowly pulled off the wrapper and nibbled at a sandwich.

'So, Anna's got to stay in until tomorrow?'

'Yes, purely for observation. She's not quite as shaken up as she was, but they want to keep her in overnight just in case.'

Christine nodded. 'I'll go down and spend some time with her after we've seen Jack.'

'She was sound asleep when I went to see her just now but I'm sure she'll wake up soon.'

Christine took another small bite of her sandwich and looked up at the ceiling. 'So do we know who rammed them?'

'All Sergeant Price would say was that the kids were in a stationary queue, having done all the right things, you know, slowing down gradually and so on, and some guy crashed into them at high speed, he reckons about sixty miles an hour. Funnily enough, he had to be checked out in A&E this afternoon too.'

Christine's eyes opened wide. 'Funnily enough? I wish he'd died. In fact, I hope he's permanently brain damaged or has some horrible disability that'll ruin his life forever.'

'The policeman said he also had a child in the car.'

Christine swallowed. 'Is the child okay?'

'Think so. The man was just a bit shaken, that's all.'

'Shaken! After nearly killing my two children!' Christine was shouting. 'I could kill him.' She gulped from her coffee cup. 'Do we know anything else about him?'

'No, and it's not important at the moment.'

'You're right, sorry.' Christine put the rest of her sandwich back in its package and pushed it away from her. 'When can we get the kids' bags and phones and things?'

'I'll phone the duty policeman later and find out. Got to see when I can go and check what's left of the car too.' He looked at the table. 'D'you not want the rest of that sandwich?'

Christine shook her head and put down her coffee while Gerry leant over to pick up her leftovers.

There was a knock at the door. Christine leapt to her feet as Staff Nurse Yates entered. 'Sorry to bother you but there's three people outside – relatives of yours – who'd like to see you.'

'It'll be Doug, Mags and Lottie,' said Gerry. 'Do you want them in here?'

'Sorry, they're not allowed in here, but you can go and meet them outside ITU,' said the nurse.

'You go, Gerry, I'm not ready to face anyone,' said Christine. 'Why didn't they just wait in Edinburgh till we gave them more news?'

'Okay,' said Gerry. 'I'm sure they'll understand.'

'Don't be long.'

Ten minutes later, the young nurse who had been by Jack's bed knocked on the door and came in, smiling. 'Mrs

Wallace, you can come and see Jack now.'

'How is he?' Christine said, rushing to the door.

'Still sleeping but we can wake him up while you're there. It'll be good for him to see his mum.'

They walked together to the ward and into Jack's room, where nurse Yates was waiting. Christine lifted her son's limp hand and clutched it to her.

'We're going to wake him up, Mrs Wallace and see how he is.'

Christine watched as Jack slowly began to respond to the nurses, his eyes opening to slits. Christine smiled at him, trying to look cheerful.

'Now, Jack, can you tell us your date of birth?' asked Yates.

'11th of February. 1990.' A tiny voice.

Both nurses looked at Christine who nodded vigorously, her eyes keen.

'Can you remember where you live, Jack?'

'9A Market Place, Durham.'

'And what about your postcode?'

Silence.

'Ask him for his home address in Edinburgh. Durham's just a student flat, he'd not know that.'

'And where do you live in Edinburgh?' urged Yates.

'31 Craigleith Avenue.'

'And can you remember the postcode?'

'EH4 3…' His voice trailed away.

As Christine beamed up at the nurses, she felt a little pressure on her fingers.

'He squeezed my hand!' she cried, elated.

The young nurse smiled and said, 'He'll need to sleep. It's the only way he'll get fully fit again.'

There was a tap on the window – it was Gerry and Doug. 'He knew his address, Gerry.' She said, beaming, as her husband entered the room.

'Mags and Lottie have gone to see Anna,' said Doug. 'But I wanted to see Jack.' His voice faltered as he looked down at Jack. 'My God, is he… How is he?'

'He's going to be fine,' said Chris, looking at Gerry. 'He remembered his birthday – and his address.'

Doug was bent low over Jack. He pressed his lips tightly together, and his eyes welled up. 'Can I touch him? I don't want to hurt him.'

'It's fine,' said Nurse Yates. 'Gently.'

Doug took Jack's hand in shaking fingers. 'He's really going to be okay? I was – we were – so worried.' He shut his eyes and bent his head down as if in prayer.

# Chapter Twelve
1872

'Elizabeth, get the bone knife oot o' the drawer. Come an' I'll show ye how to get rid o' the hairs.'

'What hairs, Mrs Malcolm?'

'Dinnae call me that, have I no' telt you often enough, it's Jessie. We're near enough family.'

'What hairs, Jessie?' They were standing in the dairy of Strathmartine farmhouse, leaning over the wooden table. In front of them was a large pat of butter. Elizabeth had just been shown how to make butter in the swing churn, then work it into a pat with wooden paddles.

'The cows' hairs. Even though there shouldnae be any, there's aye some left in there, so here's how I use the knife tae' howk them out. And only use this bone handle knife here, mind, dinnae use any others.'

She did a few then looked at Elizabeth, whose eyes were cast down, concentrating on what the older woman was teaching her. She was a diligent child, she only rarely frowned, her cheerful mien part of her charm. She loved helping Cook and endeavoured to take each task seriously. Her other duties in the laundry and around the house she undertook with relish, as if the discovery of new things was life's purpose.

Elizabeth took the knife from Jessie and continued with the task.

'You ken the mistress is wanting you to start serving at table, maybe next Sunday when they've got the minister for dinner. What d'you think tae that?'

Elizabeth's expression was eager as she looked up. She smiled at the diminutive woman who had become a mother figure to her since her arrival at Strathmartine the previous year. 'Aye, if that's what the mistress wants. I'll need to hae some lessons on how it's a' done, mind. I've never served in the big dining room before.'

'You'll be fine, she's been wanting you to serve at table for ages now, so we'll maybe get you started tomorrow morning in the breakfast room. But when there's visitors, just remember if anyone asks your age, you're fourteen.'

'Aye, you telt me, I'm not to tell anyone I'm only twelve.'

'Just as well you're sae tall, Elizabeth, you could pass for eighteen almost. And your mother's no bigger than me; dinnae ken where you got your height from.' Jessie shook her head. 'You're lucky, though you'll need tae find a giant o' a man to marry, they dinnae like to look up to us women.'

'Dinnae want tae marry, men are stupid.' Elizabeth put down her knife. 'Well, no' the master of course, but a' the others are.'

Jessie laughed and began to wrap the butter up in squares of cheesecloth.

'Will the mistress be playing the piano after dinner like she does sometimes?'

'Aye, she likely will.'

'It's just that, maybe I could be allowed tae turn the pages for her? She cannae really dae that herself, can she?'

Jessie looked at her, frowning. 'Now, what would a lassie like you ken about the piano?'

'I ken a bit, enough to follow the music. I like the piano, I really do.'

'Well, well, fancy that. I can mention it tae her if you like.'

'Thanks. Shall I go and fetch the eggs now for the bairns'

tea?'

'Aye, out you go. Mind and fasten everything up tight in the henhouse, I heard that fox roaming around again last night,' said Jessie, wiping down the scrubbed wooden table as she watched Elizabeth skip off towards the henhouse.

# Chapter Thirteen
## 2014

'Don't think I've ever seen you eat a fried egg, Chris,' said Mags, 'and you've got three on your plate.'

'Have I?' Christine was in a daze as she sat down in the hospital café. 'The woman at the servery just gave them to me. I can't remember what I asked for.'

'They'll be good for you,' said Gerry. 'Here's your coffee.'

Christine took the cup from her husband and nodded her thanks without looking at him.

It was the morning after the accident and Christine, Gerry, Mags and Doug sat around the table, eating. Very few words were exchanged. They all looked up as Lottie joined them with her tray. 'So we're getting Anna out after breakfast, Auntie Chris?'

'Yes, sweetheart.' She stroked Lottie's wavy brown hair and looked down at her plate. 'It's Jack we just don't know about.' She cut into an egg and stared at the yolk as it oozed over the plate.

'Sounds like it's just concussion now. He looked better this morning.' Gerry rammed a large bap with two sausages into his mouth.

'He looked just the same, Gerry, and he was sound asleep. We have no idea how he really is.' Christine winced as she watched her husband wipe a splatter of sausage grease off his beard.

'I'll go up with you after breakfast, if that's okay,' said Mags. 'I never saw him last night.'

She turned to Lottie, who was spooning yoghurt on her

fruit salad. 'Is that all you're having, darling?' asked Mags. 'Could be a long day, why don't you…'

'Mum, I'm fine.' Lottie's long fingers strummed against the table as she turned to Christine. 'Auntie Chris, when I'm finished, I can go and help Anna get ready. Then we can come and join you in Jack's ward later?'

'Thanks, sweetheart,' said Christine, patting her niece's hand. 'Hopefully he'll get out of ITU and into HDU later.'

'Ever upwards!' said Mags, forcing a smile. 'And you guys just say when you want us to go. We don't want to impose. We could drive back up the road and collect some things for you?'

'It's okay, Mags,' said Christine.

They finished their food in silence.

'Dad, are you okay?' said Lottie. 'You look terrible.'

Doug looked up through bloodshot eyes. 'Slept badly, Lotts. I've got a thudding head – bloody Premier Inn and their promise of guaranteed sleep!'

'I said you could have complained when that stag party started up in the corridor at three am. You'd have got your money back, it's part of the deal,' said Mags, patting his arm.

'I know, darling, but I kept thinking they'd quieten down and then…'

'And then they partied till dawn!' Lottie pushed her half-finished bowl away from her. 'Shall I go and get Anna out and you can go and see Jack, Auntie Chris?'

Mags screwed up her paper napkin and tossed it onto her plate. 'I'll come with you, Chris. Anytime you're ready, let's go.'

'Now's good,' said Christine. 'I can't eat any more.'

At the door to the ITU ward, Christine and Mags found

Doctor Ali frowning over some notes.

'Ah, Mrs Wallace, your son's just been transferred to HDU, along the corridor there. Doctor McNally's in charge, he'll tell you what the latest is.' She pointed them in the right direction and then hurried away, looking down at her beeper.

They strode along the corridor to the sign that read HDU and rang the buzzer then were taken to a bay of four beds. One of the beds was vacant and as Christine began to read the notes at the end of the bed there was a noise behind them. They both turned to see two nurses holding Jack in a standing position between them.

'Jack, darling!' Christine lunged towards her son and kissed him.

'We thought he could try a little walk before we put the catheter back in,' said one of the nurses, smiling, 'and he's done all right, haven't you, pet.'

Jack sat down on his bed with a thump then lay back against the pillow.

'How is he?' Christine whispered.

'Doctor McNally will be round in a minute, he can tell you himself,' said the other nurse, pulling the curtains round the bed. She started to fit the catheter and Mags looked discreetly away. Once it was done, Christine gently adjusted the blankets around him and Mags came to stand beside her cousin as the nurses drew back the curtains.

'Jack, you've given us all such a fright, sweetheart, but it's all going to be fine now.' Mags stroked his cropped dark hair.

Jack opened his eyes a fraction and gave his mother and aunt a flicker of a smile.

'Jack, darling,' said Christine, grabbing his hand, 'it's so good to see you awake!'

There was a rustle of curtains and they looked round. 'Hello there,' interrupted a short, stout man, his bald pate sun-freckled. 'I'm Dr McNally. Are you Jack's mum?' He was looking at Mags, who nodded over at Christine.

'How is he?' asked Christine.

'He's going to be fine,' said Doctor McNally, in his strong Irish accent. 'We have a few more tests to run, Glasgow coma scale and so on, but he should only be in here a day, then onto a general ward for a couple of days then home. We suspect he suffered a delayed concussion from rugby, exacerbated by the RTA. It's not been the serious head injuries we first suspected, but Jack has sustained a minor injury to his pelvis. It's what's known as an avulsion fracture, where a piece of bone is pulled away from the pelvis. In addition to this, he's cracked a couple of ribs. We'll give him crutches but rest and recovery at home is the best course with this.'

Dr McNally took a slim torch out of his pocket. 'Jack, can you open your eyes for me?' Jack blearily opened his eyes as the doctor shone the torch into each pupil. 'He's going to be fine. Don't worry, Mrs Wallace. A bit of physio might help too, but you can probably get him home soon.' He smiled. 'I'll be back later.'

As he left, he drew back the curtains and Christine whispered, 'I think I'm in love with Doctor McNally, Mags!'

Jack opened his eyes wide and looked up at his mother, as if checking she were still there.

'Don't worry, darling, go back to sleep now,' said Christine. 'You need to rest.'

'I've never really noticed before,' said Mags, 'but Jack's eyes are so brown, they're almost black. What a contrast to yours, Chris.'

'They probably look even darker right now because his face is so pale. Well, apart from the purple bruises.' Mags grasped her cousin's hand. 'Wasn't that brilliant what the doctor said? He's going to be fine!'

Christine gazed at her son. 'If I were religious, I'd have thanked God for answering our prayers.'

An hour or so later, Anna limped into the ward, her face still black and blue.

'Jack Duncan, what the hell happened to you!'

Jack smiled blearily on hearing his sister's voice. She rushed forward and gave him a hug.

'Watch out,' snapped Christine. 'He's all bruised.'

'And I'm not, Mum?' Anna jabbed a finger at the bruises on her face.

'Sorry, darling.' Christine took her daughter's swollen face between the palms of her hands and kissed her forehead. 'You've got to take it easy, though. Here, why don't you sit down in my seat? I'm off to the loo.'

Anna sat down. 'So how's he doing, Auntie Mags?'

'Well the doctor reckons it's just the delayed concussion from rugby, but he's still got to run some more tests. He's got two cracked ribs, and he might have a slight limp for a while as he's got a small pelvic fracture. Apart from the bruises, he looks pretty good doesn't he?'

'Better than he usually does,' said Anna, grinning. 'Oh, I was to tell you and Mum the others are coming up soon. Once Lottie's seen Jack, she and I are going to go and grab a coffee.'

'Okay, darling. When will you get your bags from the police?'

'Dad's got to go to the police station later so maybe then?'

'Hopefully.'

'Auntie Mags,' said Anna, slowly. 'Do you think… I don't know, that Mum and Dad are okay? I mean, they just seemed to be sniping at each other all the time when they were in my ward, and Lottie said it was the same last night in the hotel too.'

'It's the stress, darling; you have no idea what a fright we all got.' Mags gave Anna a hesitant hug, nervous about touching her bruises. 'Don't worry, it'll all be fine, just wait and see.'

Christine arrived back at the bedside, followed by Lottie, who bent down to give Jack a kiss on the cheek.

Mags pulled a chair forward for Chris. 'Everything's going to be okay now,' she said, taking her cousin's hand again.

'Oh, Mum,' said Lottie. 'I'm to tell you that Dad and Uncle Gerry are off to the garage to sort out the car, they'll be back in a couple of hours.'

'Okay. How was Dad?' Mags asked.

'Better. A lot calmer now that Jack's out of intensive care.'

'Yeah, Uncle Doug was a wreck, wasn't he,' said Anna. 'Dad managed to hold it together pretty well though.' Then she whispered loudly towards her brother, 'But hey, Dad never really liked you anyway, Jack Wallace!' She grinned and flicked her brother's hand with her fingers. He smiled weakly, without opening his eyes.

'Only joking, beanpole,' she said, giving his hand a squeeze.

Christine withdrew her hand from her cousin's clasp and took a tissue from her pocket. 'Some Easter this has been,' she said, shaking her head.

# Chapter Fourteen
## 2014

A week later, Mags was stirring a pan of soup in her kitchen while the sound of piano music reverberated through the house. She loved to play Lottie's piano CDs when she was cooking and this was one of her favourite composers, Ravel; perfect to peel, chop and stir to. She had just phoned Christine to suggest a visit to Register House. Mags was worried about her cousin; she was fraught all the time, even though Jack was recovering well. Gerry had told Doug she was mollycoddling him but no one wanted to tell her to back off.

Mags thought she might distract her with the family history project, but Christine had said she definitely had no time to do any more research. Mags wondered if she might go alone, to continue the search for Elizabeth Barrie.

And to think, I was the one not interested in the family history at all, she mused as she ground black pepper into the pan. She tasted the soup then added a little salt.

She took out her mezzaluna and started chopping some parsley, mulling over something Christine had said the day before.

Mags had popped in to visit Jack and catch up with Christine. Anna joined them, and they all sat around Jack's bed. Anna scolded her brother for being in bed, telling him he needed to get up and move around.

'I want to be up, it's Mum who's not letting me.'

'The doctor said you need to rest.'

'Not all day though, Mum,' said Anna.

'I'm going to start getting up at lunchtime at least. I feel fine, just a bit tired.' Jack took a sip of water from the tray on his bedside table and looked pleadingly to Christine.

'I don't want you to overdo it, Jack. Remember you said you still had a bit of blurred vision when we walked round the block yesterday.'

'*Limped* round the block!' Anna laughed.

'At least I never had puffy black eyes like yours,' he said, lying back against the pillow. He looked up at his mother's anxious expression. 'Mum, I was fine after the walk, don't exaggerate.'

'Mum, stop treating him like an invalid. Beanpole's fine. Though he's gonna become Fatboy if he lounges in bed much longer,' said Anna, smirking.

He grinned and hit out at his sister but she leapt off the bed. 'Right, I'm out of here. Meeting Lottie for a catch-up at her flat.'


Later, as Christine saw Mags out the front door, she said, 'I've been trying to find out as much as possible about Colin Clarkson.'

'Who?'

'You know, the guy who rammed their car, caused the accident.'

Mags was putting on her coat. She turned round, an incredulous look on her face. 'Why?'

Christine's blue eyes flashed with anger. 'Because he almost killed my two children. Isn't it obvious?'

Mags continued fastening the buttons on her coat then said, 'Chris, is this a good idea? What's the point? Surely there'll be a court case and he'll plead guilty and...'

'He might not plead guilty – he might not even appear in court. It's the magistrates' court in Gateshead.' Christine twisted her hands round and round. 'He lives in West Yorkshire – Pontefract – and I just have the feeling he won't attend and then...'

'What's this got to do with Jack and his recovery?'

'I want him to suffer. He can't get away with it.'

'Chris, don't talk like that.' She pulled up the collar of her coat. 'How do you know where he lives anyway?'

'We were sent the police report for our insurance company, it had all his details, including his address.'

Mags had given her cousin a hug and stepped outside, promising to phone her the next day. She had brushed off Christine's outburst as a reaction to the stress she was under, but as she stood chopping parsley she found she couldn't get Christine's twisted expression out of her mind.

The following day, Christine was in her kitchen ladling soup from a large pan into a blender. She put a tea towel over the lid and switched it on. There was a whoosh of green from the base as the lid and tea towel flew off and the contents splattered against the white wall and over the coffee machine. The thick gloop trickled slowly down the sides.

'Dammit!' She stomped to the sink and grabbed a cloth.

Anna came into the room and burst out laughing. 'God, Mum, what's with the Jackson Pollock thing?'

Christine's eyes were blazing. She said nothing, just started to wipe at the mess, fist clenched tight around the cloth.

Anna went towards her with a roll of kitchen paper. 'Here, let me help. What happened?'

'The lid wasn't on right.' She lifted the coffee machine to wipe underneath.

'What was it?'

'Organic watercress and spinach, took me ages and now it's all over the counter.'

'Mum, it's fine, and the patient couldn't care less if it's homemade, organic or a tin of Heinz. You've got to stop treating him like an invalid.'

'But he is an invalid! He was in intensive care, he could have…'

'But he didn't,' said Anna.

'Well the fact of the matter is he has two broken ribs and a fractured pelvis. I don't want him getting up unless he absolutely has to. The whole thing just makes me so angry, I could kill the man who crashed into you, I really could.'

'Mum, sit down,' said Anna, taking the cloth from her mum and continuing to wipe up the mess. 'Besides, my bruises still look a lot worse than his. Look how fetching this yellow hue is!' She pointed at the lines of bruises across her chest.

Christine started to laugh, then tears began to roll down her cheeks. 'Sorry, sweetheart, I'm just so tired I feel I've done nothing but cook and serve tea and coffee for all the visitors.'

'Well, you've got to stop being such a martyr about it all and let Dad and me help.'

'Dad's never here, Anna.'

'Mum, that's not fair, he does have a job to go to and…'

'And what about me? Don't I have a job? Just because I'm on Easter holidays.'

'Mum, you've got to try to de-stress. Let me make you a camomile tea.'

Christine's shoulders slumped and she wiped at her eyes. 'Thanks, Anna. What would I do without you.'

Christine stood up and took a tray from the cupboard, setting it with knife, spoon and plate.

'And Jack wants to get up for meals now, you don't need to take him up a tray. Sit down!'

'Well, I'll just take him a snack just now. Maybe he can come down for dinner, we'll see how he's feeling.'

# Chapter Fifteen
## 2014

Mags got off the bus in St Andrew Square and strolled down onto Princes Street. The flags on the castle ramparts were flapping in the strong breeze. As she climbed the wide steps to the entrance to Register House, she wondered how on earth she had found herself so caught up in investigating her family history; a month ago she wouldn't have cared. But since the accident, Christine had been constantly stressed; she seemed hell-bent on wreaking revenge on Colin Clarkson, even though the kids were fine.

Although Christine wasn't yet back at school, she insisted she had no time for anything apart from lesson planning, so Mags was going solo today. She sat down and took out her sheets of scribbled notes from her last visit.

Maybe if she found something interesting in Register House she could suggest they drive north to Dundee and Tannadice to see where Elizabeth Barrie had lived. Concentrating on tracking down their ancestor was surely better than trying to hunt down a stranger for dubious reasons.

Mags had just begun to look into the 1871 census when her phone beeped. She looked around, wondering if she'd be told off, but no one seemed bothered. It was a text from Doug asking where she was – he had just popped home for lunch and the house was empty without her.

'Register House. Back this aft. Quiche in larder if you fancy.x.'

A ping came back. 'Thought that said quickie.'

She shook her head and grinned. He was so predictable, but God, they were lucky – still besotted with each other, after all these years. So many of her friends were having marital problems: one was in the middle of a steamy affair and another completely indifferent towards her husband of twenty-five years. Which was worse, she wondered.

Mags switched her phone onto silent, threw it into her basket, and continued trawling through the 1871 census for Elizabeth Barrie. Eventually she found an entry that seemed to match, though again her age didn't fit. This Elizabeth Barrie was registered at a farmhouse in Strathmartine, which after a quick Google, Mags found was just north of Dundee. The farm was the home of the Patullo family – farmer John Patullo, his wife and their seven children along with a nurse, a cook and a table maid called Elizabeth Barrie, born in Tannadice.

It was definitely her, there can't possibly have been two Elizabeth Barries in a tiny village like Tannadice. But she was now said to be thirteen, which didn't tie in with either her wedding certificate or the 1881 census. And she was the only Barrie working at the Patullos', her sister was obviously too young.

Mags tried to track down a birth certificate for Elizabeth, thinking that might shed some light on the mystery of her age, but with no luck. She did, however, find Elizabeth's sister, Jane, born in April 1860 to mother Margaret and father David Barrie. She was about to print when something caught her eye. On the birth certificate, after David Barrie's name and profession – ploughman – was a cross. He must have been illiterate.

She continued trawling through births for a few years either side of Jane's dates but found nothing for Elizabeth

Barrie. So she went back to the 1861 Census and tried other Barries. When she came to Margaret Barrie in Tannadice, she gasped. The man in the next seat turned to look at her. 'Brilliant when you find something you're not expecting, isn't it!'

'Do you know what it means if it says "pauper"?' asked Mags.

'No idea, sorry. I'm stuck in 1917, Flanders. All they say is "Missing Presumed Dead"... Imagine!'

Mags shook her head in sympathy then returned to the census on her screen. There was Margaret Barrie, aged thirty-eight, widow of David Barrie, ploughman, and she was classified as a pauper. Her daughter Jane was there, aged one. Where the hell was Elizabeth?

She quickly looked back to the 1851 census and found Margaret Barrie aged twenty-eight, wife of David Barrie aged twenty-nine. No children were mentioned; so perhaps they had just got married. Their address in both censuses was simply 'the village', no street name. Mags printed everything off and went to the desk to ask the research assistant what it meant to be a pauper in the 1860s.

The earnest young man talked at length about the Poor Law of 1845, explaining that after the Act was passed, it was up to an Inspector of the Poor to decide whether applicants for poor relief were legitimate. Obviously Elizabeth Barrie's mother was suitable, otherwise she would not have had the word pauper written against her name in the census.

Pretty sad, Mags thought, but surely that wasn't the family secret?

# Chapter Sixteen
## 1871

'Why dae I have to put flowers on her grave, Ma?'

'You liked Miss Charlotte, did you no'?'

Elizabeth's head dropped and she nodded, not looking up.

'Right, so just come along wi' me and we'll hae a wee blether later.'

Margaret Barrie handed Elizabeth a little posy of snowdrops tied with a length of twine. 'Never seen snowdrops sae late, maybe the flax'll be late flowering this year an a'.'

They walked along the main road, heading out of Tannadice, the woman short and stout, the girl by her side tall and gangly. They passed the last little cottage in the main street and crossed the road. Margaret pushed the wrought iron gate and it creaked open. They both entered the churchyard and Margaret looked around.

'Look for the one wi' fresh flowers on it, that'll be her.'

Elizabeth pointed to the left side of the church, near the wall. 'Over there, Ma, is that it?'

They stepped between the grave stones and stopped at the freshly dug grave. There was no headstone, just a pottery vase of fading blooms.

'Why's she no' got her name on a stone like the others, Ma?'

'She was only laid to rest two days ago, Elizabeth. The stonemason's far too busy, she wisnae the only one taken by the influenza.'

'Where dae I put it?' Elizabeth held up her little posy.

Margaret pointed to the head of the grave and watched Elizabeth lay the snowdrops in front of the vase.

'Can we go now? I dinnae like it here.' Elizabeth began to hop from one foot to the other.

'Stand still, lassie, you're in a graveyard! And it's important you pay your respects to Miss Charlotte. Say a wee prayer for her, go on.'

Elizabeth bowed her head and mumbled a few words.

Margaret was staring at a headstone at the other side of the gravel path.

'Is that Pa over there?'

'Aye. But we're no' stopping there. Now, mind I said if you laid the flowers, that we'd hae a wee treat? We're going to tak' a walk to Auntie Jeannie in Oathlaw. We'll hae a blether wi' her then come home afore it's dark.'

Elizabeth nodded and started to walk towards the church gates. 'So when the stone's up, do I hae to come back, Ma?'

'No, you'll be awa' by then. Awa' frae the village.' Margaret took the girl's arm in hers and spoke in hushed tones as they walked out of the churchyard, along the road past the mill towards the stream and over the little, rickety wooden bridge that led away from Tannadice. They passed the pump where a half-empty bucket of water stood and continued the path that climbed steeply out of the village.

'Now you're eleven, you're old enough to go oot and work. Auntie Jeannie's sister-in-law's the cook in a big house in Strathmartine and she says they need more help now there's seven bairns.'

'But, Ma, I do work. I help you wi' your work at the manse an'…'

'This'll be a proper job and it'll mean you get to share

a bedroom wi' just one other lassie. You'll even hae your own bed, no' like our wee house where we three a' sleep together.'

'But I dinnae want to leave you and Jane.' She gazed up at Margaret, her deep brown eyes imploring.

Margaret stopped in the middle of the path, puffing. Gnarled oaks hung over the verdant moss and sprouting bracken beside the path. Behind her, down in the valley, was Tannadice. Far in the distance, the hills soared above the lush Angus glens where the black cattle grazed.

Elizabeth looked puzzled. 'And why did you make me put flowers on Miss Charlotte's grave?'

'She was always good to you.'

'But you never liked her.'

'Me and her were always different. She was a lady.' Margaret took a deep breath. 'Your sister Jane's no' as strong and fit as you are, Elizabeth. I need her tae help me at the hoose, and you go out and work.'

'But why can't I stay on to work at the manse? Is it cause Miss Charlotte's no' there any more?'

Margaret sighed. 'Sit doon.' Margaret eased her ample bottom onto a grassy bank beside a road sign that read 'Oathlaw 1 mile'. She leant her back against the wooden post and looked up at Elizabeth standing above her, unsmiling, refusing to budge.

'When my Davie – your Pa – died, Miss Charlotte was good tae you. She was starting to learn you the piano and even how to speak proper.'

Elizabeth reached up a finger into her curly mop and twisted a ringlet round and round.

'It was grand, you coming to the Manse wi' me, helping me wi' my chores and turning her pages when she practised the piano. She telt me you were doing well and she was even learnin' you to play a wee bit yersel. In fact, she was a' for getting you to sit beside her on the big organ bench in the kirk to turn the pages o' the hymns on Sundays.' She glanced up at Elizabeth, whose dark eyes were large in her pale angular face. 'And then she died.'

Elizabeth's face crumpled. 'But I still dinnae see why I have to leave home.'

Margaret reached out to the girl but Elizabeth folded her arms across her chest. Margaret struggled to pull herself up.

'The fact is, Elizabeth, now she's gone, the minister cannae bear to see you, you remind him o' her when she was a lassie. An' he's still grievin' for his one and only daughter. Now let's hurry, Auntie Jeannie'll be turnin' those scones on the girdle.'

They walked the rest of the way in silence.


'Jeannie, I was just telling Elizabeth aboot working at Strathmartine wi' Jessie.'

The three of them sat at the large kitchen table in the farmhouse in Oathlaw round a plate of scones. Elizabeth leant over to the butter dish and scraped her knife over it then smeared butter thickly on her scone.

'Aye, you'll fit in fine there. You're such a nice lassie, kind of refined somehow. Such manners she has, Margaret.'

'Aye, she's picked up a lot frae the manse.'

Elizabeth who had been silent until now, looked at Jeannie. 'How far is it tae Strathmartine?'

'Oh, no' far, aboot fifteen miles but I'll see you there myself. We'll go together on Saturday, it's my day off. That'll gie you tomorrow to get yourself sorted. And your

Ma'll come tae.'

'Dinnae want to…' Elizabeth sniffled.

'Saturday will be just fine, Jeannie, thanks,' said Margaret. 'Right, Elizabeth, we'd better be setting off home before the night draws in. Thanks for the scones.' She stood up and tied the ribbons of her bonnet.

Elizabeth put on her coat, muttered thank you to Jeannie and turned to the door, shoulders stooped.

'Where's that braw smile o' yours, Elizabeth Barrie?'

Elizabeth turned back to Jeannie and forced a smile before following Margaret outside into the chill spring afternoon.

# Chapter Seventeen
2014


Mags heard the doorbell and put down her glass. She looked up at the clock. God, it was only five o'clock, Christine would be all judgemental. She hid the wine on a shelf behind the cake tin and rushed to open the door.

'Hello, come in!' She hugged her cousin. 'I'll make some tea.' Mags led the way into the large, airy kitchen and filled the kettle with water.

'Your kitchen is fabulous when it's sunny, Mags. Look at all that light coming through the glass up there. You're so lucky,' said Christine, looking up at the clerestory windows.

'Yeah, the extension was definitely worth it, even though we're still paying off the loan.' Mags laughed. 'And will be for years probably.'

'So what did you find?' Christine asked, folding her coat neatly over her chair.

'Well, I didn't have long. They practically threw me out at four o'clock.'

Mags poured two mugs of tea and filled Christine in on her day's discoveries: Margaret Barrie was officially a pauper and a widow in 1861, and there was no sign of Elizabeth at all before the 1871 census in Strathmartine.

'Oh, I've got a nice lemon cake, want a bit?' Mags lifted down a cake tin from the shelf and opened it.

'Tiny slice please,' said Christine, catching a glimpse of the half glass of red wine on the shelf.

'Chris, you need to eat more, you've got all skinny since the accident. You need to build yourself up.'

Christine shook her head. 'That's what Gerry tells me every single night. Drives me mad!' She sipped her tea. 'So what about her mother, Margaret Barrie then? What does the pauper thing mean?'

'Well, I got the lowdown on what it meant to be officially registered in those days. It was a bit like welfare benefits, help was given towards food and rent. Anyone who was in a really bad way was sent to the poorhouse. Margaret Barrie still lived in her cottage in the village so she must have been given money by someone. Maybe the church helped the poor in the parish in those days.'

'Did you find out anything about her husband? She was a widow so young.'

'I know, terrible isn't it, but since she wasn't sent to the work house, the Inspector of the Poor must've realised it was just a temporary thing. By the 1871 census she was living in the village and was classified as a domestic servant, still a widow and Jane was eleven and living at home.'

'Anything else? Lovely cake, by the way.'

'Came to a bit of a halt, sadly.' Mags downed the last of her tea. 'Glass of wine?'

'No thanks, far too early.'

'Anyway, since I knew he must've died between 1859 and 1861, I started looking at deaths for a David Barrie in Tannadice.'

'Sorry, how did you know when he died?' Christine frowned.

'The baby – Jane – she was one in 1861, by which time David was dead.'

'Yes, of course, sorry, carry on.'

'I couldn't find his death certificate though. But we at least know roughly when we're looking.'

'Christine sipped her tea. 'They're all from Tannadice, can't be that hard, surely.'

'You say that, but look how impossible it's been to find Elizabeth Barrie. We know she must've been born at least nine months before Jane in the April of that year, so why can't we bloody well find her?'

There was a clattering in the hall and Lottie burst through the kitchen door. A young man with large geometric glasses, stood behind her, a small case in his hand.

'Come in, Peter. This is my mum and my Auntie Chris.'

He shook their hands firmly. 'Nice to meet you both.'

'Peter was on my course, he's a piano tuner now.' Lottie looked at her mother. 'Mum, remember Dad mentioned that rattly low F? Peter reckons it sounds as if it might be loose copper on the bass strings.'

'Okay,' said Mags. 'Lottie, can you pop back just for a minute once you've shown Peter into the dining room, please.'

A couple of minutes later, Lottie returned. 'Yup?'

'What about Dennis? Will he not be offended we've got someone else to tune the piano? He's always done it.'

'Don't be daft. Peter's a mate, he'll do it for nothing. And I'm not sure if Dennis is up to much anyway.'

'Is that the blind piano tuner?' Christine asked.

'Yes, we've had him for years.'

'Well, it's kind of like doctors,' said Lottie. 'Sometimes you need a second opinion.' She smiled as she followed the sound of low notes coming from the dining room.

Mags turned back to Christine. 'Where were we? Yeah, so I think we should go to Tannadice, maybe check out the churchyard, see what we can find up there?'

'Alright, how about next weekend?'

'Okay, I'm free either day. Shall we take Mum and Uncle Charlie?'

'No way.' Christine shook her head. 'A quick trip up there'd become an enormous production, walking sticks and toilet stops every ten minutes.'

'Yeah, you're right.'

'We can just take photos then go and see them when we get home, tell them all about it.'

'Cool. I love a road trip.'

Christine looked at her watch. 'I'd better be going, Gerry'll be home soon.'

'Okay,' said Mags. 'And by the way, I meant to ask you, you're not still pursuing this Colin person are you?'

Christine stood up and reached for her coat. 'No. I'm not. Definitely not.'

Half an hour later Peter was finishing up in the dining room.

'Yeah,' he said to Lottie, 'it is a problem with the bass strings. The tone sounds flat, dead, but the piano's really old, not sure I can do much apart from replace the string. Any idea what age it is?'

'No, but it's been in Dad's family for a long time. Mum's family's got one too – it's at my Granny's, even more ancient I think!'

Peter lifted an envelope from the top of his case.

'I found this tucked away inside the back.'

'It looks pretty old.'

'It was covered in dust.'

'And of course Dennis wouldn't have seen it if it was tucked away. Well, thanks for all your help. See you at the concert later.'

After seeing Peter out of the house, Lottie went back into the dining room and opened the envelope. The handwriting looked just like her dad's.

*I just wanted to say how sorry I am this all happened. It shouldn't have, we both know that. There are consequences which can't be ignored. But no one can find out. Ever.*

Lottie scrutinised the letter again; there was no date, no signature, no name on the envelope.

'Lottie, are you staying for dinner?' She could hear Mags coming along the corridor so she shoved the letter into her bag.

'No, Mum,' she shouted. 'Got to head off, seeing Peter later.'

Lottie switched off the lights and rushed towards the front door, handbag clasped to her chest.

# Chapter Eighteen
## 2014

The next morning, Lottie walked into Doug's dental practice on Ferry Road.

'Hello Lottie,' Frances the receptionist looked up from her screen, her smile highlighted by perfectly applied lipstick.

'Hi Frances. Is Dad free?'

'He's with a patient at the moment then his next appointment's a crown so that's a double. Sorry, poppet.'

Lottie bristled. Frances had called her poppet since she was little and she hated it. 'Could I just nip in after this patient for a minute, I only need…'

'Bye, Mrs Mackay, enjoy your holiday!' She heard her father's voice booming down the corridor and saw an elderly lady with a stick heading for the door.

'I'll just nab him now, Frances, if you can delay the next patient,' Lottie said, running into Doug's surgery.

He was chatting with the dental nurse, who was arranging instruments on the tray. In fact, he was flirting with her, even though she only looked about twelve, with her ponytail high on her head.

'Dad, have you got a minute?'

Doug swivelled round and the grin on his face disappeared.

'Is everything okay? Jack all right?'

'I need to speak to you, won't be long. Couple of minutes, tops.'

Doug looked up at the large clock on the wall. 'I've got

two minutes before the next patient, so fire away.'

Lottie nodded at the dental nurse's back.

'Sorry, Amy,' said Doug. 'Would you mind?'

As she closed the door behind her, Lottie removed the letter from her bag and handed it to him. He opened it, glanced up at her then read the note.

'Where did you find this?' His voice was croaky.

'In the piano.'

Doug stretched his head from side to side.

'Dad, stop doing your bloody neck exercises and tell me what this is about.'

'I have absolutely no idea. Who wrote this?'

'It's your writing, Dad!' Lottie jabbed at the paper in Doug's hand.

'It does look a bit like my writing, but I never wrote this, it doesn't make sense.' He stared at it again. 'Maybe it was my dad, his writing was like mine. You wont remember, you were only little when Grandpa died.'

'Dad, you're lying, I can tell,' said Lottie. 'Were you having an affair?'

'What? No, of course not.'

'So what was it then? Drugs? Murder?'

'Don't be ridiculous. I told you, I didn't write this.'

'You're a fucking liar.'

'Lottie, let's not discuss this now. I'm at work. There's nothing else to say. I know nothing about this note. God knows how it got inside the piano.

'I don't believe you. I'm going to tell Mum about this.'

There was a knock at the door then a loud whisper.

'Sorry, Doug, will you be long? Mrs Davidson's anxious about her crown.'

'One minute!' shouted Doug. 'Look, Lotts, please don't

tell Mum. Let me think about it for a bit.' He pocketed the note. 'Something might come back to me.'

Lottie glared at her father. 'Fine. But I want an answer, Dad.' She opened the door and marched out.

Mags sat on the sofa between two of her friends, closed books on their laps. It was their monthly book group and, having fully discussed their latest read, they had moved on to gossip and wine.

'So is that us done with discussing *Big Brother*?' asked Jeanette.

'God, yes, such a depressing read, it'd put you off eating for life!' said Suzanne, sipping from her glass.

Fiona leaned forward for the bottle and passed it round. 'Anyone want tea or coffee or shall I just get more wine?'

'Wine, please. After that book, we need something to dull the memory!' Mags laughed as she downed her glass.

An hour or so later, the book club stalwarts were still there, more sprawled than before. Jeanette took a fistful of salted nuts, chomped noisily then sat up straight and announced, 'So, last night, Ben got home at midnight. Again. And there was a definite smell of perfume this time.' She swigged from her glass as the others stared at her, waiting. This was not the first time they had heard her suspicions.

'I know you all said last time I told you that it must be my imagination, but, well, he can't be in the office every night that late, can he?'

He's chief exec of some huge company and earning millions, Mags mused. Maybe he's actually got to work late so his wife can buy yet another bloody Mulberry handbag.

'Have you confronted him yet?' Suzanne asked.

'What could I say that doesn't make me sound like a

deranged, obsessive wife?'

'Just ask him why he's suddenly working so late and why the hell he smells of perfume.'

The others all chipped in with suggestions but Mags remained silent.

'Don't you agree, Mags?' said Fiona. 'Confrontation is the best policy, isn't it?'

Mags was beginning to feel quite drunk, which normally made her even more garrulous. But though she felt sympathy for Jeanette, she didn't want to get involved. Gossiping about celebs was one thing, but this was someone she knew and it was no one else's business.

'Not sure any of us are in a position to advise,' she said, gulping some wine.

'Just because gorgeous Doug only has eyes for you,' said Suzanne.

Mags didn't say anything. She was so sure that Doug would never stray, she didn't know how to react without sounding smug.

'None of us should take our husbands for granted,' said Jeanette. 'Not even you, Mags.'

'Doug won't even indulge in a bit of playful flirting. Believe me, honey, I've tried!' Fiona cackled. 'Still, I do reckon no marriage is rock solid. Can't trust any of them, all men are bastards. I mean, look what Mike did to me.'

Here she goes, back to her own problems, thought Mags. And if we hear one more time about how the bloody divorce lawyer screwed her over...

'God, is that the time? I'm on the first shuttle to Heathrow tomorrow,' said Suzanne. 'Sorry ladies, got to go.'

At the door, they hugged then headed off up the road.

'Oh, it's my house next time, I'll email you which book

to read!' shouted Mags as she staggered off in the opposite direction.

Mags clumsily inserted her key in the lock and stepped into her dark house, tripping over the doormat as she did so. She switched on the hall light and looked at her watch. Shit, it was already half past twelve. How had that happened? The next day she had to be up first thing to prepare an outside catering buffet she'd agreed to at the last minute. She'd meant to be home by eleven at the latest.

As she locked the door behind her, she remembered Jeanette's comment, directed at her, about not taking husbands for granted. Though she tried to laugh it off, she knew Doug wouldn't stray. God, Doug had even told her, all embarrassed, about Fiona flirting outrageously with him at that dinner; Mags had found it hilarious. But Jeanette's comment lingered; had she heard something from that awful friend of hers, the one who was a dental nurse?

Mags tiptoed into the dining room to put the book back on the shelf. A slice of moonlight cut through the open curtains; the polished rosewood of the piano gleamed. Mags stopped and frowned. Something looked different.

There was red on the keys, a long brushstroke, leaving a narrow trail down the middle of the white notes. Mags touched a key then lifted her finger to her nose. It was blood.

# Chapter Nineteen
1868

'Can I really stay a' day, Ma?' Elizabeth skipped along the road towards the manse beside Margaret Barrie.

'Mind how you're cawin', Elizabeth, you just skelped me wi' yer rope.'

'Sorry, Ma. So, can I stay? Can I?' Her eager, smiling face would melt even the hardest heart.

'Aye, if you behave. You'll gie me a hand in the morning then Miss Charlotte wants you to help her wi' something in the afternoon. Something tae dae wi' the piano.'

Elizabeth beamed, her dark eyes shining. 'So will we tak' oor dinner there an a'?'

'We'll see. Agnes is mindin' Jane at home so we might be able tae.'

They arrived at the tall, wrought-iron gate. As it creaked open, Margaret turned to Elizabeth. 'Put the rope awa' now. Here, put it in my basket. The minister's no' wantin' tae hear bairns playin' when he's writing his sermon.'

Elizabeth gazed at the imposing stone house as she looped her rope into a coil. 'Ma, what's that bird up on the chimney? See how black it is?'

Margaret looked up, squinting against the bright morning sun. 'It's a corbie. There's a poem aboot it.'

'How does it go, Ma?'

Margaret frowned then recited,

*'A corbie sat at the top o' yon tree*
*An he's looking at me wi' his black, black ee*

*An he's crying oot wi his caw caw caw...'*

Elizabeth looked up, expectantly.

'Cannae mind the rest. Yer Pa kenned it a'.' Margaret looked up at the bird.

'I'll ask the dominie to write it doon for me, Ma, when I gang tae school on Monday. I'll learn it for ye.'

Margaret laughed. 'You've got the look o' a corbie yourself, wi your black, black ee.' She headed round the back of the manse towards the kitchen door. 'Come away now, lass and mind good manners if ye want to stay a' day.'

Charlotte Whyte sat down on the piano stool and pulled the skirt of her beige dress up a little so her feet were clear of the heavy silk, resting her heels on the floor in front of the pedals. She pinned a strand of blonde hair into her bun then smoothed down the cream tatted collar around her high neckline.

'Elizabeth, there's something I need you to do when my father has left for the church, please.' She stretched her neck and sat up tall.

The girl sat on a little piano stool alongside and gazed up at her. Miss Charlotte's neck was long, like that swan's the dominie had showed them in the picture book.

'Aye, anything, Miss Charlotte.'

'Try to say yes, not aye, Elizabeth, please. I've told you before how my father is about language.' She sighed and began to leaf through the pages of her music book. 'Which tune would you like now?'

'*While Humble Shepherds Watched Their Flocks.*'

'That's a Christmas one,' Charlotte said, smiling, 'but I can play it for you. Why do you like it?'

'It's got the angel and the shepherds and the sheep and the dominie telt us there was a big star too.'

'There certainly was.' Charlotte stroked Elizabeth's curls. 'I shall play this one for you then it will be my choice next. Is that agreed?'

'Aye, er, yes, thank you, Miss Charlotte.'

Elizabeth stared at Charlotte's long elegant fingers as she started to play. She lifted her hands in front of her and stretched out her stubby fingers, calloused from work.

Charlotte's back was rigid and her head did not move as she concentrated on reading the music. She had just started the last verse when the door was flung open. Charlotte looked round and Elizabeth jumped down off the stool.

'Is it Christmas already?' boomed a sonorous voice.

'No, Father, but it was Elizabeth's request.' Charlotte pushed her skirt down so that her ankles were covered.

'Oh, was it now.' Charlotte's father – tall, gaunt and dressed all in black – glowered at her. 'Perhaps you could play something more appropriate,' he said, sneering at Elizabeth's tattered dun dress and scuffed boots. 'Charlotte, do you have the music for *Dear Lord and Father of Mankind*? The new hymn I told you about. You are forever trying to persuade me to introduce new hymns.' He stood in the doorway, his balding head almost touching the lintel.

Charlotte reached for the pile of music on top of the piano and lifted out a sheet. 'I have it here, Father. Would you like to stay while I play?'

'No, I would not. I did not come here with the luxury of time to spare. As ever, there are many parish matters to which I must attend. It was but the sound of the piano that drew me here. It would be fitting if both of you listen not only to the music but to the words of this hymn.' He strode over to Charlotte, snatched the music from her and read aloud, 'Dear Lord and Father of Mankind, forgive our foolish ways, re-clothe us in our rightful minds, in purer lives our service find.' He looked up from the page and continued, each sibilant S a hissing sound as he bared his long teeth. 'And in the last verse there is such judicious choice of language in these exhortations for our daily lives.' He peered at Charlotte and Elizabeth, his haughty gaze never leaving them as he recited the rest from memory. 'Breathe through the heat of our desire, thy coolness and thy balm.'

Charlotte stared down at the ivory keys. Elizabeth's dark eyes, too, were downcast. She stared at the black chenille tablecloth. The grandfather clock struck two.

'I must be on my way. It pleases me that you are teaching the child hymns and psalms.' He turned towards the door then addressed the room, reaching for the handle. 'Tell Cookie I shall be back for tea. Farewell.'

The front door slammed and Elizabeth sidled back onto her stool. The sheet of music was trembling in Charlotte's hand.

'Are you going to play that one, Miss?'

Charlotte looked down at the yellowed keys then took a deep breath. She threw the sheet of paper on top of the piano. 'No, I am not,' said Charlotte. 'Now that Father has gone, I can indulge in another piece. But first I need you to stretch your arm along the back of the piano to retrieve the music I hid down there last week when Father came in here unexpectedly.'

Elizabeth leapt up and went to the back of the piano. She stretched her arm along the wall behind the piano. She strained and shut her eyes, forcing her arm further.

'Got it!' she cried triumphantly, withdrawing her arm and presenting Charlotte with her sheet music.

'Thank you, Elizabeth. I have attempted several times to extract this but could not succeed.' She shuffled upright on her stool, yanked her skirt up over her ankles then turned her head towards Elizabeth. 'You are in for a treat, dear child. Chopin's Etude, opus 10, number 5.' She turned the page to open it. 'I do hope I am not very much out of practice.'

Elizabeth stared at Charlotte's long neck and at her profile, the neat snub nose and the dimple in her cheek. She ran her finger along her own nose, wishing it were as pretty as Charlotte's. She poked a forefinger into her cheek, then smiled and her eyes lit up as she found a tiny dimple in the plump flesh.

'I shall nod when I need the page turned, Elizabeth. Is that understood?'

'Yes, Miss,' she said, beaming.

Charlotte leant forward and began to play. As the music progressed from playful to fiery, her expression changed from one of deep concentration to one of pleasure. The crescendo increased towards the climax and she closed her eyes and stretched back her head.

The final bars rang out, the tumbling sound of the octave scale passage loud and passionate. Charlotte kept her eyes shut for what seemed like forever. Then she turned to Elizabeth and whispered, 'Is that not the most beautiful piece of music?' She was breathless.

The room had changed. It had been cold before, but Elizabeth felt a fire had just been lit and she was sitting directly beside the flames.

'Yes it is, Miss, that was fine, really fine.'

Charlotte smiled and leant towards Elizabeth. She held her rosy cheeks between her palms and was about to give her a kiss when the door opened.

They both turned to see Margaret Barrie standing there, rigid. 'Excuse me, Miss, it's time to take Elizabeth home.' She gestured to Elizabeth to join her at the door, her face sombre.

'Oh, Margaret, I'd hoped to take her to the kirk while I practise the organ for Sunday.'

'That willnae be possible, Miss.' She nodded to Elizabeth. 'Out now, go and fetch your bonnet frae the kitchen.'

Charlotte stood up to her full height at the piano.

'I thought it was just psalms you were playing for her, Miss?'

'Psalms, hymns and other things, Margaret. There is surely no harm in that?'

'As long as you play music for her that your father would approve of, Miss,' Margaret said, a sour expression on her face.

'Yes, Margaret.' Charlotte sighed and removed the music from the stand.

Margaret slammed the door behind her as she left.

# Chapter Twenty
## 2014

'Why did the farmers decide to ruin the landscape with all those fields of rapeseed?' Christine sneezed as she looked out her window at the passing mass of yellow.

'I know, hideous isn't it,' said Mags. 'What would they have grown here in the past?'

'Well, the flax for Dundee's linen industry was all grown locally, here in Angus.'

'Flax flowers are that gorgeous blue colour, aren't they? That must have looked awesome, fields of blue everywhere.'

They came to a signpost and Mags veered left. 'Let's stop for a coffee in Forfar. I've got some brownies with me if the baking's rubbish.'

'You can't take your own food into a café, Mags,' Christine tutted.

'Watch me,' said Mags, parking the car.

As they walked towards the coffee shop, Mags said, 'I keep meaning to ask you this, Chris. Now that Jack's doing so much better, are you going to stop pursuing that man from Pontyprydd who drove into them?'

'Pontefract, Mags. Colin Clarkson. Yes, I told you already I'm going to let it go. Always hated the name Colin anyway.' Christine sighed. 'Jack still gets pretty tired. It's taken its toll, you know. And he's still got a bit of a limp. Every time I see him it breaks my heart.'

Mags couldn't read the expression on Chris's face; she had no idea if she would really stop this quest for revenge. But she'd had enough of pandering to her bossy cousin's moods since the accident. She'd always been a bit obsessive, but now she was almost paranoid about that Clarkson man. And her constant fretting about Jack had to stop. Most of it was in her imagination, he'd hardly any limp at all.

And Chris never asked how Mags was doing. Mags thought this trip might be the time to talk about her own worries over her cake business. Or even tell her about the drunken discussion at book club, but she doubted Chris would be interested; she'd become totally self-absorbed.

Inside the café, Mags peered at the cakes in the glass stand. 'Are the scones freshly baked today?'

'Not sure. Think so. If not I can heat one up for you. Butter and jam?' The young girl gave her a look her mum would have described as 'glaikit'.

'Er, no thanks, just a coffee for me, please' Mags turned to Christine. 'You want something to eat?'

'Just a coffee. You go and get a seat, Mags, I'll get these.'

Mags wandered over to the window table and sat down. She watched Christine take out a bottle of water from her handbag, pop something in her mouth and tip her head back as she swigged down the water. Mags idly flicked through the local newspaper that was in front of her.

Christine arrived with the coffee and sat down.

'You okay, Chris? Saw you popping pills just now.'

'Oh, just a bit of a headache, good old Nurofen,' she said, patting her handbag as she placed it down beside her. 'Anyway, here's the coffee. I don't hold out much hope for it though.'

Mags delved into her capacious basket and brought out a foil package and started to open it.

'You're not going to eat your brownies in here, are you?' Christine whispered.

'I sure am. There's no way those scones are fresh, they look as tired as the fruit cake.' Mags handed her cousin a square of brownie.

Christine looked around and took a surreptitious bite.

'Mmm, gorgeous. What's in these ones?'

'Cardamom. Good aren't they? I know you like the clove ones but they're too Christmassy for June.' Mags flicked open the property section in The Forfar Dispatch on the table as she slurped her coffee.

Christine took out her Ordnance Survey map and unfolded it. 'What was that place you said had a good pub for lunch?'

'The Drovers Inn in Memus, it's meant to have great food and...' Mags stared at the paper more closely. 'Bloody hell, look at this,' she said, pointing to a photo. 'The Old Steading, by Tannadice, one bedroom, one bathroom, one kitchenette. Offers over ninety thousand.' She looked up at Christine. 'Pretty cheap isn't it? Imagine the equivalent size in Edinburgh, it'd be three times that!'

Christine was staring at the photo of the house.

Mags sat up in her seat and beamed. 'Let's go and see it after we've been to the cemetery.'

'Why?'

'Because Doug's family used to own it! His parents bought it as a holiday cottage, to get away from their surgeries and patients in Aberdeen. In fact, Doug and I used to go there from Dundee when he could borrow his flatmate's car.' She smirked. 'Scene of many a dirty weekend.' Mags tilted her head back and chuckled. 'God, Chris, not seen you bite your nails for ages.'

'I know, sorry, disgusting habit.' Christine stood up. 'Let's get some fresh air, it's too stuffy in here.'

Mags coughed loudly as she tore the page out of the paper and slipped it into her basket.

'You can't do that,' Christine hissed.

Mags ignored her and headed for the door. 'Nothing to do with being stuffy,' she whispered, 'it's the pot I put in the brownies working its magic already!'

Christine glared at her cousin.

'God, woman. Chill! I was joking.' Mags laughed. 'You take life way too seriously!'

Ten minutes later they turned off the main road at a sign that read Tannadice.

'How will we know where the graveyard is, Mags?'

'If we blink we'll be through the village, can't be that hard. There's the church, let's park there.'

Mags edged into a space and switched off the engine.

'Did you have time to Google it?' asked Christine.

'Yes, this building's from 1846 but there's been a church here for centuries so there'll be old graves too.'

They got out and crossed over the road towards the church.

'Not exactly buzzing, is it?' Mags said, looking down the deserted road.

'It would've been so different in Elizabeth Barrie's day,' Christine said, pushing open the gate to the graveyard.

Yew trees lined the wall along one side of the pathway. When they came to the church, they stood looking south towards a large grassy area of gravestones, many sloping forwards, bent with age.

'Not too crowded is it?' said Mags.

'Well, no, I suppose not, but it's a huge graveyard for such a tiny village.'

'It would've served all the surrounding area, the parish is probably enormous,' said Mags, leaning down to inspect a headstone.

'Let's split up to look for any Barrie graves. I'll go down to that area down there, though the stones all look more modern than these ones.' Christine crunched along the gravel path, stopping to inspect the headstones along the way. Mags removed her jacket and tied the sleeves round her waist. The sun was beginning to peek out from the clouds and warm the spring air. At the back of the churchyard, the trees cast long shadows across the weathered stones. She began to find recurring family names, many Craiks, Andersons, Robbies and Mitchells. There were no Barries.

Along the fence at the back, nearest the church, were two large family crypts, with iron gates, padlocked with heavy chains. Mags peered into these and saw that they were all Nicolls, presumably one wealthy family.

Most of the people in these grand crypts lived to about eighty years, though one child had died aged four. As she moved back towards the smaller graves for the poor, she realised that they lived to only about sixty, seventy maximum.

There was a lone headstone on the other side of the gravel path. Mags stooped down to read it and immediately shouted for Chris. 'Come here, look what I've found!' Mags beamed as she got out her notebook and pencil and started to scribble.

Christine hurried over, and Mags pointed to the inscription on the stone. 'Barries. We've found them at last.'

'There's three of them in there,' said Christine, then read aloud in her teacher voice, 'In Memory of John Barrie, died at Corrie, 16th January 1855, aged sixty-eight years. Also of his wife Lorna Mackie, died at Corrie, 3rd July 1860, aged sixty and of their son David Barrie.'

'That's Elizabeth's father, isn't it?' Mags interrupted.

'Think so,' said Christine. 'David Barrie died at Tannadice, 25th June 1860, aged thirty-nine years.'

'God, he died young. And just a month before his mother. Is that not strange?' Mags thrust her pencil through the bun at the back of her head.

'An unfortunate coincidence, maybe. Are there any more Barries up here? I couldn't find any.'

'Just got those ones over there to check,' she said, pointing.

The two women wandered over to a cluster of three crumbling gravestones close together and then towards a grand headstone ornamented with a panel and a large cross.

Christine read, 'In memory of Maud Euphemia Whyte, wife of the Reverend Charles William Whyte, died at The Manse, Tannadice, 4th June 1860, aged fifty-seven. Also of their daughter Charlotte Ann Whyte, died at The Manse, 27th March 1871, aged thirty. And of the Reverend Charles William Whyte, Minister at Tannadice, who died at The Manse, 22nd August, 1889, aged eighty-four.'

'No wonder this is such an impressive headstone and so near the church,' said Mags. 'God, the poor man. His wife and daughter died so young.'

'Awful,' said Christine. 'And the wife died in 1860 as well, same as David Barrie and his mother. D'you think there was maybe some disease going around – typhoid or something?'

Mags shrugged and Christine continued, 'I suppose there was always some danger lurking, they died of a bad cold in those days, didn't they. No sign of Margaret Barrie,

Elizabeth's mother?'

'Maybe they didn't bury paupers in churchyards,' said Mags. 'I'll ask my new best friend when we go back to Register House. Anyway, at least we know roughly when Elizabeth Barrie must've been born since her father died in June 1860.'

They stood on the path, looking from the simple Barrie gravestone to the minister's grandiose monument.

'What's that flower engraved beside Charlotte Whyte's name, Mags?' Christine pointed to a floral design.

'Looks like lily of the valley. What do you reckon?'

'Yes, think you're right. Wonder what that symbolised in Victorian times.'

'Something else to research, we can Google it at lunch,' said Mags, pulling the pencil from her hair and scribbling once more on her notebook.

'Are we finished here?'

'Reckon so, just let me take some photos of the Barrie grave and then we'll go check out the Old Steading.'

Christine headed for the gate.

'Oh, I'm going to take a photo of the minister's grave too, in case the lily of the valley means anything. Awesome, isn't it?'

'Told you, Mags!'

'Do we have to go to this house?' Christine sat down in the passenger seat and strapped in.

'Yeah, I want to go, old times' sake for Doug and me. I'm pretty sure I'll remember the way, but we always came from the other way, from the Dundee-Aberdeen road. Let's have a look at your map.'

Christine unfurled the Ordnance Survey map and Mags

traced the route from Tannadice.

'Yeah, that's where we'll go off the main road. See, we used to come in from here. We parked at the end of the track and walked. I've no idea if you can drive now.'

Mags handed the large expanse of map back to Christine and started driving.

'But surely there must be someone living there,' Christine said, folding up the map. 'We can't just pop in.'

Mags shrugged. 'Let's see.'

They drove slowly for a few minutes south-east then Mags came to a halt. 'Check the map, Chris, would you. Is the turn-off before or after that bridge?'

'Hang on, um, after I think. It's here, there's the track!'

'So it is, and looks like you still can't drive along there. I'll park on the verge and we can walk.'

Mags beamed at Christine and jumped out of the car. 'Cheer up, woman. Why do you look so bloody miserable?'

'Sorry Mags, my hay fever's bothering me,' she said, sneezing. 'Must be the rapeseed everywhere.'

They set off along the track and soon came to a clearing. The vegetation underfoot was damp and Christine looked down at her feet. 'I'm going to ruin my suede shoes, do we have to keep going?'

'Not much further,' Mags said.

Christine nodded and set off to her right.

'No it's this way, between those two trees over there. I'm sure I remember it being there.'

'Oh, okay,' said Christine, stepping gingerly over the wet grass to join Mags who was inhaling deeply.

'Can you smell the wild garlic, Chris?' Mags pointed to the plants all around. 'Did you know, the leaves are the same as lily of the valley, but there's one difference: the lily's are deadly poisonous.'

They picked their way towards the trees, but there was no sign of a cottage. 'Oh, wait,' said Mags, 'it must be the other way, my memory's shot.'

They walked back to the clearing then off to the right. 'Look,' said Mags. 'There it is. It's so cute, like a gingerbread house in the woods.'

'Lets just hope there's no witch inside.'

The little stone cottage was a perfect oblong, with two little chimneys poking up at either end. It looked like something a child would draw if asked to paint a cottage. There was a wooden door in the middle and two windows, with chipped grey paint, on either side. A vine grew up one side, creeping up and over the low doorway.

'That's an impressive climbing rose,' said Mags. 'It must be pretty old, it's so thick and gnarled. I wonder if it still flowers.'

'Well,' said Christine. 'You've seen the cottage. Can we go back now?'

Mags ignored her cousin and rapped gently on the door. When there was no answer, she peered close into the window, palms of her hands at the side of her head, outstretched against the pane.

'There's no one in,' she said. 'It looks so different. They had furniture from Doug's gran's house in it before. It was like entering a time warp, stepping back to the 1930s.'

'Let's go. I'm peckish.'

'Christine Duncan, I don't think I've ever heard you say you're hungry in your life. I'm always the one who's ravenous. But fine, let's go. I can't wait to tell Doug about this.'

Christine immediately strode back towards the clearing,

but stopped when she realised Mags wasn't with her. She circled round to the back of the house, where she found Mags standing at the foot of a huge, knotted oak tree.

'I just remembered about this enormous tree. They kept saying they'd chop it down because it made the back room so dark. There used to be a swing or something on it.'

Christine looked up through the sturdy branches and slender twigs to the sky.

'No,' said Mags, grinning. 'I remember now, it was a tree house.' She pointed to a couple of rotting planks of wood wedged between the branches. 'There's the remnants of it there. It used to be a proper little house, a tiny tree house. Doesn't look in good shape now though, what a pity.'

'Must have been a storm,' said Christine starting to walk away.

Mags joined her, 'Yeah, when was that? Late eighties?'

'1989 here in Scotland. Down south it was '87,' said Christine staring straight ahead as they strolled towards the clearing.

'Amazing the facts you teachers have at your fingertips,' said Mags, looking at her watch. 'Right, I'm going to phone Doug when we get to the pub and tell him about it. He'll be so excited, he might even want to buy it!'

They arrived at the Drovers Inn pub and parked in the large car park. The sun was now blazing in a cloudless blue sky.

'It's turned into a gorgeous day, hasn't it?' said Mags. 'Let's sit outside,'

'Right, why don't you grab this table, then? I'll get us drinks at the bar.'

'Diet coke for me, please.'

When Christine was gone, Mags delved into her basket for her phone and tapped in Doug's number. While she waited for him to answer, she put on her sunglasses and sat with her face raised towards the bright sun.

'Doug, hi, just a quick call. Guess where we went today? The Old Steading in the woods, remember?'

She nodded thanks at Christine who had just put down a coke in front of her.

'Yeah, it's up for sale so we thought we'd check it out, hasn't changed a bit. Well, inside it has, but that huge tree's still there in the garden with the tree house, it's all wrecked now though... What? Yeah, of course Chris was with me. Okay, I'll see you later. Love you.'

Mags ended the call and smiled at Christine. 'I still think it's amazing we saw the remnants of that little tree house. I used to have this dream, long before Doug and I were even married, that we'd take our kids there to play in the woods. I must've read too many Swallows and Amazons books; Dad used to have the whole set at home, remember?'

'And did you?' Christine asked without lifting her eyes from the menu.

'Did I what?'

'You and Doug, did you take Lottie there?'

'Yeah, we took Lotts up a couple of times when she was a toddler. We kept saying we'd repair the tree house but never got round to it. Doug loved it there though.' She smiled and picked up the menu. 'Right, what looks good?'

'I fancy the asparagus tart with salad.'

'Oh, good shout, it'll probably be from that farm down the road. I noticed a sign when we passed.'

Christine got out her phone and began to Google. 'I'm checking what lily of the valley signifies on a Victorian grave.'

'Good idea.' Mags pressed her thumbs to her temples. 'Can I have one of your Nurofen, I can feel a headache coming on.' She stretched out her hand.

Christine opened her mouth to speak but instead leant down to pick up her bag, and rummaged inside. 'Sorry, I must have had the last one in the café.'

'Never mind. Maybe some food will help. I'm just going to nip to the loo.'

Christine watched until Mags was inside the pub then abandoned Google to write a text, typing and pressing 'send' quickly. She then returned to Google.

'I gave the man at the bar our order,' said Mags, sitting down. 'Did you find anything?'

'Here we go,' said Christine squinting in the sun. 'Lily of the valley on Victorian gravestones symbolised innocence, purity and virginity.'

'Oh, bless her, her father must have wanted that on her grave. How sad.' Mags tore off a crust of bread. 'Maybe the Victorians didn't know the leaves are also lethal.'

Christine's phone vibrated. She glanced at it then slipped it into a zipped pocket in her bag.

'Bring on the food!' said Mags. 'I am bloody ravenous!'

# Chapter Twenty-one
1866

Elizabeth sat on a high stool at the manse's kitchen table podding peas, her grubby feet dangling as she bent her head over the trug. She put down an empty pod and turned to the elderly woman standing at the stove.

'Cookie, can I eat just one pea?'

'If you say please, I might let you.'

Cookie walked over towards the child who was mouthing 'please,' and tickled the back of her neck. 'You can even have two, Elizabeth.'

'Thanks, Cookie!' she said, picking up two tiny peas, one in each chubby hand. She popped them into her mouth one after the other and smiled. Her dark eyes glinted in the sunlight that was flooding through the window.

'Come on, you've got to carry on podding those peas, lassie, or the Minister and Miss Charlotte willnae hae anything to eat for their lunch.'

There was a knock at the back door and in walked Margaret Barrie. She wiped her feet on the mat, removed her bonnet and dropped it on a chair at the door.

'Hello Elspeth, I hope Elizabeth's behaving?'

'Come away in, Margaret,' said Cookie, 'she's podding peas for the Minister's lunch."

'It's awfie good of you to have her here. You'd say if she got in your way, wouldn't you?'

'Margaret, it's a pleasure, she's guid company.'

'Why've you no' got yer shoes on, Elizabeth? You look like an urchin!' Margaret pointed at her feet, mucky with soil.

'Och, she's fine. She was helping Grieve oot in the garden.'

'Aye well, you let me know if she's too much trouble.'

'You ken Miss Charlotte likes when she's around. She wanted her to go to the drawing room wi' her this afternoon and hear her piano practice. She's got a recital in the kirk hall next week and she's been practising a' day long.'

'Oh, please, Cookie!'

'I dinnae think that's suitable, Elspeth. Look at the state o' her.'

'Dinnae be daft, Margaret. I'll gie her feet a good scrub in the big sink an' put her shoes on again. It'll dae her good and the Minister's to be oot all afternoon.'

Elizabeth swivelled round and looked at Margaret. 'Please, Ma. Please?'

'Well, if Mrs Anderson disnae mind, then that's fine. It'd gie me more time for my work. Thanks Elspeth.'

'Ma, why d'you call Cookie Elspeth?'

'Because that's her name, Elizabeth. And you shouldnae be calling her Cookie. It's Mrs Anderson to you.'

'Leave her alone, Margaret, I'm fine wi' Cookie. Besides, Miss Charlotte used to call me that when she was a bairn. She still does sometimes, I like it.'

Margaret scowled then said to the child, 'Just dinnae call her that when the Minister's around.'

'Nae chance o' that, Margaret, he never comes into my kitchen.' Cookie wiped her hands on her apron and retied the knot round her ample waist.

'Just as well.' Margaret sidled up to the Cookie and whispered, 'I saw him last week glaring oot the windae as the bairn came to meet me at the gate. He looked like the devil himself standing there in his black. You'd no let her oot o' yer sight, would ye?'

'Dinnae be daft, Margaret, he's…'

The door at the far end of the kitchen swung open. A slim young woman, wearing a long, cornflower-blue dress and matching ribbon in her wispy blonde hair stood at the entrance.

She nodded at both women then turned towards the large table. 'So, Elizabeth, how are you today? Are you helping Mrs Anderson prepare my lunch?'

'Aye, am podding the peas frae the garden and…'

'Elizabeth, get doon from there and greet Miss Charlotte properly, like I telt ye,' Margaret scolded.

The child hopped down from the stool and bobbed in front of Charlotte, who laughed and said, 'My, you make me feel like Her Majesty the Queen herself.'

Charlotte picked up a couple of peas from the bowl and popped them into her mouth. 'There is nothing like fresh peas, is there. A quintessential taste of summer, don't you think, ladies?' They hesitated then nodded in unison as she continued, 'So Margaret, is it convenient if I keep Elizabeth after lunch and play her some music?'

'Aye, Miss, I suppose that'll be fine. She'll put her shoes on, she willnae bring any dirt into the house.'

'Good.' Charlotte straightened her back and looked out the window to the garden. 'Why doesn't Grieve walk her home once he has finished in the garden?'

'If Grieve disnae mind.' Margaret stood at the door, sullen.

Since Charlotte didn't say anything further, Margaret picked up her bonnet, knotted the ties under her chin, and opened the back door. 'See you later, Elizabeth. Mind an' behave!'

After the door had closed behind Margaret, Charlotte turned to Cookie and clasped her hands together at her waist. 'You know Margaret rather well, I believe. It is not something I can ask her myself, but do you think she would mind if I started teaching Elizabeth the basic elements of proper speech? I already try to correct her when we are alone together, simply trying to eliminate all these ungainly ayes and dinnaes from her vocabulary.'

'I'm sure that will be fine, Miss. Oh, look at the time, your father wanted lunch at a quarter to one today as he has a funeral at two o'clock. I should be getting on.'

'Well, I shall see you after lunch then,' Charlotte said to Elizabeth, leaning down to stroke her cheek gently with the back of her fingers. 'Such soft skin.'

Elizabeth's eyes looked larger than ever as she gazed up at Charlotte. 'Thank you, Miss Charlotte,' she said, clambering back up onto the stool. 'Will you learn me the piano too?'

'Will I *teach* you the piano, Elizabeth?' Charlotte's eyebrows arched. 'Yes, indeed I shall. It would give me great pleasure.'

Elizabeth stared as Charlotte swept out of the door, her dress swishing against the wooden frame, before turning back to the trug full of peas on the table.

# Chapter Twenty-two
2014

Lottie sat at the kitchen table watching her mother kneading bread. Mags pressed down the dough with the heel of her hands, turned and lifted it, then slapped it back on the table to begin again.

'I don't see why you bake your own when that new baker just down the road's got the best bread in town. Even you said so, Mum.'

'I know, their sourdough's awesome, but your dad's always loved my homemade bread and I thought I'd try to be nice to him. He's so stressed at the moment, I don't know if it's that extra batch of NHS patients on his list or what.'

'Well, it's what he's paid for, Mum. And bloody well paid compared to lots of other people.' Lottie went over to the kettle and flicked it on. 'Cup of tea?'

Mags nodded and plopped the dough into a large bowl. She covered it with a tea towel and took it to the airing cupboard.

'True,' she said, shutting the cupboard door, 'and thank God. I mean, the little I get for my cakes and things, I could hardly support anyone.'

'Exactly. And I've only got about twenty pounds left till the end of the month.'

'Darling, I can give you some.'

Lottie filled the mugs from the kettle. 'No, it's fine, I should get my cheque from Mrs Hardy tomorrow, she's owed me for Dan's lessons for about three weeks now.'

Mags removed a plaster from a fingertip and stared at a small cut. 'That's healed up nicely, but I'm always terrified blood gets into my cakes.'

'Mum, that's gross.'

Mags folded her plaster over and flung it into the bin. 'Speaking of which, do you know of any reason why I might find blood on the piano, Lotts?'

'Where on the piano?'

'I found a long streak of blood all down the white keys the other night. Didn't like to ask Dad in case he got even more stroppy with me.'

'Show me?'

In the dining room Lottie sat down on the piano stool and raised her hands over the keys. 'Which notes?'

Mags pointed at Middle C then ran her fingers up the white notes a couple of octaves. 'Somewhere about here?'

Lottie stood up and lifted the lid of the piano stool where the music was kept. She rifled through the sheet music and, after selecting something, sat back down and raised her hands over the keys again.

After a few bars, Lottie turned her right hand to the side, so her palm was uppermost, laid her fingertips on the keys and slid her fingers up two octaves. She played, using the same movement of her hand after another few bars, nodding at her mum. After a couple of minutes, she finished and sat back, shoulders relaxed.

Mags stood smiling, as she always did when her daughter played.

'It's the glissandi, Mum. Dad goes berserk when he plays a glissando in this Debussy prelude. I've noticed his fingertips bleeding before. I told him he should change technique and do it like this.' Lottie demonstrated the same movement but with her thumbnail. 'But he insisted on doing it his way, using his fingertips, so the top knuckles bleed. Though it's a long time since I've seen him do that. Last time was ages ago when he was in a foul mood.'

'A bit like how he's been for the past few days,' Mags said. 'So does this bleeding fingers thing happen to everyone who plays that Debussy piece?'

'No, it depends how sensitive your fingertips are, and Dad's are really sensitive. That's why I didn't think he ever played this piece now. Wouldn't look good delving into a patient's mouth with scabby fingers, even with those plastic gloves on.'

Mags looked down at her hands and wiggled her fingers. 'Never realised that about glissandos.'

'Glissandi,' Lottie corrected, raising an eyebrow. 'They're usually played from top to bottom but Debussy was always a bit different. Do you not remember that undergrad concert you and Dad came to and I'd to go on after Phoebe Begbie playing her Debussy? She'd left so much blood on the piano I had to wipe it off with my sleeve before I could start. It was disgusting.'

'I've never noticed blood like that after Dad's played though.'

'He must be especially stressed right now. It's really satisfying doing one, just bloody painful.'

'Reckon I'll stick to cakes,' said Mags, heading back towards the kitchen. 'Wish I knew what's bugging your dad though, Lotts.'

Christine walked up the steps to Register House and turned to look at the imposing statue of the Duke of Wellington on his rearing horse below. She heard someone calling her name and looked up to see Mags standing at the front door, waving at her. Well, that must be a first, she thought, Mags arriving before her. She trotted up the final steps and hugged her cousin.

'Fancy a quick coffee first?' Mags asked. 'We need to discuss our strategy.'

Christine pulled back her sleeve and checked the time. 'Well, it's only just after ten, but yes, okay, a quick one. We need to chat about that funeral Dad and Auntie Peggy want us to go to.'

'Whose is it again?'

'Their second cousin, I think. Jimmy someone. Never met him.'

The two women made their way to the café.

'And it's this Saturday?' asked Mags.

'Yes,' said Christine.

'We won't know many people,' said Mags. 'Auntie Bella will be there though, I imagine. She's a hoot.'

'Yes, larger than life, isn't she? She used to smoke a pipe.'

'And I can still remember at a family party not long after I got married – think it was Mum and Dad's silver wedding or something – she asked me if I actually enjoyed sex. I was so stunned I couldn't reply but she carried on regardless and told me she never really liked it but put up with it till her husband had that operation.' Mags burst out laughing. 'Way too much information!'

Christine smiled and spooned up the foam from her cappuccino, then placed the spoon neatly on the saucer. 'Right, let's drink these quickly then get to work!'

An hour later, Mags turned to Christine at the next

computer.

'Why the hell can't we find her birth certificate? Did she actually exist?'

'I don't know. I suppose she might have been born in England, or Canada even. How on earth would we find her then? What've you been typing in?'

'Just Elizabeth Barrie and her parents' names, but I've been trying further afield than Tannadice and Dundee. Still nothing.'

'Unless they weren't both her parents? Did they go in for adoption in those days?'

'No idea.' Mags leant back against her chair and looked up to the ceiling. 'I'll try searching for Elizabeths in the general area around Tannadice.'

Ten minutes later she prodded Christine's arm. 'Look,' she hissed. 'Read that!'

Christine peered over and read out loud, '1860 births, Parish of Oathlaw in the County of Forfar. Surname Whyte. Name of baby Elizabeth, born February 29th at Corrie.' She looked at Mags and shrugged. 'So? Still no Barrie. Why do you think this is connected to…'

Mags jabbed the screen with her finger. 'Here, look. Name of father – David Barrie, farm servant. And then right below it says illegitimate. God, look what's written here at the side, Chris.'

In the left hand margin, written in the same hand, was an extra paragraph. It looked out of place: none of the other babies registered had anything written there.

*In an action relating to the paternity of a female child born 29th February 1860 named Elizabeth Barrie at the insistence of Charlotte Whyte of Corrie, Parish of Oathlaw, against*

*David Barrie, farm servant, Tannadice. The Sheriff Court of
Forfar on the 4th day of June 1860 found that the said child
was the illegitimate child of the parties aforesaid. Signed George
Stewart, Registrar. June 18ᵗʰ, 1860.*

Mags smiled at her cousin. 'Reckon your dad was right,
Chris. That must be the secret!'

'Yes, but hang on, something's ringing bells about the
name. The mother's name is Charlotte Whyte, and it's
an unusual spelling. Was that not the name on the grave
with the lily of the valley? She was the minister's daughter,
remember?'

'God, yeah, but don't be daft, it can't be the same person.
I mean, what are the chances of a farm labourer having it
off with the minister's daughter in those days.' Mags shook
her head. 'We should try to find David Barrie's death
certificate next.'

The search did not take long.

*Death certificate 1860*
*Name: David Barrie, male*
*Address: The Village, Tannadice*
*Parent's names: John Barrie, farmer, deceased and Lorna
Barrie née Mackie*
*Spouse name: Margaret Barrie, née Harris*
*When died: June 25ᵗʰ 1860, Tannadice, Parish of Oathlaw*
*Cause of death: acute kidney failure as a consequence of
accidental poisoning*
*Buried in Tannadice Churchyard*
*Signed George Stewart, Registrar*

'Poisoning! God, I need another coffee. Let's go over to the Balmoral and have one there, at least it'll be made from proper beans.'

'Unbelievable,' said Christine, grabbing her coat.

# Chapter Twenty-three
## 2014

The wind had picked up since earlier, canopies were flapping over shops and everyone was rushing, heads bent down towards the pavement. The flag above the Balmoral Hotel's grand entrance was taut against the freezing easterly wind. Mags and Christine hurried through the revolving door and into the hotel lobby, a haven of calm from the storm. The concierge smiled. 'Can I help you, ladies?'

'Yes, please, where do we go for coffee?' Christine tucked her hair behind her ears and smoothed down her skirt.

'Up the stairs straight ahead.'

'Thanks,' said Mags. 'Could you please let Trish Hay in HR know that her friend Mags is in there? In case she has time to pop in and see us.'

'Certainly, Madam.'

Trish was an old school friend of Mags, who had recently moved back to Edinburgh from London.

They had just ordered coffee when a tall woman with flame-red hair rushed in.

'Mags, hi!' she said, embracing her friend. 'And Christine Duncan, look at you, you've not changed a bit!'

Christine smiled. 'Think that's a slight exaggeration, Trish. It's been about thirty years! It's good to see you.'

Trish leant in towards them and whispered, 'I was just hearing some gossip from the receptionist about an American businessman – mega rich of course – who's a regular guest here, no names obviously...' She looked round at Mags and paused, as if for dramatic effect. 'Anyway, he has his mistress staying with him for three nights; she arrives with him at the weekend. But he insists she's not to be registered, no passport, nothing. Then she leaves on the morning of the fourth day and that very same afternoon his wife arrives and stays another five nights, same suite and everything!'

'Bloody hell, what if someone had said something?' Mags said.

'He'd already asked the manager to brief the staff to say nothing about his previous guest to his wife and because he's a platinum card holder, everyone has to respect his wishes.'

Mags looked amazed. 'But how could he keep that from his wife?' She shook her head. 'Bastard!'

'I know! Men!' Trish smiled. 'Anyway, how's your handsome husband, Mags?'

'Oh, fine. Bit fatter than he was but just the same old Doug. Do you want to sit down and join us?'

Trish shook her head. 'I'm meeting the boss in ten minutes.' She stood back to let the waiter serve their coffees. 'How about a glass of bubbly too?'

'Oh yes, please,' said Mags, beaming.

'Well, we've got to get back to Register House soon, it's just a quick break and…'

'For God's sake, woman, chill,' Mags snapped at Christine.

Trish perched on the arm of Mags's leather armchair and waved to the barman who came to take her order.

'And the kids? How's Lottie? I've forgotten how many you have, Chris.'

'Two. Jack and Anna.'

Mags reached into her basket for her phone. 'I've got some photos here.'

'How's your mum?' asked Trish, as Mags scrolled through the photo album on her phone.

'She's great, thanks, just the same. Never misses a trick. When I said you were back in town, she wanted to know if you can still do the splits!'

Trish burst out laughing. 'I've not tried for some time, but I'll let you know. Right, who's who?'

Mags pointed to Lottie in the first picture then flicked to a photo of Lottie with Jack and Anna.

'Is that Doug's sister's son?' asked Trish.

'No, that's Jack, Chris and Gerry's son.'

Trish squinted at the photo. 'Oh. Something about the eyes reminded me of Doug.'

'Hmm. I suppose they've both got brown eyes. I don't really see it.'

'I remember that night you met Doug, it was at that party at Katriona Mack's house,' said Trish. 'Feels about a million years ago now. Chris and I both really fancied Doug but he was only interested in the beautiful Mags.' Trish smiled.

Mags chortled and leant back as the waiter approached with a tray of two tall glasses.

'I don't think so,' said Christine. 'It was you who was trying to chat him up.'

'Didn't work though, did it,' said Trish, ruffling Mags's dishevelled hair. She looked at her watch and stood up. 'Anyway, I've got to dash. Enjoy the champers!'

'Cheers!' said Mags and Christine, waving goodbye.

'Hilarious,' said Mags. 'Why would she think you two fancied Doug?'

'No idea, she was the one who was after him,' said Christine, eyes focused on the champagne bubbles. 'As you say, hilarious!'

'God, if Doug heard that it might make him slightly less grumpy. I almost feel like telling him.'

'Why's Doug grumpy?'

'Wish I knew. Lottie agrees with me, he's been crabby and irritable for days now, daren't ask him why. He's usually so laid-back.' Mags downed her coffee then reached for her glass. 'Anyway, what a discovery this morning. So it looks like Elizabeth Barrie's father was David Barrie but her mother was this Charlotte Whyte. And you don't think it could be the same one from the manse then?'

'Impossible I'd say, but let's look at the censuses later. And what about David Barrie's death by poisoning?' Christine sipped her champagne. 'What could that have been?'

'No idea, but it said he was a farm hand so maybe something used on the soil?'

'No,' said Christine. 'They wouldn't have used chemicals back then, would they? Maybe some sort of food poisoning?'

'Suppose so. We can mention it to Uncle Charlie at the funeral, see if it jogs his memory. Oh, are you going to drive us there or shall I?'

'I'll drive,' said Christine. 'You drive far too fast on motorways; it'd give the old folk heart attacks. I'll pick you up at 8.30, then swing by Dad and Auntie Peggy.'

'Sounds like a plan,' Mags said. 'Though I don't drive that fast.'

Christine shook her head. 'Ninety on a motorway is fast, Mags!'

Mags glanced at her cousin then leant over the table, twiddling with the stem of her glass. 'What's the latest on Connal from Ponteprydd?'

Christine placed her glass on its coaster on the table and pushed it away from her. 'You do that just to annoy me, don't you? It's Colin from Pontefract. Anyway, I had an email from Sergent Price. *Colin*' – she emphasised the name – 'is pleading not guilty at the magistrates' court hearing next week.'

'Not guilty? How the hell can he do that? Weren't there loads of witnesses?'

'Yes, three witness statements and photos of skid marks and all sorts.'

'You're not thinking of going to the court are you, Chris?'

'No, of course not. What's the point.' She looked at her watch. 'Right, Register House shuts early on a Saturday.'

Mags raised her glass which still had some bubbles. 'I'm not rushing this Bolly, Chris.'

Christine pulled her coat onto her lap. 'Come on, get that down you. We need to get back over the road. Those censuses beckon, Mags.'

# Chapter Twenty-four
1865

'Is a penny bun like a scone, Miss Charlotte?' Elizabeth stood in the clearing in the woods and looked up at the tall, slim figure who held her hand tight. Charlotte's chin was tilted up as she gazed at the morning sun breaking through the branches.

'No, it's a mushroom, Elizabeth, and we are looking for some for the Minister's supper.' Charlotte strode over to a tree stump and beckoned to Elizabeth, who skipped over the dead leaves to join her. 'Look round here.' Charlotte poked round the trunk with a stick. 'This is where I found them last week, a clutch of lovely penny buns. I was going to cook them for supper but Father went out unexpectedly and refused to eat them the next day even though they were fine.'

'Why did Cookie nae cook them, Miss Charlotte?'

'Why did Cookie *not* cook them.' Charlotte raised her eyebrows. 'She is permitted some free time now and then. Indeed, tonight is her night off again so I thought I would try once more to cook them for Father, as a treat.'

Elizabeth tugged on Charlotte's grey dress. 'Look, Miss, over there!' She scampered towards the edge of the clearing, the skirt of her brown cotton dress flapping behind her. Charlotte stepped towards her and poked her walking stick into the moss. 'Well done, Elizabeth Barrie!' She laid her basket on the ground and took out a small knife. 'Watch, this is how we cut them.' She held the tops and deftly cut them off at the base. 'These are truly fine penny buns, look how pretty they are with their fat creamy stem and curved brown cap.'

'Aye, they're like the ones the fairies live under.'

'Precisely.' Charlotte smiled and gazed down at her charge. 'Elizabeth Barrie, I do believe your eyes get browner by the day. The colour of glossy black treacle.'

The child smiled up at Charlotte, before a rustle from under a beech tree behind them made her start.

'It might be a rabbit, let's go and see,' said Charlotte.

Elizabeth jumped over a couple of broken branches and looked down. 'Here, Miss Charlotte,' she shouted, 'some mair penny buns.'

'Some *more*, Elizabeth, not mair!' Charlotte crouched down to where the child was pointing. A smile played on her lips, 'This is more like the place the fairies live, Elizabeth. These are more toadstool than mushroom. Some mushrooms are not suitable for eating. Do you understand? They are poisonous.'

'But I thought mushrooms were for the Minister's tea.'

'Yes, but some are not edible. That means they must never be eaten – ever. And that includes these ones here. If you are ever in the woods without me, do not touch them.' She stood up tall. 'Why don't you run over there, you will find a little cottage through the woods. I will follow presently.'

Elizabeth picked up her skirts and scurried off, over the damp foliage and through the trees. Charlotte watched her go, then crouched down to scrutinise the mushrooms at her feet.

Soon she was striding off in the direction Elizabeth had headed, the basket on her arm covered with a cloth. She got to the little cottage just beyond the clearing and stood still, waiting to hear the child's voice. She surveyed the front, the wooden door and window frames freshly painted. The roof was newly tiled and the chimney stack looked recently pointed, the mortar silvery grey against the sombre brick. And there was the climbing rose growing up the side of the door, with one deep red bloom. She leant towards the flower, shut her eyes and inhaled.

Then she realised she couldn't hear Elizabeth.

'Elizabeth, where are you?'

Silence. There was a caw of crows and she looked up to see a flock of dark birds swoop from a large tree up towards the low, drifting clouds. She shivered. It did not feel like September, it was chilly even in the middle of the day.

'Elizabeth!'

She walked round the back of the cottage and looked all around.

'Miss Charlotte, I'm here!'

The little voice came from the branches of the beech tree.

'Someone's gone and made a wee house up here!'

Charlotte picked up Elizabeth's little boots from the base of the tree. She leant one hand against the large trunk and, peering upwards, could see Elizabeth sitting on a wooden board that had been placed across two branches, her bare feet dangling as she swung her legs back and forth.

'I can't get up there with this dress on. But I can see you.' Charlotte stretched up onto her tiptoes and saw a second board placed higher up. 'And look, can you see the roof above your head?'

'Aye, just like a real house, Miss Charlotte.'

Charlotte stretched up on her tiptoes. 'It is rather splendid, isn't it? I used to love being up there. What can you see?'

'I can see into the windaes o' the wee cottage, cannae see anyone inside though. Who lives there?'

'No one for now, but I believe there are to be new tenants moving in soon. It was owned by a farmer; it was for his woodcutter before he died. Corrie Cottage it was called, after the farm steading.'

Elizabeth began clambering back down towards the ground, her little feet placed firmly on each branch. She jumped down the last few inches and sprang to clasp Charlotte round the knees. 'Well, if I owned that wee cottage I would let the fairies live up there in the tree. It's like a magic treehouse.'

'It is enchanting, isn't it. Anyway, put your boots back on, I must be getting you home.'

They strolled back through the woods, hand in hand, until they reached the road. Charlotte released the child's hand and said, 'Now, just walk beside me. Mrs Barrie will be watching out for us.'

A figure emerged from one of the cottages on the main street. Margaret Barrie was untying her apron as she bustled down the street towards them.

'I was wondering where you'd got to,' she muttered, her face pinched. 'Poor wee Jane's still no' well.'

Charlotte inclined her head. 'I am sorry to hear that. Is there anything we can do to help?'

'No, that willnae be necessary, Miss Charlotte, thank you,' snapped the older woman, spying the basket. 'You been picking brambles?'

'No, Ma, we didnae go that way. We got penny buns for the Minister's tea!'

Elizabeth started to tug at the cover over the basket but Charlotte spun round. 'Yes, penny buns!' She held the basket up high and held a finger to her lips. 'But hush, we don't want to disturb the fairies, do we?'

Margaret scowled. 'Fairies, eh?'

Elizabeth started to jump and hop back along the road, playing hopscotch on imaginary markings. Margaret bellowed after her, 'Elizabeth, have you thanked Miss Charlotte for taking you for a walk?'

The little girl hurtled back towards them, coming to a sudden stop in front of the women. She looked up at Charlotte and said, 'Thank you, Miss Charlotte. Can we go back soon so I can play in the tree house again?'

Margaret glared at Charlotte. 'What tree house?'

'You know, the one at Corrie Cottage.'

'What were you doing there?'

Charlotte shrugged. 'We were on the quest for fairies living under mushrooms. And you must agree that the cottage is rather enchanting.'

Margaret gave her a withering look and began retying her apron with calloused hands. 'Come away, Elizabeth, there's work tae be done.'

Elizabeth leapt to the side to avoid Margaret's grasp, and waved at Charlotte. Charlotte smiled and blew the girl a kiss, but Margaret yanked Elizabeth away by her elbow before she could blow a kiss back.

Charlotte sighed and walked back towards the manse.

She went into the hall and slotted the walking stick back into its usual place in the hat stand. She noticed a letter addressed to her on the hall table, in her father's handwriting.

She put down the basket and ripped it open.

*Charlotte, I have been called away unexpectedly on a Presbytery matter to Forfar. I shall not be back until late, therefore shall not require any supper. Your father.*

Charlotte stamped her foot. She picked up her basket and trudged along the corridor to the kitchen. She went over to the fire, stoked it up with the poker then, one by one, tossed in the mushrooms from her basket. She ran to open the back door and flung the windows wide as the toxic smell began to fill the kitchen.

# Chapter Twenty-five
## 2014

Christine parked her car at the end of the road and marched towards the house, her bulging bag of jotters over her shoulder. She glared at the cars parked outside her house. Why was she never able to park there herself, why did every single neighbour need two cars? She lifted up the lid of the green bin at the gate and glanced at the bulging bin bags; yet again they hadn't been lifted.

But she had too many things on her mind to bother chasing that up with the council. School had been a nightmare: Ewan Rutherford had been sick all over his desk just before morning break and the classroom had smelled awful all day.

And this was the day Colin Clarkson was appearing in court. She had agreed with Sergeant Price she would phone him for results after four o'clock.

On the drive home from school, she had thought about nothing else, turning over, yet again, the events at the hospital that day. Was he one of the people she had seen in the A&E waiting room? There had been a man there, with the shiny suit, and he had a child with him, a little girl who looked about ten. That must have been him, she was sure of it. She had been in the same room as the man who had nearly killed her children, and she hadn't even realised it.

God, if she could go back...

Well, he wasn't going to get away with it.

Christine walked up the path to her house, shaking her head at the white plastic window frames glinting in the sun.

So ugly. She would love to have beautiful wooden ones like Mags's, but Gerry said they couldn't afford it.

She rammed the key in the lock, hung her jacket on the banister then headed for the kitchen. From her handbag she produced a large envelope, on which she had written *CC/ Pontefract*. She placed it in front of her, with a pen and a pad of A4 paper alongside.

She dialled Sergeant Price's number and cleared her throat.

'Sergeant Price here,' he answered, in his broad Geordie accent.

'Hello, Sergeant Price, it's Mrs Wallace here, Jack's mum, from Edinburgh. I was just wondering how it went at the magistrates' court today?'

'Mrs Wallace, good to hear from you. How's Jack?'

'He's better, thanks, but there's still a way to go. He gets very tired.'

'Understandable.' There was a noise of papers being shuffled. 'Well now, I'm sorry to say nothing happened today. The defendant didn't turn up at court.'

'What? How can he do that?'

'It's rescheduled for next month, the 30th. His lawyer might be playing for time.'

Christine leant back in her chair and looked up at the ceiling. 'That's so disappointing. How dare he. So nothing for another month?'

'Sorry, Mrs Wallace.'

'Does he ever ask about Jack?'

Sergeant Price cleared his throat. 'He didn't mention it last week when my colleague and I went to see him.'

'You went to see him? What's he like?'

'I'm not really at liberty to say, Mrs Wallace. But Jack's on the mend, that's the important thing.'

'He nearly killed my two children!'

'Yes, I understand. We went to see him to challenge his premise that he'd been trying to avoid a minibus and that it was not his fault.'

'Minibus? What a load of rubbish! None of the witnesses mentioned a minibus, did they?'

There was silence on the phone.

'Sorry, Sergeant Price, I didn't mean to shout. It's really good of you to take time like this.'

'You're all right. As I said to you last time you phoned, Mrs Wallace, the facts speak for themselves. It's all delaying tactics. In terms of witness statements and photos, he's not got a leg to stand on.'

'Good.'

'Now then, I'd better be getting on. Why don't you phone the magistrates' court yourself after the next hearing?'

'Can I do that? '

'Yes, anyone can find out results from court proceedings. It's due at 10am, so you could phone after dinnertime.'

'Thank you so much, Sergeant Price.'

Christine placed her phone on the table then pulled her diary from her bag. She flicked to the 30th and wrote, '10am. CC! Phone court after lunch.'


At six o'clock the noise of the front door interrupted Christine, who was stirring a Bolognese sauce in the kitchen.

'Chris, where are you?'

'Kitchen!'

Gerry strolled in, beaming, and threw his car keys on the table. He crossed over to give her a peck on the cheek.

She flinched. 'You're freezing Gerry! And I wish you'd trim that beard, you're beginning to look like a hippy.'

He rolled his eyes and headed for the fridge. 'Good day?' he asked, taking out a beer.

'Not really.' She turned as the can opened with a sharp hiss. 'Actually, I'd like a drink too, Gerry.'

'Oh!' He looked up at the wall clock. 'Not like you to imbibe this early. Glass of wine?'

'Please,' Christine said, putting the lid on the pan. 'Why are you home so early?'

'I was meant to be going to the pub with Doug but he called it off. I don't mind, he's not good company these days, so bloody grumpy.'

Christine took her glass from Gerry, took a sip and glanced up at her husband. 'Why's he grumpy?'

'God knows. I did try to ask him but he just got more crabby.' He took a swig from his can. 'But tell me about your day.'

'Colin Clarkson refused to turn up and it's delayed till next month.'

Gerry scratched his beard. 'Colin who?'

'Are you not interested in the outcome of our children's accident? Colin Clarkson who rammed them at sixty miles an hour did not turn up at court today. And he is trying to invent lies to cover his actions!'

Christine's face was bright red. Gerry set down his can and looked directly at her.

'Chris, look at you. This isn't healthy. Why the hell are you trying to wreak revenge on this man?'

'Because, unlike you, I believe in Old Testament judgement, an eye for an eye, a tooth for a tooth.'

'But the kids are both fine.'

'He could have killed them, Gerry. And I could murder him for that.'

'Did you not say it's a magistrates' court? So that means he'll get something like three points off his licence and maybe a hundred quid fine. That's all.'

'Not if I can help it!'

Gerry put his hands up. 'What the hell are you going to do about it? Take the law into your own hands? You've got to trust in the process of law, Chris. Now calm down and forget about Callum.'

'Colin!' she shouted as she stormed out of the room.

'So, when'll you be back tonight?'

'Not sure. Tea time I imagine. Depends on the traffic.'

'Okay, text me when you're leaving the restaurant. Where is it you're meeting her again?'

'York, kind of halfway between us and London where she lives now.'

'Oh yeah,' said Gerry, stirring eggs in a pan. 'Sure you don't want some scrambled eggs before you go?'

Christine picked up her jacket from the back of a chair. 'I'm fine, thanks.'

'Okay. Have a good time with Jenny. Must try to meet her some day.'

'Yes.' She peered at the eggs. 'You'll need to soak the pan before you wash it.'

'Okay, boss.' He smiled. 'Still reckon you should have got the train.'

'I told you, Sunday timetable's a nightmare.'

He nodded. 'Drive safely.'

Four hours later, Christine slowed down at the end of

a street and parked the car. She got out her phone and checked the address. Where was it? She remembered the type of car from the police report so scanned the cars parked down this tree-lined suburban street.

Number twenty-six – there it was, a small red-brick semi. She removed the sturdy black leather case she had brought with her and put it on her lap.

She'd had the entire morning to think as she drove south. She had felt a frisson of something – was it fear? – as she drove past Gateshead on the A1, knowing that was where the kids had had their accident. But now here she was in Pontefract, and she was still undecided about what to do. She looked up and down the street but could not see his car. She looked at her watch; twelve thirty, maybe he was out at the shops. She would sit and wait.

Twenty minutes later she noticed a blue car approach in her mirror. She didn't move as she watched it drive along the road and park directly outside the house. It was the Nissan. Christine peered through the window. A man got out. He was about forty and dressed in a shiny suit and garish orange tie. The passenger door opened and she could see an elderly lady sitting on the seat.

Christine unclasped the binding on the leather case and removed the binoculars. She lowered her window and looked closer. The lady, smartly dressed in a navy coat and matching woollen hat, looked about her dad's age. She was swinging her legs out from the seat in slow motion; the action reminded her of Auntie Peggy emerging from a car, cautiously, knees first. The man rushed round to her side and handed her a stick; leaning on his arm, she pulled herself to a standing position.

She heard the back door slam and a girl with two bouncy

bunches in her hair appeared on the pavement. The man pointed inside the car and the girl picked up two books. The girl skipped along her garden path and up the steps to the front door. Christine adjusted the binocular lens and saw that the books were identical; black and thick. Bibles. They must have been to church.

The man guided the old lady slowly up the path and into the house. The little girl reappeared a couple of minutes later and sat on the doorstep with an ice lolly. She removed the paper and licked. The man came out, patted her head then took the paper from her before going back inside.

Christine felt numb. This was not how she had imagined things to be when she saw Colin Clarkson. Though she hadn't had any idea what would happen, this pleasant domestic scene was unexpected – returning from church with a lady that could have been her aunt and a child that could have been her daughter at that age. Christine felt her heart begin to race. He was a father, why the hell did he not feel more remorse for nearly killing her two children? And why was he driving like a madman with a little girl in the car? Surely he could at least have apologised, asked about Jack… She let out a long breath then slowly raised the car window and rammed the binoculars back into their case. She scrabbled in her handbag, found a pill and swigged it down with some water, then turned the key in the ignition and began the long drive home.

# Chapter Twenty-six
## 1864

Tannadice church was packed. Easter Sunday was a time when every single member of the parish was obliged to attend. Charlotte took her seat on the wooden bench at the brand new organ and checked that her book of psalms and paraphrases was at the right page. Her father's selection of music was nothing if not traditional. *'Christ the Lord is Risen Today'* was an obvious choice for Easter and Charles Wesley a safe lyricist, but her father would not contemplate it, even though she had been telling him about the abundance of new hymns being written.

She had hoped that, since he had at last bowed to pressure from the kirk session to replace the old piano – not with a new piano but with an organ – he might also consider new music. But when she had told him the congregation were sure to enjoy these new hymns, he had sneered. 'Our traditional psalms have served us for aeons, why should we change? Furthermore, the *enjoyment* of my flock is not why I was called to serve the Lord, Charlotte. Our established music will suit us fine here in Tannadice.'

As ever, he made her feel naïve and irrelevant.

She looked around at the congregation and noticed the daffodils and snowdrops that adorned some modest bonnets throughout the pews. In the front rows all the ladies seemed to have on new outfits for Easter. She was certain she had not seen Mrs Mackay in that shade of green before. And Miss Grant had never worn anything other than black in church; that silver colour at least matched her straggly grey hair. In the side pew, Lady Munro was resplendent in black and cream stripes.

She was not sure what her father would think of these fashionable dresses in the kirk. He had told her so often that she was permitted to wear only dark colours. A fortnight earlier, she had arrived in the vestry before the service wearing a dark grey dress with a cream lace collar and he had ordered her to hurry home and change into something more appropriate.

It was five minutes to go till the beadle ushered him in so she straightened her back and shuffled on the bench. It was so uncomfortable, but she wasn't permitted a cushion. She was about to start playing when a jostling a few pews behind her made her look round. A woman was urging two little girls in plain bonnets and drab fawn frocks to squeeze into the narrow wooden pew. The woman skelped the back of one of their little heads then shoved them along. The girls sat with heads tilted up, looking up at the empty pulpit and the huge bible opened upon the lectern. The woman kept her head down, as if seeking anonymity.

It was Margaret Barrie with Elizabeth and Jane. Charlotte took a deep breath then looked up as the beadle bowed deeply and her father entered the sanctuary. The congregation stood and she began to play the first hymn.

After an hour and a half of her father's sonorous voice thundering from the pulpit, she played the final amen, then saw Margaret Barrie stand up and gesture for the little girls to follow.

She finished the tune then smiled at the choirmaster. 'Mr Ferguson, I need to speak to one of Father's parishioners. I shall return presently to collect my music.'

The elderly man nodded and she darted past the choir

and out the back door of the church. Round at the front of the building she craned her neck to see over the emerging congregation. Past the yew trees, she could see her father at the door, greeting his adoring flock.

He was nodding in acknowledgement of their approbation as his congregation filed past. Charlotte noticed, not for the first time, that his aloof expression and affected manner made his attempts at a smile more of a sneer. She was reminded of the last verse in Robert Burns' poem, Holy Willie's Prayer:

*But Lord, remember me and mine*
*Wi' mercies temporal and divine!*
*That I for grace and gear may shine,*
*Excell'd by nane!*
*And a' the glory shall be thine!*
*Amen! Amen!*

'Ah, Charlotte, that was an enlightening sermon, was it not?' Lady Munro stood at her side, smiling through black teeth. She had heard someone suggest, unkindly, that the discoloured teeth were due to the claret she consumed on a regular basis.

'It was, Lady Munro, perfect for this beautiful Easter day.'

'Indeed, the zeal of your father never fails to impress.' She inclined her head. 'Good Day, Charlotte.'

'Good day,' she said and stretched her head up to look again towards the door.

There they were at the foot of the steps. She rushed over, though she knew Lady Munro was watching.

'Mrs Barrie, it is indeed good to see you back in the village.'

Margaret Barrie looked up, unsmiling, at the tall figure. She glanced over at Lady Munro who raised her chin and walked on ahead.

'Aye, well we couldnae stay much longer wi' my cousin Jeannie when her man took sae ill, so we're back. I've got some work in the village.'

Charlotte was not concentrating on what the woman was saying, she was gazing at the girls. One had curly hair and large brown eyes, pools of molten chocolate. Her lips were rosebuds. The other, whose hand Margaret held, had lank hair and freckles. As Cookie might say, not a bonnie child.

'The girls?' she whispered.

'Aye, here's Jane and this tinker's Elizabeth.' She took hold of the pretty girl's ear lobe and pulled her towards her. The little girl winced but said nothing. 'Say guid morning to Miss Charlotte, girls, then we must be away home.'

The girls obediently murmured their greeting, Elizabeth twisting a ringlet round and round her finger as she looked up, entranced, at Charlotte.

'May I call upon you one day, Mrs Barrie?'

'If you must.' The small woman scowled. 'Ye ken the auld cottage in the main street, that's where we are.'

'Thank you. I would love to perhaps take them for a walk or...'

'I'm no' sure the Minister would like that. He just aboot ignored us at the door the now.' Margaret turned to leave and shoved the girls forward. 'Goodbye, Miss Charlotte.'

The woman headed towards the wrought iron gate, the plain girl skipping beside her. Elizabeth, however, stood still for a moment, gazing up at Charlotte, her little bright face animated, before turning and running full pelt towards the gate.

# Chapter Twenty-seven
2014

The church was freezing. Christine took her dad's walking stick and put it in the umbrella stand at the end of the pew. 'Can't you keep your bonnet on, dad? You'll get a chill!'

'Christine, all men must remove their hats in church.' He tutted and turned to his sister sitting alongside.

'Look, there's Bella,' said Peggy, turning fully round to stare down the aisle. 'Goodness me, she's put on weight since I last saw her!'

'Mum!' Mags hissed, 'you're speaking far too loudly.'

'And I'm not sure you should wear red at funerals,' said Peggy, pointing at Auntie Bella waddling down the aisle, dressed in bright scarlet.

Bella took her seat in the opposite pew. When she noticed the four of them sitting so close to her, she beamed. She opened her mouth to say something then stopped as the undertaker asked the congregation to stand.

The coffin passed the end of their pew and they all glanced towards it.

The funeral wake was a jolly affair. The older guests clung onto their sherry and whisky glasses as the waiters weaved around offering refills. Auntie Bella was one of the few women drinking whisky and every time she came back into the room after a cigarette break outside, she called over a waiter to top her glass up. Now she was sitting by the buffet table, legs akimbo, her woollen skirt stretched, taut between her knees.

Beside her was the table laden with food. Mags and Christine had watched the elderly guests all pile their plates high the moment the waitress had said, 'Help yourselves.'

Mags whispered, 'God, you'd think all the old folk hadn't eaten for days. Look at them!'

'I know and half of them are on their third or fourth dram.'

There were half-empty plates of sandwiches, sausage rolls and cakes beside her. Bella picked up a scone, peered at it over her glasses, then took a large mouthful. The cream and jam smeared on her lower lips so she licked them and took another bite, before putting it on the plate balanced on her lap.

Christine and Mags approached and Bella slapped the chairs beside her. 'Sit down, girls. Tell me your news!'

After they had told her about their children, Christine said, 'Auntie Bella, we're doing some research into the family history. It's fascinating, isn't it, Mags?'

Mags nodded and smiled.

'Anyway, we've done really well, got back to the nineteenth century easily but then we came to a complete standstill for Elizabeth Barrie, your granny. We can't seem to find a birth certificate.'

'Yeah, she only comes into existence from 1871 when she's fourteen and a domestic servant in a big house in Dundee,' Mags added.

'Has your dad not told you, Christine?'

'Told me what?'

'Well, about her secret?'

Christine's eyes lit up. 'He kept saying there was a secret but couldn't remember what. Auntie Peggy said he was talking nonsense.'

Christine and Mags dragged their chairs nearer.

'Well, it was on Granny's deathbed. She called in her children – my mother Annie and your Grandpa Douglas'

'And what did she say?' Mags was impatient.

'Well, this is what Ma told me about Elizabeth Barrie. Her father was married to someone else and her parents had had an affair. But when Elizabeth was born, for some strange reason she was brought up by the Barries instead of her real mother, even after David Barrie died young.'

'So it's true,' said Christine. 'But Auntie Peggy didn't know anything about it.'

Bella shrugged. 'Maybe your Grandpa Douglas only told Charlie. Or, more likely, he told neither of them and Charlie eavesdropped.'

'Well that would explain why he can't quite remember all the facts,' said Christine. 'Is there anything else you remember?'

'Let me think,' said Bella, picking up her empty glass. 'Oh, Mags, would you be a good girl and get me another dram. Someone must have drunk mine.' She handed Mags the tumbler.

'Don't say another thing till I come back, Auntie Bella!'

A long draft of whisky later, and Bella started again. 'There was something else, now what the heck was it…'

'Something about Elizabeth's real mother?' asked Mags.

'No, we definitely never knew that.' She screwed up her eyes. 'There was something to do with the church or the churchyard or something, now what was it?'

'Well, we've seen her father David Barrie's grave in the Tannadice cemetery there. Is that it?'

Bella nodded. 'Yes, that must be it.' Bella drained her glass and leaned in close to Mags and Christine. They could see the fine white whiskers round her wrinkled mouth.

'Now, girls, I wonder if you could do something for me?'

'Of course,' they both said.

'I'm eighty-eight years old and as you know, I like a dram and a cigarette. Life's been good to me, even though Kenny's not with me now to enjoy it.'

They nodded in sympathy.

'But there are still some things I'd like to do before I join Kenny.'

'Like a bucket list?' Mags suggested.

'Not really. I don't plan on going bungee jumping in New Zealand or anything. No, what I want to do before I die is to try some dope.' She looked at Mags. 'Can you get me some, please?'

Mags's mouth dropped open. Christine was staring at Bella, wide-eyed.

'I'm not going to become an addict or anything, but I could never have tried with Kenny around, you know what a puritan he was! So just a wee go at some cannabis would be the business. And seeing you here, Mags, I just thought you'd be the one to get it for me.'

'Well…'

'Christine, Mags,' called Peggy. 'Charlie's keen to get going before the traffic gets bad. Is that okay?'

'Okay, Mum, just give us a couple of minutes,' said Mags. She turned back to Bella. 'Let me see what I can do and I'll give you a ring. Can't make any promises though.'

'Thanks, dear.' She smiled. 'Life's for living you know, girls. Make sure you fill yours to the brim.'

# Chapter Twenty-eight
## 1861

'There was a meeting of the kirk session yesterday evening, Mrs Barrie, and we have decided upon a resolution to your situation,' said a short, stout man dressed in black, standing at the door of the Barries' tiny cottage in Tannadice.

'And what's that then, Mr Lamb?' Margaret stood at the door, adjusting the straps of her apron. There was the sound of crying from inside.

'Might I be permitted to enter, Mrs Barrie?'

'If you want, it's a right guddle though. The bairns dinnae look after themselves.'

He removed his tall black hat, bent his head down and stepped inside. The cottage smelled of the mutton broth that was stewing in a pot on a swee over the fire. He turned towards the noise and saw two infants on the floor. A chamber pot poked out from under the bed.

'Sit doon if you want, Mr Lamb,' said Margaret, dusting off some crumbs from the only armchair in the room. 'The girls are just starting to eat oatcakes, they mak' a bit o' a mess.'

'I shall remain standing, thank you. I do not wish to be a burden.' He pressed his chalky white hands together as if in prayer.

Margaret shrugged and went over to the little girls, one of whom was trying to crawl towards Mr Lamb. Margaret picked her up and put her at the other side of the bed, away from the fire.

Mr Lamb coughed. 'Mrs Barrie, ever since the tragic

death of your husband and your consequent status as pauper we, as a kirk session, have endeavoured to ameliorate your position by giving you some financial aid on a monthly basis. This obviates the need to approach the Parochial Board as per the Poor Law of 1845. And as you may or may not be aware…'

'Mr Lamb, I dinnae hae all day, please can you just say what you have to say and in language I can understand.' Margaret picked up the second child and gave her a finger to suck.

Mr Lamb grimaced. Margaret's finger was filthy.

He continued, 'To summarise, we have found a position for you to take up and we conclude that this is the best solution for you, for the children and also for us as a parish.'

'And what would that be then?' She began jiggling the child up and down on her hip and glanced towards Elizabeth, who was crawling towards the chamber pot. 'Elizabeth! Dinnae touch!' She ran to the other child who had her hands outstretched towards the grubby chamber pot. She glowered at the infant who frowned back.

'You are to go to live with your cousin Jean Mann in Oathlaw. There you will assist her with her own children while she starts work as a cook at Oathlaw Farmhouse for Lady Munro's daughter Mrs Nicholson who, as you may be aware, left the family estate to live there after her recent marriage.'

'Does Jeannie ken aboot this?'

Margaret grabbed Elizabeth by her arm and dragged her back to the other side of the bed. The little girl sat down with a thump and raised a chubby little hand to her head. She began twisting a finger around a ringlet while staring up at Mr Lamb, brown eyes open wide.

'Yes, she does, and she is more than happy to accommodate you and the two children. This will mean the kirk session will end its payments to you.'

'An' whit about this place? It's been in the Barrie family for years.'

'This cottage will remain yours and you may keep the few items that are yours here until such time as it is deemed fit for you to return to live in Tannadice.'

Margaret sighed and went over to the bed to deposit the child on her hip. She hauled the other one up from the floor and put her alongside. 'Am I right in thinking this is the Minister's doing?'

Mr Lamb glared at her. 'As you know, everything the kirk session decides is sanctioned by the Reverend Whyte. He has also been in communication with Lady Munro in Oathlaw. You may leave here as soon as possible, Mrs Barrie. Mr Grieve has a cart he can carry your belongings on. Perhaps this Saturday would be a convenient day?'

'I dinnae believe I hae any say in the matter, dae I?'

Mr Lamb put on his hat, inclined his head and stepped outside.

# Chapter Twenty-nine
## 2014

Doug peeled off his latex gloves and washed his hands, peering into the mirror as he did so. God, what a fat slob he was these days. He really should be giving up beer and starting to run again.

'Bye, Amy,' he called, as his dental nurse opened the door of his surgery to leave. 'See you tomorrow.'

He picked up his jacket from a hook by the door and switched off the lights. In the reception area, Frances was talking on the phone. He waved goodbye but she put up her hand for him to wait.

He stood at the window and watched a car reversing into a space outside. It was a flashy silver Mercedes, just like Gerry's. In fact, it was Gerry's car, he was sure of it. A woman with cropped black hair and large sunglasses got out. She smoothed down her short skirt, locked the door and rang the surgery door bell. Frances buzzed her in and the woman strolled into the reception area, without glancing at Doug, handed the car keys to Frances and walked right back out again, her high-heeled boots clicking behind her. She knew Doug was watching her.

'Who was that?' asked Doug, as Frances put the phone down.

'Oh, that's Angie. She cleans at Gerry's surgery so he sometimes lends her the car to get about. He asked her to leave it here as he's meeting you for a pint round the corner. You're to take his keys.'

Doug frowned. 'Do I recognise her?'

'Yes, she's cleaned here too when Bev's been off ill. Agency cleaning, so she picks and chooses. Doesn't want her husband to know as he doesn't like her going out to work.'

'Oh, right,' said Doug, looking at his watch. 'What was it you wanted, Frances?'

She burrowed into her handbag for lipstick and a compact mirror then proceeded to apply two thick red lines. 'Two things,' she said, lipstick hovering. 'Don't forget you told Mrs Owen you'd be in at eight tomorrow for her root canal.'

He nodded and showed her the back of his hand across which he had scrawled a marker-pen reminder.

Frances shook her head. 'In this day and age, could you not use your Blackberry?'

'Not as much fun.' Doug winked. 'Always gets a rise from you, Frances.'

She tutted. 'And Lottie phoned to tell you to be home sharp as she's cooking dinner for the three of you for Mags's birthday.'

'Okay.' He turned to go. 'Thanks, Frances. And thank God you reminded me about the date on Friday, she couldn't believe I'd got her a card and a present this morning!'

'All in a day's work, Doug,' she said, smiling at him adoringly.


'The usual, Gerry?' Doug nodded as his friend entered the bar.

'Please. What a day!' He sat down beside Doug on a high bar stool then said, 'Actually can we go and sit at a table, my back's killing me.'

Doug followed with two pints of beer and they sat down.

'You know I've told you before about this elderly patient, she's about eighty, the one who's got chronic periodontitis. Anyway, she refuses to have the seat reclined even a fraction and I have to do everything at a really awkward angle as I can never get my stool high enough. Today she was in for a double appointment and by the time she left I could barely straighten up.' He placed his hand at the base of his spine and rubbed.

'These old buggers, why don't they like lying prone?' Doug said, chuckling. 'Too many nights at the swingers club, I reckon!'

'That'll soon be us, mate,' Gerry said, sipping from the glass.

Doug raised an eyebrow.

'The getting old bit, not the swingers.'

Doug put down his glass and fished in his pocket for the car keys. 'So what's with the tarty cleaner in the mini skirt driving your car around town?'

'Ah, Angie, she's great, isn't she! Did Frances tell you about her? Her husband's really old-fashioned and wants her just to sit at home looking after their house and making his tea, but she gets cleaning jobs here and there so she can have her own cash.'

'Yeah, I get that, but the car thing? What would Chris say if she saw tarty cleaner driving her husband's Merc?'

'Tarty cleaner is called Angie. I just gave her the car to help her out today.' He frowned. 'Mind you, I've never thought about what Chris would say, good point. Should I tell her?'

'Nah, not sure she'd take it well.'

'You make it sound dodgy and it's really not!'

The lines round Doug's eyes crinkled into a smile. 'I believe you, mate. It's just, Chris might not. You know what she's like.'

Gerry nodded. 'She's certainly got a jealous streak. She got all emotional once when I told her about Debbie Kennedy.'

'Christ, what did you tell her about Dynamo Debs for?'

'Dunno, she asked me about girlfriends at uni.'

Doug shook his head. 'Sometimes best to avoid telling the whole truth with things like that, especially to jealous types like Chris.'

'Good thinking. Anyway, enough of me. Good to see you're a bit less bloody grumpy today.'

Doug smiled. 'I know, sorry, I've been just a bit down lately, but I'm fine now. Anyway, I can't stay long. Lottie's cooking for Mag's birthday and I daren't be late. The wrath of my daughter is something to behold!'

'Yeah, Anna's the same. How come we have such stroppy daughters, but Jack's Mr Chill?'

Doug lifted his glass and downed his pint. 'A mystery, Gerry.'

Gerry walked down the road from the bus stop, turning into his street in Craigleith. It was a cold night and not a cloud to be seen, just bright stars everywhere. He'd get out his binoculars later and that book on stars he'd been given for his birthday. It fascinated him, he really ought to have studied astronomy instead of dentistry.

He turned the key in the lock.

'Kitchen!' Christine shouted. He went through and saw the table set as usual, napkins neatly folded and the water poured even though she knew he always preferred to run fresh water from the tap.

He leaned towards his wife for a kiss, but even though he had trimmed his beard, she swung away so that his kiss only brushed her cheek.

'Presume you knew it was Mags's birthday, Chris?' said Gerry.

'Of course I did! I'm taking her out for lunch on Saturday. Are they doing anything special tonight?'

'Lottie's cooking one of her specials so Doug was rushing home to be on time. Though he said he was tempted to have a pie at the pub as she'd probably be doing one of her mung bean flummeries.' He jingled the coins in his pocket. 'Thought a flummery was a pudding?'

'That's just Doug being funny, Gerry!' Christine snipped the top off a bag of broccoli and tipped the contents into a pan. 'How's he doing these days? Less moody?'

'Yeah, back to normal, no idea what that was all about.' He looked over to Christine at the stove. 'Give me five minutes and I'll be right down. Smells good. What is it?'

'It's only a Markies' cottage pie.'

'Lovely.'

Christine placed her knife and fork together on her empty plate and began strumming her fingers on the table. 'I hate living in a new-build house on an estate. I can't stand living in a modern box, Gerry. No character at all and we're all so close together. We are just far too near Phyllis next door. I mean, if she pokes her head over the fence for a chat one more time, I will actually kill her.'

'Don't be so mean, Chris, she's just lonely, she's a widow. And she's interesting. I chatted to her for ages at the weekend about vitamins, you know she used to run that health food shop before it shut down?'

'Yes, she's told me, more than once.' Christine finished her water and looked around her. 'Why is our kitchen not huge and light and airy like Mags's?'

Gerry sighed. 'They got that house in Trinity years ago before the area became trendy. And don't forget, running an old Victorian house has its downfalls. Remember all that money they had to pay for those roof repairs, and the new kitchen cost loads.'

'Yes, but they can afford it.'

'He inherited it from his parents' estate when his mum died. What, would you rather Charlie was dead so you were wealthier?'

'Of course not, don't be silly, but it's just... Well, it's not just their new kitchen, they've also got those lovely tiled fireplaces and the original wooden floors rather than our horrible lino, and...'

'God, Chris, you should hear yourself. You'd think you were jealous of them.'

Christine grabbed Gerry's plate and stood up.

Gerry sat back in his chair and swirled the remnants of wine in his glass. 'Let's change the subject.'

Christine stood at the table, plates in hand, listening.

'You know that woman Angie who I told you was doing our cleaning? Well, I've lent her my car a couple of times to get about town. Remember I said she had that husband who doesn't let her go out to work?'

'Yes, that's nice of you, Gerry. So?'

'Well, I was telling Doug and he said you might not be too pleased about the car thing and...'

'Why the hell not? It's not like you've bought her a brand new Mercedes - or you're having an affair or anything.'

'Precisely! Sometimes I wonder if Doug's overly sensitive about these things.' He frowned. 'Do you reckon he's ever had an affair?'

'How the hell would I know, you're his friend. Don't think that's the kind of thing Mags would confide in me.'

Christine picked up their empty glasses and bent down to load the dishwasher. 'That Angie woman, was she not the one you introduced me to when I had that crown fitted? Bit older than me, grey hair, dumpy?'

Gerry glanced at his wife's back at she stacked the dishwasher. 'Er, I can't remember exactly if she was in that day, possibly. Yes, she might well have been.' He brought over the last of the dishes. 'I'll do these. You go and get the telly on.'

# Chapter Thirty
25th June 1860

Margaret Barrie lifted her head from the pillow and looked at her husband curled up beside her, sound asleep. She slipped out of bed without disturbing the sheets and tugged the curtain back a fraction. A low mist hovered over the fields of blue flax and a weak sun was breaking through the clouds to the east. She tiptoed towards the wooden cot where the babies lay, back to back. Jane snuffled and thrust her thumb into her mouth. Elizabeth lay on her side, unmoving. Margaret had to admit she was a bonnie baby, but she could never love it, not like her own. Margaret stretched her hand down towards her nose to check she was breathing. A light, warm puff of breath tickled her hand.

She went to the door, pulled on her boots and her coat, picked up the basket and unbolted the lock slowly. She slipped outside and pulled the door behind her.

She looked east and calculated that it must be about five o'clock; David got up about six, so she had enough time. She walked along the street and crossed the main road into the woods. She stepped over fallen branches and grass moist with morning dew. Soon she found what she was looking for around the mossy tree trunks. The long, broad leaves were damp, still covered with tiny droplets of water. Margaret took care to remove any flowers before she put them into the basket. She spread a cloth over the top.

She looked towards the clearing. She would meet him in the cottage later. He would have a bowl of soup and if he had time, perhaps a seat in the garden first, with his pipe, gazing at the tree house. The tree house he said he had built for her, but she knew it was really for the other one, the one with long slender legs to climb up there. How could she, his wife, with her great fat thighs, possibly climb a tree?

Margaret hurried back out of the woods and over the road, checking to see if anyone was up yet in the village. A wispy plume of smoke puffed up from the cottage at the end of the street but everyone else would soon be cleaning out their grates and setting their fireplaces to light.

Then she spotted Bob Grieve, the gardener from the manse, emerging from his cottage next door. She paused, but he headed in the other direction, up the road towards Forfar. Margaret continued with caution up the street, wary of seeing another neighbour. She quietly opened her front door. Silence. Good, the girls had not yet woken.

'Are the bairns still sleeping, Margaret?' He glanced over his steaming porridge to his wife, who was standing at the sink washing the pan and spurtle.

'Aye. That new one seems to calm Jane doon, dinnae ken how.'

David picked up his horn spoon to dip again into his bowl. 'Did you say you'd meet me at the cottage wi' my dinner? Mak' it easier for me to get back quickly to the farm if you could.'

'Aye, I've tae mind Agnes's wee boys a' morning so she'll mind the girls when I bring you your soup.'

'Grand. Thanks, Margaret.' He pushed back the rickety chair from the table and went to the door. 'See you at the cottage then.'

She nodded and took his bowl to the sink. She looked over at the cot, hearing one of the girls begin to stir, then bent down to pick up the basket of leaves and hung it up high on a hook.

In the little cottage in the woods, she lit the fire she had set the day before and began to chop onions. She had dug up two big ones the day before to provide the oniony flavour that ramsons should give. She peeled the potatoes, chopped them up small and plopped them into the pan. She had probably about an hour before he arrived so she had to work fast. The wee boys had been playing up and Agnes took longer to settle them so it had been later than expected when Margaret was able to leave the girls at her cottage.

She rolled up the leaves and sliced them as finely as possible. They were thicker than ramson leaves so would need to cook a little longer. The fire was burning nicely and she had just put the water into the pan when she realised she had forgotten the salt. Why was there nothing like that in this cottage? She would have to hurry home.

When David's father had died, his estranged elder brother had tried to take the cottage, but, having then pilfered the family's meagre savings, he headed for Canada. So his mother remained at the farm steading at Corrie and David kept this cottage, though Margaret had removed much of the furniture for their own home. She had only used it a couple of times, but once the girls were older, she would bring them out here to play in the woods.

She stirred the last of the leaves into the pan, set it on the swee which hung over the fire and rushed out the door. She hesitated then decided to lock it, just in case. She put the key deep into her pocket then strode through the trees before running quickly up the road towards home. Puffing, she poured some salt into a little poke of brown paper then retraced her steps. Fortunately there was no one about, the men all out working in the fields, the women all busy in their homes. She noticed a couple of small children playing at the other end of the street, but that was the only sign of life.

As she reached the glade, she heard someone approaching from the other direction. Margaret recognised the distant sound of a man whistling; it was him. She ran to unlock the cottage, shutting the door behind her. The tiny kitchen smelled good, a strong onion smell. Adding that piece of cow heel to the soup had been a good idea, it looked really appetising now. She added the salt and reached for the wooden spoon to taste. The spoon was at her lips when she remembered. With a start she dropped the spoon and rushed to the door where he sat on the step.

'Why did you shut the door, Margaret? I thought it was locked.'

He sat there, muck from the fields on his hands, his boots filthy.

'I like it here fine enough, but I still wonder about intruders. You ken those folk frae Oathlaw will be oot soon looking for mushrooms.'

He shook his head. 'Food o' the devil.' He pulled off his boots, stood up and came inside.

'That's a fine smell, Margaret. Is it ramson soup?'

'Aye,' she said, glancing at him then turning quickly back to the stove. 'Aye, ramson soup. Sit doon, I'll get you a bowl.'

He sat down at the little wooden table on the only chair in

the room. 'Got to get another chair for this place, Margaret.'

She nodded and ladled out a brimming bowl of soup. She carried it over to him then stood at the door, looking out into the sun-speckled woods.

'It's late for ramsons, is it no'?'

She shrugged and looked round at him. He was spooning in mouthful after mouthful of soup. After a morning working in the fields he always ate like a starving man. She clasped her hands tightly together and looked away.

First she heard the thunk as the spoon dropped to the floor. Then a long, guttural cry of agony. She turned and saw him drop to the floor, clutching his stomach. 'Cannae see! My stomach,' he groaned. 'Gonnae be sick…'

She rushed to get a cloth and put it under his head and he vomited into it, writhing like a mad animal.

She spun round and went to the front door.

'Margaret,' he croaked, 'Dinnae leave me…'

She walked round into the garden and looked up at the tree house, wringing her hands. She nodded, affirmation before her that she had done what needed to be done. This was where the two of them had come, 'just to learn, like at the school', he had said. Davie was bright enough but his reading was atrocious and he could barely write his own name. She had taught him about books, helped him with his reading, he insisted it was nothing more.

But no one would make a fool of Margaret Barrie. Charlotte Whyte might be seen as superior to her, but she was no true lady after what she had done. And she, Margaret, had the upper hand: she was the one Elizabeth would call Ma, not Miss Charlotte, and that served her right. For she must have been a willing victim, not just an innocent seduced by her husband.

Margaret shivered as she thought of the two of them together in the cottage. The minister's daughter and her Davie who she'd always taken for a good, noble man. Well, he's paying for it now. She tipped her head to the side and listened. Silence. Slowly she rounded the corner to the front door and peered in. There was blood mixed in with the vomit by his head. His eyes were open, but she knew he was dead.

She pulled him towards the door, cursing the fact he was so heavy. She dragged him over the moss and grass to the leaning hazel tree opposite. Here she stopped, beside the fresh colony of mushrooms she had spied earlier. She let go of his hand and his arm dropped to the ground like a corpse on a hangman's noose. All the way back to the cottage, she kicked up the vegetation to hide her tracks.

She retrieved the pan of soup and deposited the contents in the mulch underneath the large beech tree in the garden. She piled some branches on top then went back inside and took a pan of boiling water and scrubbed the wooden floor so there was no mark on it other than the odd burn from fallen candles.

She raked over the fire then opened a window just a crack, went to the front door and stepped out. She locked the door behind her and, empty basket in hand, trod her weary way home. She got inside, scrubbed her hands, stoked up the fire then went next door to fetch the babies.

It was not yet dark but the sun was low; there was a chill in the air. Margaret pulled her shawl round her shoulders and went next door to Agnes's to ask if she could listen in for the girls crying – she wanted to go through the woods to look for Davie. He should have been home ages ago.

Agnes's husband Billy said he would go with her and they set off down the road together. Grieve was just coming out of his house with his pipe.

'Fine evening, is it no'?'

Margaret said nothing. She stood, her head stooped, eyes fixed on the road, as Billy explained what they were doing.

'I'll come along wi' you.' He glanced up at Margaret's face, pinched into a frown. 'He's maybe had a pint over in Corrie and fell doon into a ditch.'

The three of them entered the wood, murky in the dying light. They tramped swiftly over the damp vegetation. As they approached the clearing, Margaret slowed down. She began to look around as if she could hear something.

'I thought there was a noise, but it's maybe just a rabbit.'

Billy and Grieve headed towards the leaning hazel tree.

'Look! Here! And he's…'

They both knelt beside him, and Grieve touched a hand to Davie's cold forehead.

Slowly, Margaret walked towards them. She breathed deeply then bent over him. 'Davie!' She clapped both hands to the sides of her face.

Billy pointed to the mushrooms. 'They're deadly webcaps – he must've thought they were penny buns!'

Margaret nodded. 'What will I dae, what will I dae now, these two babies and…'

'But Margaret…' Grieve stood up and looked at her. 'You ken Davie hates mushrooms, he wouldnae touch them, never mind eat them.'

'No, you must been thinking o' someone else,' said Margaret. She stood up straight and said, matter of fact, 'Shall we try an' get him home?'

A couple of hours later, the body of David Barrie was laid out on the wooden table in his cottage in Tannadice village. There were four men around him, a dram in each of their hands. Agnes from next door and Elspeth, the cook from the manse, were sitting beside Margaret on the bed. The babies had been awake all evening with the commotion, but both had finally fallen asleep in Agnes's arms and were now tucked up in their cot.

There was a knock at the door.

Grieve answered it. As he opened it, the candlelight flickered to reveal a tall black figure.

'Mrs Barrie, I have come to pray for your husband's soul.'

Margaret and the women sprang to their feet and the men slipped their drams behind their backs.

'Thank you, Mr Whyte. Come away in, please.'

The minister removed his hat and strode over to her, mouth pursed in zealous resolve. 'Mrs Barrie, before we pray, I feel it incumbent upon me to talk about his burial. He shall be buried in the churchyard alongside his father, if that is satisfactory?'

There was silence in the room as everyone looked at her.

'That is kind, thank you.'

A low buzz of conversation resumed in the dingy room. He leant down to speak to her close. 'I think perhaps we might find this is for the best. Now we may all be at peace.' The long hiss of a sibilant S lingered then faded away.

She looked up at him and felt his eyes penetrate her soul.

# Chapter Thirty-one
2014

Mags went upstairs to the study in the attic and wrinkled her nose. What on earth was that smell? It was reminiscent of joss sticks burning at student parties. She went to the window and found it was open a couple of notches, then picked up a box of matches from the desk. She started searching through drawers till she found what she was looking for. Cannabis. Doug had stopped years ago, before Lottie was born and vowed he would never smoke dope again. But he was obviously so fraught, he was smoking to try to calm down. What the hell was he so bloody stressed about?

He had just left ten minutes before in Gerry's car and hadn't said a proper goodbye as he rushed out the door, even though they wouldn't see each other now until Sunday. Mags tucked the package back where she had found it, underneath a packet of staples, and decided she would speak to him about it once he was back from the dental conference.

Christ, was he even going to a dental thing, hadn't he been to one just before the kids' accident? Was he having an affair? She shook her head. She was sure he wouldn't ever betray her, yet he'd been acting so strangely recently. She headed for the window, opened it wide then stomped downstairs.

In the kitchen she looked around for something to distract her. She picked up the folder of family history research and sat down to look at it. They had got so far, but still couldn't find any record of Elizabeth Barrie before 1871. Would Chris ever get her mind off this fixation on the court case and back onto this? She doubted it. She closed the folder and looked at her watch. Might as well open a bottle, it's that time of night, she thought, heading for the wine rack.

Lottie sat cross-legged on the floor of Anna's Newcastle flat and proffered her empty glass to Jack, who lay sprawled across the bed. They all had their coats on and Lottie had her scarf wrapped round her neck, as the heating had packed in.

The three of them had just finished their take-away pizzas and Anna was ramming the cardboard boxes into the overflowing bin with her foot. She gave a final thrust then went to take the bottle of red from her brother. 'Does Auntie Mags ever get really arsey with Uncle Doug and just bawl at him the whole time?' she asked Lottie. 'That's what Mum and Dad were like last time I was up. They were so snappy, weren't they, Jack?'

Jack frowned. 'Er, no actually, Dad was fine. It's Mum, she gets so cross with him. No idea why, he's just trying to be helpful.'

'She's been pretty grumpy since the accident, hasn't she?'

'Well,' said Lottie, 'she can't be worse than my dad is right now. He's so bloody stressed these days. I mean, he looks terrible, really rough, like he's got a permanent hangover.'

'Uncle Doug could never look rough. You know my friends Mia and Jen really fancy him even though he's ancient,' Anna said, grinning.

Lottie smiled and picked up her glass. 'Is there any more wine, Anna? It's warming me up.'

Anna poured the dregs of the bottle into Lottie's glass.

'Thanks. Anyway, change of subject from parents – you know that girl Katie I babysit for? She's thirteen, doesn't really need a sitter but her mum wants me there. Anyway, she was starting work on some project on genetics and I told her about a fact I remembered from somewhere.'

She went over to Jack and took his chin in her hand. She tilted his face up and looked at him. 'Yeah, you've got brown eyes, so Uncle Gerry's must be brown too as I know Auntie Chris's are really blue.'

Anna shook her head. 'Nope, Dad's are blue too, though not as kind of turquoise as Mum's.'

Lottie sat down beside Anna. 'Well, according to the Google search I did with Katie, it's impossible for two blue-eyed parents to have a brown-eyed child.'

'Oh yeah, that sounds kind of familiar, but is it not the other way round? Two brown-eyed can't have a blue?' Anna produced a slab of chocolate and broke it into pieces, offering it round.

'Oh, yeah, maybe,' said Lottie, taking a piece. 'I'll get some more info for Katie online. Her teacher's an idiot so I said I'd help her with it.'

'Any more wine?' asked Jack.

Anna lifted up the covers hanging off her bed and peered underneath. 'Nope, that was one I pinched from home anyway. No booze left. Let's go down to the pub, might be warmer there.'

When she got back to Edinburgh the next day, Lottie went to visit her mum. She opened the kitchen door and saw Mags standing at the stove, wooden spoon in one hand, stirring a sauce, glass of wine in the other. She shook her head and grinned. 'Look at you, Mum, your favourite pose!'

She gave Mags a kiss. 'Did you have a good time, darling?' Mags put down her glass and the spoon and gave her daughter a hug. 'How are they both?'

'They're both good. Jack is completely recovered, according to the doctor, so no excuses if he fails his exams!'

Mags laughed and pointed to the wine bottle.

'No, thanks. I've got to teach later. I'll have a green tea.' She headed for the kettle. 'So it's closure on that horrible accident for them all. Everything's completely back to normal.'

Mags tasted her sauce then put on the lid and switched the gas off. 'Well, apart from Chris's obsession with revenge on the guy who rammed them, it's really not healthy but she won't let up.'

'Is he not going to court?'

'He didn't turn up, so they've rescheduled. But she's really consumed by it all, even though the kids are fine.' Mags shook her head.

Lottie told her mum more about her visit to Anna's then she got onto Katie and her genetics project. 'So is it two brown-eyed parents who can't have a blue-eyed child?'

Mags shrugged. 'No idea, darling. You know I've never had any interest in science. Ask your dad, he was always into that sort of thing.'

Lottie had already booked a dental check-up for the next day with her dad, who was now back from the conference. Doug turned round from the computer in the corner as his daughter entered the surgery. He smiled and pointed to the dentist's chair.

'Hop up.' Amy handed her a large plastic bib to put

round her neck as he tugged on his latex gloves.

He pressed his foot on the pedal to lower the back of the reclining seat. 'So what have you been up to?'

'Well, remember I was down in Newcastle and...'

'Open wide,' he said, peering into her mouth. 'Hmm, got a bit of plaque build-up on the molars. You're still using that electric toothbrush I gave you, aren't you?'

She nodded, mouth wide.

'Well you need to use it more at the back. But don't go mad, like Mum does, it's bad for the gums. Let the brush do all the work.'

He picked up an instrument and she relaxed her mouth. 'Anna and Jack are both fine, by the way, fully recovered after the accident, according to the doctors. We were chatting about genetics so Mum said to ask you about the eye colour thing. You know how two parents with the same eye colouring can't have a child with a different colour, but I can't remember which way round it is. Can two browns not have a blue?'

'Bollocks, that whole eye colour thing, really common misconception. Right, open wide!' Doug stood over her, instrument in hand, concentrating on her teeth. Lottie looked up at the ceiling which was bare, apart from a glaring strip light. Why did dentists never have interesting things up there to take patients' minds off the trauma of the violation on their teeth?

She returned her focus to her father and looked straight up at him as he scraped at her teeth in silence. God, he was a bit jowly these days, that was obviously all Mum's fab food, though it could be the beer too. She stared up into his eyes. As she did so, she took a sharp intake of breath.

'Sorry, Lotts, was that sore? Your gums are a bit sensitive

there.'

She gaped at the deep brown eyes and did not move.

'Are you all right, Lottie?' Amy asked. 'You've gone a bit pale.'

She nodded slowly and clenched her hands tight together on her stomach. She had seen eyes exactly the same just the day before. Her cousin Jack's.

# Chapter Thirty-two
18th June 1860

The clip-clop of the horse announced her arrival. The cart drew to a halt outside the imposing stone edifice of the manse and everything was still, apart from a snorting as the horse shuffled its head back and forth. It was early morning and a light summer mist hung low over the village.

The driver leapt down, creaked the manse gate open and ran along the path to the back door, which was ajar. Soon a figure wrapped in a large shawl emerged and walked silently down the path.

'Here, hand the wee one tae me, Miss Charlotte, while you get down by the loupin'-on-stane here.' Cookie pointed to the set of five stone steps built beside the wall for easy dismounting from horse or carriage. There was another at the other side of the manse, by the gate to the churchyard.

Charlotte handed the swaddled baby down to Cookie then descended the steps and stood gazing at the manse. This had been her home since she was born but for the past few months she had lived at Corrie with her beautiful child. But now her father needed her back at home. He had decreed it was not fitting that a minister should live there without a lady and since he now had no wife, his daughter would have to suffice.

She looked down the road and considered what she was about to do, something that would pain her more than childbirth itself. She shuddered as she peered through the morning haze.

'Shall I tak' your bag intae the manse, Miss Charlotte?'

'Thank you, Grieve, that would be kind. Cookie and I will be back presently.'

Charlotte stretched her arms out for her baby, then snuggled the bundle close to her breast. 'She's sleeping, Cookie. I fed her before we left. Are you sure Mrs Barrie has enough milk for two babies?'

They walked along the road past the little village houses, some with faint lights from early morning candles. 'Margaret Barrie has such a bosom on her, Miss Charlotte, she could nurse a' the bairns in Angus. That wee one o' hers is a skinny wee soul, so she's plenty milk left for your baby.'

Charlotte began to sniffle. 'I cannot imagine how life will be without her, not yet four months old but such a joy. How will I find the strength to endure each day?'

'I'm sure that, wi' a bit o' time, he'll let you see her. I mean they're just doon the road and…'

Charlotte stopped walking, and brushed her fingertips across her daughter's plump cheek. 'He will not. The shame of everyone talking about it would be too much. He has said I am to be confined to the manse, penance for the disgrace I have caused, and for bringing about my mother's demise. If I am allowed out, it will be to the garden or along the path to the church. He said he needs me at home now Mother is gone, but truly, I believe he wants to keep me a prisoner.'

'You mustnae think like that, Miss. And you didnae cause your poor mother's death. She was always a wee bit poorly and prone to a' sorts. He said it was the shock that did it, but I'm sure it was just her time.'

'Cookie, she was only fifty-seven years old. If you had seen her face when she looked at Elizabeth that day, you'd know I caused her death.' Charlotte looked up at the sky, which was beginning to brighten. 'And so I must now atone for my transgressions. It is God's will.'

They came to a halt outside a house that had a wisp of smoke emerging from the low chimney.

Charlotte bit her lips as Cookie rapped on the door.

'He won't be here, will he?' Charlotte whispered, panic in her voice.

Cookie shook her head. 'The men have already a' gone tae the fields', she said then nodded as Margaret Barrie opened the door. She stood in a ragged brown dress on the doorstep and for a moment did not move. She eyed Charlotte up and down, assessing how she had changed in the past months. Still tall and slender by the looks of her but less well kempt, her frock was a little ragged around the hem, and her eyes were red-rimmed and weary.

'I willnae ask you in, wee Jane's still sound asleep.'

'Is the cot big enough for two babies?'

Margaret glowered at her. 'Aye, plenty big. And there's certainly nae problems wi' feeding the both o' them.' She paused to press a forearm across her large breasts and squirmed. 'I've tae much milk, they're sore a' the time.'

Charlotte nodded and looked down at Elizabeth, who was still sleeping, her long black lashes throwing a slight shadow across her perfect skin. She planted a kiss on her nose, before Cookie gently reached forward to take her baby away. Charlotte screwed up her eyes as if in physical pain as Margaret snatched the baby from Cookie. 'She's heavier than Jane but maybe my Janie'll overtake this one soon.'

She turned to go back inside.

Charlotte leant forward, trying to see where her child was

to live. 'Mrs Barrie, you'll let us know if there's anything you need?'

'I'll let Elspeth ken if there's anything.' She nodded gravely at both women and shut the door behind her.

Charlotte's legs buckled and she collapsed onto Cookie's shoulder. The older woman put an arm round her and walked her along the road. 'There, there, it'll be fine, Miss Charlotte. Margaret's no' a bad woman, just a simple country wifie. The wee one'll be fine. At least she's just doon the road – mind the other option was for her to gang far away and you'd never see her ever again. It's for the best. Now let's get you home and straight tae yer bed.'

Charlotte's sniffles were now sobs, uncontrollable gasps that wracked her whole body as she leant against Cookie's shoulders.

They shambled along the road to the manse where a dim light emerged from the study. As the gate scraped open, a curtain was drawn a fraction and the women saw a black figure peering out, eyes blazing in a haunting pale face.

# Chapter Thirty-three
2014

Lottie stumbled into the car park outside her dad's dental practice and pulled out her phone. She typed out a quick text, asking him to meet her at the pub next door when he finished. It was an abrupt message, 'Meet for drink at five, pub next door.' No kisses. She knew he would do as she asked.

Now she had an hour to kill, but she couldn't go home, to her parents' house, until she had seen him. She couldn't face her mum and pretend everything was normal. She felt dazed.

Lottie decided she would wait in the pub and have a drink while waiting for him, to try and calm her nerves.

Mags had texted Christine earlier asking her to call if she had a minute during her lunch break. In the middle of unloading the dishwasher, her phone rang.

'Is everything all right?' asked Christine.

'Yeah, I just wanted to run something past you.'

'Fire away.'

'I'm a bit worried. You know I've mentioned before how stressed Doug is? Well, there have been other signs, I won't go into them now but, the thing is… God, I can't believe I'm about to say this. I think he's having – or has had – an affair.'

Silence.

'Did you hear me?'

'Yes, sorry, a P2 boy's just tripped and fallen headlong, but Eileen's there. So, why do you reckon he might be?'

'He's unbelievably grumpy and distant, and has been for ages now – Lottie's noticed it too – and, well, he doesn't seem to fancy me any more, he's barely touched me in weeks. I don't know what to do.'

Silence.

'Do you know something, Chris? Has Gerry said something?' Mags's voice was urgent.

'Heavens no, sorry. No, listen, I think he's maybe just going through some kind of weird midlife crisis. I mean, I thought Gerry was having an affair with his cleaning lady, Angie, till I realised she's about ninety and the size of a house.' There was forced laughter. 'I think we're all just too stressed at work. I know I am.'

'Yeah, well I wish I was stressed at work too but I've got hardly any to do these days.'

'Mags, you are so talented, that big cake contract will come your way. Just wait!'

'Hmm. Maybe I just have too much time on my hands right now, and I'm overthinking everything.'

'I'm sure that's all it is.'

'Yeah. Doug wouldn't stray, would he?'

Silence.

'Are you still there?'

'Yes. Sorry, Mags, I've got to go, but no, I think he's fine. The men just need a bit of space to work through their midlife crises. He'll be back to normal soon, you'll see.'

Mags came off the phone and went to the back door to get some fresh air. She opened it wide and stood on the step listening to a harsh squawking noise. She looked towards the pair of apple trees in the garden where two large crows were cawing menacingly at each other.

Doug wove his way through the tables towards the bar, acknowledging fellow drinkers with nods or quick exchanges of pleasantries. It was like watching a celebrity negotiate the paparazzi on the red carpet, such was the adulation for her handsome father from the locals.

'What can I get you, Lotts?'

She looked up at him, taking in the thick mop of hair, greying at the sides, the heavy, dark eyebrows. And those eyes.

'I'll have another wine,' said Lottie, pushing away her empty glass. 'Red.'

Lottie watched her father banter with the barman as he pulled a pint. Doug brought the glass to his lips and sipped through the foam, waiting as the barman poured Lottie's large glass of red.

'Cheers!' he said, sitting down and raising his glass to her. 'So, tell me more about your weekend. You said the doctor's given them the all-clear. Is Jack a hundred per cent now?'

Lottie sipped from her glass of wine then put it back on the beer mat. 'Yup, fully fit, they're both well.' She brought her chair closer to the table and looked directly at Doug. 'Anyway, I'd started to tell you about Katie and the genetics project. I'd told her I thought a couple with blue eyes can't have a child with a different eye colour.'

Doug took a long draught of beer. 'Like I said, Lotts, it's a complete myth. Put that girl straight before she gets marked down. It's not common, but it's certainly possible for two blue-eyed parents to have a brown-eyed baby. Something to do with the blue gene being a broken one.'

Doug swigged from his glass and glanced over at Lottie, whose features were set rigid.

'Dad,' She leaned in so she was just inches from his face, 'whether that genetics thing is true or not, I want you to answer me straight. Is Jack your son?'

He stared at her for a moment too long then laughed, a little too loudly. 'What? Whatever makes you think that?'

She said nothing, and kept staring at his eyes. He looked away and downed his pint.

'Want another one, Lotts?'

'No. I want you to answer my questions truthfully, or…'

'How's it going, mate?' A hearty clap on Doug's back. 'Not seen you for ages.'

'Bill, how're you doing? This is my daughter Lottie. Want to join us?'

Bill stretched out his hand to Lottie. She shook it and said, 'Sorry Bill, nice to meet you but we're having a kind of planning meeting, a secret family thing.'

'No worries. See you later, mate.'

Doug stretched his neck from side to side, still avoiding his daughter's gaze.

'Dad, you can do all you want to get off the subject, do your physio in the middle of the pub if you like, but I'm not moving from here until you tell me the truth.'

Doug opened his mouth then put up his finger. He turned to Bill at the bar and shouted, 'Bill, get me a pint, mate, would you?'

Bill nodded. Lottie and Doug were silent, Lottie finishing her wine while staring at her father, Doug clapping his hands together silently as if trying to get warm. Bill delivered the beer and left.

'Well?' said Lottie. 'Is Jack your son?'

'Don't be ridiculous.'

'The letter in the piano was definitely your writing. I

looked in my old photo album and saw Grandpa's writing – it's nothing like yours. And Jack's eyes… Dad, they're just like yours.' She strummed her fingers on the table.

'Eyes can be similar, of course they can.' Doug looked down at the table. 'Christ, Lottie, how many glasses have you had? You're becoming like your mother, drinking too much. Talking nonsense.'

Lottie leant forward again and spoke in a low voice. 'If you don't tell me the truth, Dad, I'm going to tell Mum about my suspicions.'

'Don't. Please, Lotts, don't mention a thing to Mum.'

'Why not? If it's not true then there's nothing to worry about.'

Doug put his pint down with a thud. 'You can't. Please. It's not as simple as that. The truth is… It's not what you think. It wasn't like that. It wasn't an affair, it wasn't.'

'What the fuck do you mean?'

'What I mean is, it was all an accident, she ensnared me, it was a trap and it should never have happened.'

Lottie's eyes opened wide. 'Who's she? Auntie Chris?'

'Obviously. She's his fucking mother.' He took a long drink and set down his glass again. His hand was shaking.

'So it's true. That note at the back of the piano was from you to Auntie Chris?'

His shoulders slumped. 'Yes, I'd forgotten all about it. God knows how it ended up in there, I must have been trying to hide it. But you can see by what I wrote that the whole incident meant nothing. I never loved her. I love your mum, I always have. Always will.'

He shut his eyes and leant back. Lottie said nothing so he opened them and whispered, 'Please don't tell her.'

'Give me one good reason why I should be on your side!

You've kept this secret for all these years. And doesn't Jack have a right to know?' She gasped. 'That's why you were so emotional when he had the accident, wasn't it? I can't believe this.'

'Please. Just don't tell Mum. Please. I'm begging you, I'll do anything, Lotts.' He bit his lip.

Lottie stood up and picked up her glass. 'If this still had wine in it, I'd fling it in your face. You are nothing but a fucking liar. I hate you.'

She stormed towards the door and Doug strode after her. 'Lotts, please, please don't tell Mum,' he whispered. 'Give me time, I'll explain it all to you.'

She wrenched the door open, refusing to look back at him as she strode out.

# Chapter Thirty-four
4th June 1860

Maud Whyte emerged from the dim courtroom into broad daylight and blinked. She stretched out an arm to lean against the solid granite wall of Forfar Sheriff Court. She was trying to control her breathing, as the doctor had told her to do so often, to slow her racing heart.

'My dear, shall you sit down to recover?'

'I cannot sit down in the middle of Forfar High Street, Charles!' she muttered to her husband.

'I shall ask Grieve to fetch the carriage and you may sit there until the proceedings end.' He raised a slender hand upwards and pointed one bony finger heavenward to beckon the driver.

'I will be back presently.' The Reverend Whyte turned and re-entered the court, his long black frock coat swinging wide behind him.

'Madam, will you sit up here awhile?' Grieve extended his hand to Mrs Whyte and gestured to the loupin'-on-stane. With his help, she managed to ascend and soon she sat back in the carriage, her powder blue dress gathered around her and her dark bonnet perched on top of her tight grey bun. She continued repeating the breathing exercises Doctor Macleod had taught her.

She really ought not to have come. Charles had tried to forbid it but she insisted, even though she knew her health was not up to it. But he was forever controlling her and she decided that, for once, she would do as she herself wished and would attend, for the sake of her daughter.

Even though she was permitted no contact with Charlotte, she could at least be there in the court for her. Maud felt a sudden sweat envelop her face and she rummaged in her bag for her smelling salts.

'Is there anything I can get you, Mrs Whyte?'

'Nothing, thank you, Grieve,' she whispered, her voice as feeble as her body. She took out her fan and attempted to cool her face. When she shut her eyes, the frightful scenes she had just witnessed inside the court room loomed up once more.

She still did not understand why her husband had insisted on the paternity suit. The ignominy and shame of the whole situation had been bad enough, why he had demanded that David Barrie be named as the father on a legal document was beyond her comprehension. It was mystifying, but no one, not even his wife, dared to question his decisions.

Charles had always asserted his authority over her in everything, from what she was permitted to wear to whom she could invite to the manse for tea. And with her fragile health, it was simply too much to cause discord by attempting to disagree with him.

She was still surprised that he had consented so readily to her suggestion that she accompany him this morning to Forfar and to the court. But as she sat there in the carriage, eyes still tight shut, heart pounding, she contemplated the prudence of her action.

A noise from the courtroom entrance made her open her grey eyes and turn round. Her heart seemed to race faster, if that was at all possible. It was Charlotte, alone, about to cross the road towards a woman standing with a bundle in her arms. That must be the child! She watched as her daughter rushed to the woman and swept the baby into her arms.

Could she do this? Before he came back out from the court room, would she be able to see her grandchild, even though it was strictly forbidden? He would never forgive her, but there was surely time…

'Grieve! Go and fetch Miss Charlotte. At once!'

Grieve nodded, jumped down from the carriage and sped over the road to speak to her. Maud saw Charlotte's bewildered expression, but she followed Grieve and came to stand by the carriage. The baby was snuggled in tight to her chest. Maud took in her daughter's face, her slate eyes lacklustre and her hair bedraggled. She reached out her hand and tucked a loose strand of hair behind her daughter's ear underneath her bonnet.

'Mother, how are you?' The concern in her voice conveyed to Maud how dreadful she must look.

'I am not well, Charlotte, but I had to come. Let me see the child. Please, before your father arrives.'

Charlotte glanced round to the courtroom entrance then turned the baby round to face Maud.

Charlotte tickled her chin. 'Oh, Charlotte, look at her.' There was such sadness in her mother's faint voice. 'Are you managing at Corrie?'

The baby stirred, and opened her large eyes, gazing straight at Maud.

'Oh, look. How beautiful her eyes are, my love.' Maud smiled then put down her fan and peered closely at the child. Suddenly she drew back, with a sharp intake of breath. 'The eyes, they are so brown, so dark…'

Maud panted for a few moments while Charlotte tried to pat her mother's narrow back, as she had been doing for years when she had an attack. But Maud's wheezing worsened. She struggled for breath, trying desperately to draw air into her tight chest. Her bony shoulders rose as she took one last strained gasp for air and slumped back onto the seat.

Charlotte put her hand on her mother's brow. 'Grieve, fetch a doctor. Now!'

Bob Grieve set off, running full speed up the street. A kerfuffle at the courtroom door drew Charlotte's attention. It was her father.

She took one last look at her mother then bolted across the road back to the waiting woman and they both hastened away down the street. At the end, she turned back to see her father stride towards the carriage, three members of the kirk session behind him. They were all in black, tailcoats flapping; a murder of crows.

# Chapter Thirty-five
2014

Christine and Mags were in Mags's garden with a cup of tea, sitting on the wooden bench in a bower framed by two coral-pink rhododendron bushes.

'Those apple trees give us too much shade at this time of year,' said Mags. 'I've asked Doug to chop off some of those high branches but he keeps wittering on about his fear of heights.'

'Oh, I think it all looks gorgeous out here. You're so lucky to have a well-established garden. Our hedge is so short, there's no privacy from the nosey neighbours.' Christine looked to her side. 'Are those lily of the valley over there? I thought they were a spring flower?'

'No, mine flower till July. The garden's north facing so maybe that's why. They're on the wane.' Mags sipped from her mug. 'Are you looking forward to the summer holidays? I can't believe it's that time already, it feels like it was Easter just recently.'

'I know! I thought we might do another visit to Register House if you're up for it? See if we can pin down Elizabeth Barrie and try to check if her mother was the same person who was the minister's daughter, the one with lily of the valley on her tombstone.'

'That's just so unlikely, Chris, and the more I think about it, why on earth would you have a paternity suit if it wasn't for the money. You know, alimony. And surely a daughter of the manse wouldn't need any? It's not like they'd be paupers or anything.'

'True, unlike the woman we thought was her mother, what was her name again?'

'Margaret Barrie.' Mags took a mouthful of brownie. 'You've not tried these brownies yet – there's a new flavour today, guess what's in them?'

'You know I'm rubbish at this.' Christine nibbled on a corner. 'Cinnamon?'

Mags nodded. 'Yeah, your taste buds are improving! I was going to bake a different batch this afternoon. Why don't I give you a couple to take down to Gateshead tomorrow? You can have them with your coffee, take your mind off the court thing.'

'Thanks, that'd be great.'

'I'll pop round with them tonight.' Mags glanced over at her cousin. 'Chris, are you still positive you want to go to the hearing tomorrow?'

'Definitely, he's got to turn up tomorrow. That's twice he's not attended so it's his last chance. And with the witness statements, he's really got no option but to plead guilty.'

'Are you sure you don't want me to come with you?'

'You'd just get cross with my driving,' said Christine.

'Well, you are a bit slow.'

'I'm not slow, I'm safe. And better that than cause the kind of accident that nearly killed my two children.'

'You're right. Sorry.' Mags frowned. 'Okay, I won't come. But you're not planning anything are you? You won't confront him or anything?'

'No, I just want to see him being sentenced. That's revenge enough.' Christine looked at her watch. 'Right, I should go. I need to fill the car with petrol on the way home.'

They picked up the tea tray and went back into the house. 'I'll pop round tonight with brownies for your journey,' said Mags.

'Brilliant, they'll be my breakfast.'

They hugged each other and Chris headed for the gate before turning back. She called back, 'How's it going with Auntie Bella's bucket list?'

Mags grinned. 'The thought of an octogenarian smoking dope still kind of freaks me out, but hey, if that's what she wants, I'll ask around. See you later.'

Mags tidied away the things from the tea tray then unfolded the ironing board and picked up the overflowing laundry basket.

She had just finished folding the shirts and putting them away upstairs when she heard a shout from below.

'I'm home, darling!'

It was Doug. She looked at her watch. Strange, he was very early.

She went downstairs and wandered along the corridor towards the kitchen. He came towards her and gave her a kiss. 'My last two patients cancelled so I thought I'd just come home. Have you got much on this afternoon? We could go and do something together?'

She looked at him quizzically. 'Like what?'

He shrugged. 'I dunno, go for a walk or... Oh, what about a cycle down to South Queensferry or something?'

She wound the flex round the iron. 'If you want, though Lottie said she might pop in as she's got the afternoon off too.'

'Lets just go now, Mags. We can have a late lunch somewhere.'

'Well…'

They heard the front door slam shut, and Lottie strode into the kitchen.

'Hi, Mum.' She glared at Doug.

'What's wrong?' asked Mags. 'Why are you looking at your dad like that?'

'I'll let him tell you.'

'Tell me what? Doug?'

But Doug was silent, his face grey.

'Tell me what?' Mags repeated.

Lottie hesitated, briefly, then looked at her father. 'He's a lying, cheating bastard.'

There was a deathly hush.

Doug looked at Lottie, eyes imploring.

'What are you talking about?' Mags bit her lip.

'Sit down, Mum.'

Mags sat heavily on the chair that Lottie pulled out for her. Doug remained standing by the ironing board.

'It all started when I found a letter hidden inside the piano. Then that story Anna told me about genetics, even though it's not true, it got me thinking. And Jack's eyes, they're just like Dad's.'

'What the hell are you getting at?' Mags asked. Doug's face was haggard; he had the look of a condemned man.

'I found a letter from Dad to someone,' said Lottie. 'To Auntie Chris.'

'Stop!' shouted Doug.

'Dad is Jack's father.' Lottie's shoulders slumped and she leaned forward to take her mother's hand.

Mags burst out laughing. 'Don't be ridiculous, Lotts, just because they've both got brown eyes.' She turned to her husband. 'What's this all about, Doug?'

He looked at the floor and said nothing. 'I'm sorry, Mum,' said Lottie. 'But it's true.'

'Is this some kind of sick joke?'

'No,' said Lottie, staring at her father. 'It's true. He and Auntie Chris had a fling and the result is Jack.'

Mags swallowed. 'Get me some water.' Doug darted to the sink and filled a mug with water. He placed it carefully on the table beside her and she downed it in a couple of gulps.

'Doug, tell me it's not true?'

Doug looked up at the ceiling. 'I'd love to, Mags, really I would, but what Lottie says is true. Jack's mine, but it was *not* an affair. We've kept it a secret from you all for so long now, I hoped it would all just go away and...'

Mags opened her mouth wide. 'Go away? So all that stuff you've told me about finding Chris unattractive over the past twenty-five years has been rubbish. You've lied all this time to me and to Lottie and to... God, does Jack know? And how about Gerry? Anna?'

'No. Nobody knows.'

'And is Chris aware we know?' she asked Lottie.

'Not yet.'

Mags slumped onto the table and buried her face in her hands.

No one said a thing until Mags sat up straight and looked at her husband. 'Doug, get out of here. Now.' She looked at her daughter. 'Lottie, don't tell anyone about this, not a whisper, do you understand?'

Lottie nodded.

'Mags, darling, I can explain everything. It's not what you think.'

'Ha, I'm sure it's not.' She picked up her mug and hurled

it at his head. He ducked and it shattered against the pale cream wall.

Doug snatched his car keys and slunk down the corridor and out of the house.

'Want a glass of wine, Mum?'

'Yes, that… No, actually, I won't. I've got things to do.'

'What can I do?' Lottie said, walking towards her and reaching out her arms for a hug.

Mags shivered and said, 'Nothing, darling, just play me something lovely on the piano, please.'

'Soothing or loud?'

'Music I can rage to.'

# Chapter Thirty-six
4th June 1860

Charlotte Whyte had just sat down in the seat allocated to her in Forfar Sheriff Court when a noise behind her made her turn. It was her father dressed in his minister's vestments and on his arm was a stooped old lady, head bent low. Charlotte peered round and realised this was no old lady, it was her mother. She looked ghastly. Why had she come, had he forced her? She tried to snatch another look but they sat down and she could see only him, his steely gaze taking in the stark courtroom and finally settling on his daughter. She cast her eyes down to her lap, brushing at her skirt as if it were covered in dirty stains.

She was as bewildered as she had been three days before when her father's man Mr Lamb had delivered the letter summoning her to court. The letter with its legal phrases made little sense to her but it was easy to see her father's malevolence behind it.

*Sheriffdom of Forfar*
*Initial Writ*
*-In Causa*
*-Charlotte Whyte, Corrie, Parish of Forfar, Pursuer*
*Against*
*-David Barrie, The Village, Tannadice, Parish of Forfar, Defender*

*-The Pursuer craves the court:*
*To find and declare that the defender is the father of Elizabeth*

*Barrie, an illegitimate child born to the Pursuer on 29 February 1860.*

How was this necessary? She knew her father had registered the birth, but she had never seen the birth certificate.

When Mr Lamb had brought the letter, she had asked why the kirk session was doing this, for she had neither asked for this nor given her consent. And why had her daughter been named Barrie rather than Whyte? He remained silent, merely pointing to the document.

She had tried to read the writ but could get no further than the statement that she and the defender had had carnal knowledge out of wedlock and that she had given birth to an illegitimate child. How could her father be so cruel to expose her to such public humiliation?

When Mr Lamb eventually spoke, his reply gave no comfort. 'The Defender denied paternity of the child, Miss Whyte, so the case will be heard at the Sheriff Court on the 4th of June. Your father shall arrange transport for you and I need not add that the baby must not be brought to court. No doubt you can make arrangements to have her minded?'

Charlotte felt sick. She glanced up at the ruddy face and thick whiskers of Mr Lamb. 'My father is insisting upon this?'

'He is, Miss Whyte.' He left the room, taking his stale stench of sweat with him.

Charlotte was startled from her thoughts by the wigged clerk calling out her name. 'Charlotte Whyte against David Barrie,' he announced to everyone.

'This is an action of paternity over an illegitimate child, my Lord. It is tabling today so it is a first calling; there is to be a hearing.'

Charlotte could hear an indefinable rustling from the gallery and glanced up at the audience. Behind the wooden railings were the public benches and a couple of rows of people, presumably locals keen to witness the spectacle. Mercifully she recognised no one from the village; that would have heaped even more humiliation upon her.

The proceedings seemed to have no more to do with her than the writ her father had lodged without her agreement. The Sheriff on the high bench in front of her was addressed by a lawyer in a gown, apparently her advisor, though she had never spoken to him. Presumably her father had instructed him as to his daughter's 'wishes'.

'I represent the pursuer, Charlotte Whyte, my lord. The defender is unrepresented. The defender denies paternity, so a trial will be needed.'

'Is that correct, Mr Barrie?' asked the Sheriff. 'You deny being the father of this child?'

'Please stand,' the clerk ordered.

David stood up, folded his arms in front of him and looked straight at the Sheriff. Speaking softly and slowly, he said, 'I *am* the father of the bairn, Elizabeth Barrie, I dinnae deny it, sir.'

Charlotte gasped. She leant forward to look at him, and for a brief second their eyes met. Those beautiful, deep-set eyes of his. She saw the compassion in them as he tried to smile at her. She shook her head and mouthed 'Why?'

David looked back two rows towards where the minister and his wife sat. He stared, features rigid with loathing.

'You understand what this means, Mr Barrie?'

David nodded and the Sheriff said to the lawyer, 'I will find him as confessed but you have not asked for in-lying expenses for the birth of the child or for aliment to support the child.'

'No, my lord.'

'Very well,' said the Sheriff, turning back to David. 'David Barrie, in terms of your confession I will grant the Pursuer's Plea in law and declare you to be the father of Charlotte Whyte's child, Elizabeth Barrie.'

At that, the clerk pronounced the court dismissed and Charlotte heard a rustle behind her. She turned to see her mother stumble out from her seat and stagger towards the door.

# Chapter Thirty-seven
2014

Christine placed her handbag and the little basket from Mags on the passenger seat and turned the key in the ignition, peering at the dashboard to check the time. Eight o'clock, that should give her plenty time to reach the court in Gateshead by eleven, when the hearing was due to start.

As she took the slip road out of Edinburgh onto the A1, she thought through the implications of the text she had received from Doug the previous evening.

It had been about nine o'clock and she was sitting on the sofa beside Gerry, who was engrossed in the football. Seeing Doug's name on the screen, she turned her back to her husband as she put on her glasses and read. The message was full of typos and there was no punctuation; he must be drunk, extremely drunk. It read, 'tje secrets out say notjing til we cam corobbrate storys be in toucj later'. She stared at it, not moving a muscle. Gerry was still staring at the screen, his fists clenched as he watched a player running for the goal. She slipped off the sofa and stole towards the door, running upstairs to try and call Doug. It went straight to answer phone. She paced up and down the bedroom, trying again and again.

What part of the secret was out? And who knew? She went to the bathroom and splashed her face with cold water then grabbed a towel. In the mirror her eyes were wide with fear.

She went downstairs and sat down beside Gerry, who

had not moved.

The doorbell rang.

'I'll get it!' She rushed to the door. Please don't let it be Doug, she thought.

She opened the door and there stood Mags, beaming, a little basket in her hands.

'Oh, Mags.' Christine faltered. 'How are you?' She scrutinised her cousin's face.

'Fine.' Mags looked a little strained but she smiled again. 'Here are your brownies for the journey tomorrow. New flavour, think you'll like them.'

'Thanks. Do you want to come in?'

'No, I don't have time, got a cake to ice for a catering job.'

'Oh, brilliant! Well done.'

There was an awkward silence. Mags handed the basket to Christine. 'Right, must go.' She looked into her cousin's eyes, a strange expression on her face, and said, 'Goodbye, Christine.'

She turned quickly and headed towards the gate. Christine shouted goodbye, but Mags didn't look back.

Funny, she thought, Mags hadn't called her Christine for years.

All the way to Berwick-Upon-Tweed, Christine mulled it over: Doug's text then Mags's strange visit.

Doug's phone was still switched off, so she decided to concentrate instead on the court hearing. She was trying to imagine how Colin Clarkson would appear in court. She thought about first seeing him in A&E with his daughter and then more recently on that Sunday she had seen him outside his house. Would he have on that same shiny suit?

She shivered as she thought of the day of the crash, the

worst in her life, no question.

A large road sign indicated that it was nine miles to Alnwick, and a small sign just past it read 'Brownieside'. Why had she never noticed that name before on her journeys south to see the kids? It was like something from Enid Blyton. And then she remembered Mags's brownies, and realised she was starving.

Keeping her eyes on the road, she removed the cloth from the top of the basket with her left hand. She smiled as she laid the cloth neatly over her lap. How well Mags knew her: she hated crumbs in her car, and had always forbidden the kids from eating anything on journeys apart from boiled sweets, to much consternation from Gerry who said they would rot their teeth.

Christine lifted back the foil in the basket and picked out a large brownie. She bit in; they were gorgeous as ever. Mags had told her it was all about the quality of the chocolate and the dark brown sugar – and was it duck eggs that made them even richer? Anyway, these were really delicious. What on earth was the flavour? They were incredibly more-ish.

She had a couple of swigs of water from her bottle then picked up another large brownie and dug in her teeth. Was that a hint of mint in there? Or was it ginger? Another bite. No, maybe rosemary; but how could Mags get the flavour of rosemary without the coarseness of the leaves? These were so smooth and buttery. Mags really was a great cook. Compared to herself, she had to admit, her cousin was a genius in the kitchen.

Christine settled back into the seat and arranged her head into a comfortable position against the headrest. She felt quite sleepy, actually. It must be the stress of everything that had been happening. Today was a big day. Christine put on the radio but switched it off after a while – it was all too dull for such a beautiful day. The sun was out and white clouds dotted the sky like fluffy marshmallows. She smiled as she glanced at the fat lambs grazing beside their mothers in the fields to her left; to her right she saw a bird of prey, perhaps a kestrel, hover then swoop to the ground.

It was a glorious day. But soon she would come face to face with the man who had so nearly killed her two children, and this time there was no elderly mother or cute child to influence her feelings. But she felt surprisingly calm – pretty relaxed, in fact. Today would bring some closure. And once she'd seen Colin Clarkson get his punishment, that would be that. No more vengeance.

She leaned forward and checked her face in the mirror. She looked dreadful, she had aged. Even though she had carefully applied her eyeliner, her eyes looked tired. She couldn't be bothered carrying on with this revenge thing, it was taking too much out of her – and making her a crabby old bitch.

Life was too short, she thought as she nestled back comfortably into her seat again. She bit another chunk of brownie, then rammed it all inelegantly into her mouth. Heavens, she'd never eaten two huge brownies for breakfast before.

She was starting to feel queasy, but still her left hand hovered over the basket. She jerked her hand away and said aloud, 'No, you greedy old bag, two brownies are enough for breakfast.'

She was still feeling rather sleepy, when she needed to be alert and make good time down the road. She didn't want to be late. She put her foot down hard on the accelerator.

'Just get yourself to Gateshead!'

She swerved into the overtaking lane and drove past the little blue Golf in front. How slowly some people drive! She veered left again and found herself stuck behind a slow-moving lorry.

She strummed her fingers on the wheel and glanced at the clock. She needed to hurry. Down went the foot, pressing hard on the floor as she veered sharply to the right. She glanced down at the speedometer and chuckled: amazing how this clapped-out old banger could get from fifty to seventy so quickly! Maybe Mags was right, driving fast was a lot more fun! She was halfway past the lorry when it became clear this was no longer the dual carriageway and there were only two lanes. Another colossal lorry was hurtling towards her, head on.

# Chapter Thirty-eight
29th February 1860

Lorna Barrie jolted awake to an unusual sound. Not quite a cry, not quite a wail, it was coming from downstairs. She sat up and threw the wide shawl she used as a bedspread around her. She lit the candle on the bedside table and went to the door.

'Miss Charlotte?' she shouted into the gloom. 'Where are you?'

The reply was another groan. Lorna descended the stairs as fast as she could, thinking of the time three months previously, when Davie had persuaded his mother to take Charlotte in before she showed, so the parishioners need not know. She hadn't realised how difficult it might be having a lady stay in her modest farm steading, just the two of them. Of course Charlotte was polite, grateful and well-mannered but their lives were so different. And Margaret, Davie's wife, had not taken too kindly to the situation at all, which was hardly surprising.

In the kitchen a lamp was lit and Charlotte sat at the table leaning back against the chair, arms outstretched towards the table, white-knuckled fingers grasping the edge. She was panting heavily.

'Oh, Miss Charlotte, the baby's coming, you must get back up the stairs.' The elderly woman pulled her shawl tight round her. 'Why are you doon here?'

'I was so thirsty and then suddenly I was wet and…'

'Come now, my dear, let's get you up yon stairs then I shall rouse young Johnnie to go and fetch Ma Craig.' She put an arm round Charlotte's back and guided her to the stairs, holding the candle aloft.

At the top of the stairs, Charlotte stooped and started panting again.

'Now then, lass, it will all be fine,' said Lorna, patting Charlotte's back. She managed to get her along the corridor to her room and into bed. 'Dinnae move frae here, I'll be back presently to light the fire.'

Lorna Barrie, although only sixty, stooped like a much older woman. Because of her heart, she had always taken her time to do even the simplest of tasks. Before Davie's birth, she had been perfectly healthy but he had been such a big baby, the delivery had nearly killed her. The howdie wife said she had never brought such a big bairn into the world.

She moved down the stairs as quickly as she could, with a grimace on her face. 'Why's it aye the middle o' the night?' she muttered.

She went into the kitchen and to the door where she thrust her feet into a pair of boots caked in dry mud, then opened the door into the chill air. She turned towards the stable and banged on the door.

'Johnnie! Get up, Johnnie, I need ye to gang and fetch Ma Craig!'

She heard a sigh from inside, and the door creaked opened a little. 'I'll just get ma clothes on, Mrs Barrie.'

'You better be quick, the bairn's on its way.' She turned to go back to the house then shouted over her shoulder, 'If ye dinnae get a move on, it'll be you helping me wi' her upstairs!'

She was kicking off her boots at the kitchen door when she heard a door slam. Good, for once the lad was aware of the urgency. She started her weary ascent of the stairs. 'I'm here, Miss Charlotte, dinnae fret. I'm on my way.'

A couple of hours later, there was a blazing fire in Charlotte's room. Johnnie had been left to light the fire in the kitchen and his next job was to boil water.

'Get that pan o' water up the stairs, Johnnie Bell!' Ma Craig bellowed out the door into the murk. 'An' bring up another lamp.'

There was a low moan from the bed as Charlotte's contraction took hold. The two women held her arms down so she wouldn't fall out of the narrow bed as she writhed in agony.

'Mop her broo, Lorna,' said Ma Craig.

Once Charlotte had stopped shifting about, she said, 'Miss Charlotte, I'm gonnae hae a wee look doon there now as the pains are comin' faster. Dinnae think it'll be long.' She turned to Lorna and told her to hold the lamp near.

She fumbled to remove the covers and Charlotte shouted, 'I need to push, now!'

'Wait, lass, wait till I say.' Ma Craig gestured to Lorna to hold down her arms while she took the lamp to see better. 'Where's that lad wi' the other lamp?'

A thump at the door announced his arrival. 'Am leavin' the pail and the lamp oot here,' he bellowed. There was a scampering of footsteps heading downstairs.

Lorna opened the door and grabbed the lamp.

'Now, Miss Charlotte, now it's time to push.'

A long wail followed and the two women waited. Charlotte's eyes were shut tight in agony.

An hour later, Charlotte lay in a freshly made bed, the baby in her arms, wrapped in a white sheet and woollen blanket. She gazed at the sleeping child and stroked her soft downy head. 'Are babies always so peaceful when they are newly born, Mrs Craig?'

'No' always, Miss Charlotte, but this yin's a big, healthy bairn, she's nae need tae girn. Has she opened her eyes yet?'

'Not fully, no, but her lashes have fluttered open and shut. She's so beautiful.' She looked at both women. 'Thank you both very much. It's the middle of the night, Mrs Barrie. You must be tired. But please would you fetch my purse from the dresser over there so I might pay Mrs Craig?'

Lorna stretched her neck and stood up slowly, rubbing her back.

'That willnae be necessary, Miss Charlotte.' Ma Craig shook her head.

Charlotte looked up from her baby. 'But surely you must be paid for your work?'

'It's a' been taken care of.'

'What do you mean?'

'The kirk session's dealing wi' it, Miss Charlotte.' Ma Craig stood up and picked up her bag. She turned to Lorna. 'You'll be a' right here tonight?'

The other woman nodded.

'I'll be back here in the morn to check them both oot. I've tae check on Bessie Grant over by the smithy first thing but I'll come on after that.'

Charlotte nodded at Ma Craig as she left. Lorna went with her to the top of the stairs and bellowed for Johnnie to see her home.

When Lorna returned to the room, she noticed a tear trickling down Charlotte's cheek.

'Are you well, Miss Charlotte?'

She nodded at Lorna then leant down to kiss the top of her baby's downy head. 'Even at my baby's birth,' she whispered, 'he controls me.'

# Chapter Thirty-nine
2014

Gerry took off his dental tunic and reached for his coat. He didn't usually take much of a lunch break, but everything was ready for the afternoon so he planned to go over the road to the barber and have a quick haircut and a trim of his beard if possible. Chris was always moaning about it being bristly.

He walked along the corridor and, as he passed the reception area, saw two policemen talking to Patricia, the receptionist.

'Gerry,' she said, 'these policemen want to see you.' Patricia was frowning as she peered over her glasses at him.

One of the policemen moved towards him. 'Is there anywhere quiet we can speak, Mr Wallace?'

'You can come up to my surgery,' Gerry said, glancing over at Patricia who was pursing her lips and frowning.

'It's not one of the kids, is it? Is one of them in trouble?'

'No, Mr Wallace.'

The three men entered the surgery and Gerry switched on the light.

'I'm Sergeant Bowman and this is Police Constable Singh.'

Gerry reached out his hand and said, 'How can I help you?'

Sergeant Bowman coughed. 'Mr Wallace, I'm afraid there's been an accident.'

Gerry felt his stomach muscles tighten. 'But you said the kids are fine.'

'It's your wife, Christine. She was involved in a road traffic accident on the A1 south of Berwick. She was airlifted to Newcastle Royal Victoria Infirmary but she was dead on arrival. They could do nothing for her. I'm sorry.'

Gerry stumbled, reaching for the dental chair to prop himself up. He shook his head. 'It can't be Chris, it can't be.'

Sergeant Bowman took out his notebook and continued, 'I'm sorry, Mr Wallace. We've checked her ID and we got your details from her phone.' He went over to the sink and picked up a plastic cup which he filled with water. 'We're here to take you down to the hospital,' he said, handing Gerry the cup. 'And we'd like your permission for our colleagues to contact your two children. I believe they live in the Newcastle area?'

'Yes, the kids.' He nodded. 'No, I should tell them, I'll do it, I'll phone them.'

Gerry looked away from the policemen, towards the window. He always told his patients the view was the best in the city, looking south to Edinburgh Castle, which today was resplendent against the blue sky, high clouds scudding east in the summer breeze.

'Shall we go, Mr Wallace?'

Gerry nodded, stumbled to his feet and followed them downstairs. Patricia was waiting at the door of the reception. She put her hand to her mouth when she saw Gerry's face. 'Anything I can do, Gerry?' she whispered.

Gerry continued walking, as if in a trance. He turned at the door and mumbled, 'Cancel the patients.'

Gerry wanted to do the mortuary visit alone. It wasn't fair to put the kids through that trauma, he decided. The nurse shut the door quietly behind him and he walked into the large room where she was laid out on a high bed in the middle. The only other furniture was three chairs alongside, incongruously low.

Her face was covered in bruises and cuts; he was grateful he had decided the kids should not see her. Despite the injuries, she looked calmer and more serene than he had seen her for a long time. Her thick hair was pulled off her face; it looked as if someone had just brushed it. A long navy woollen blanket covered her up to her chin. Gerry resisted the urge to pull it down; she hated the feel of wool on her face.

He went to touch her then retracted his hand quickly as if burnt. He remembered touching his father when he had died; he had hated it.

He pulled a tissue from his pocket and wiped the tears streaming down his face. He had to keep himself in control, if only for the kids. He turned and shuffled towards the door where the nurse was waiting for him.

'Sergeant Bell says the children are in the family room. Can I get you anything, pet?'

He shook his head and allowed her to lead him from the mortuary. Through the glass door to the family room, he could see Jack's lanky figure folded up tight, as if in pain. His body was shaking with sobs. Anna sat rigid, staring straight ahead, face wet, eyes black with smudged mascara. She put her arm round her brother and patted his back. They both looked up as Gerry entered and Anna burst into tears, rushing to embrace him.

The following day, the three of them sat in the same family room in front of Sergeant Bell, who was ticking things off in his notebook.

'So, that's the rough timeplan outlined for you. We need to get the results of the post-mortem, then when that's done we can release the body for the funeral.'

'Do you have any idea what might have happened, Sergeant?' Gerry asked, holding Anna's hand tight.

'According to the witness statements, it looks like she was overtaking a lorry and another lorry was coming straight at her on the other side. The dual carriageway had ended just a half mile or so before, so perhaps she had forgotten there was no overtaking lane.'

'But Mum's such a good driver, she was always so careful,' Anna mumbled. 'I just don't get it.'

'Why was she driving down the A1 anyway?' Jack's voice was quiet. 'She wasn't coming to see us.'

'It was the trial at Gateshead,' said Gerry. 'She wanted to see that man get his sentence.'

Sergeant Bell coughed. 'Do you two kids want to go grab a coffee? There's something I'd like to discuss with your dad.'

Gerry was waiting for Anna to insist on staying but she stood up, and pulled on her brother's arm. 'Okay. Dad, we'll bring one back for you.'

Once they had left the room, Sergeant Bell said, 'Mr Wallace, this is rather a delicate matter.' He paused and looked down at his notebook. 'Though the post-mortem is still to be done, I have to tell you that, in the initial blood tests, there was a high level of cannabis in Christine's system.'

Gerry leant forward. 'Cannabis?' He shook his head. 'There must be some sort of mistake, my wife never took drugs. I mean, she hardly even drank...'

'I'm sorry, there is no mistake, definitely cannabis.'

Gerry slumped back into his seat. 'This makes no sense, none of it does.' He looked up at the policeman. 'So what does this mean?'

'We'll find out more from the post-mortem and take it from there. I'm sorry,' Sergeant Bell said again.

Gerry had told the kids after the meeting with the policeman that he wanted to go and walk in the hospital gardens to make a couple of calls. They were going to get the train to Durham to pick up Jack's things and collect the car, then Jack's flatmate would drive them to Anna's flat in Jesmond for her things.

Gerry pulled his phone from his pocket and tapped in Mags' number. Though upset, she had been a great support, reacting calmly and rationally to the news. She said she would take care of everything up in Edinburgh for now, much to Gerry's relief.

'How's Charlie?' he asked.

'Not great, but that's hardly surprising.' Mags voice was a monotone. Gerry could hardly recognise her without the usual cheerful lilt. 'Mum's staying with him for now. How're the kids?'

'Not good at all.'

He could hear Mags breathing out loudly, but she said nothing.

'I tried Doug's phone but can't get through to him. Any idea where he is?'

Mags cleared her throat. 'No, I texted him yesterday so I'm sure he'll phone you. What happens next?'

'They've got to do a post-mortem so the body won't be released for a few days. But actually there was something I wanted to ask you, Mags.'

'Yes?' Her voice was strained.

'Well, the policeman told me earlier that – well, you won't believe this, but it seems Chris had a high level of cannabis in her blood when she died. I just don't understand.'

Silence.

'Mags, are you still there?'

'Yes, sorry. What?'

'Cannabis found in her blood. I know how you and Chris had had that chat with Great Auntie Bella about sourcing her some hash before she died. Did you ever get it?'

'No, we didn't do anything about that crazy request. So, no leads there. Sorry.'

'No. It just seems so out of character.'

'Yes.' Her voice faltered. 'It does.'

'Sorry. Forget this whole conversation, please, it's as if you're implicated somehow and you must be feeling as...' He stopped, trying to regain his composure. 'As bereft as I am.'

'Yeah,' whispered Mags.

'Better go now. Thanks for looking after Charlie.'

'No problem,' she said, hanging up.

Two days later, Mags went round to Gerry's house with a casserole and an apple pie. She hadn't wanted to invite them to her house as she hadn't seen Doug since she threw him out and knew it would be awkward explaining his absence.

When Mags rang the doorbell, a policewoman answered the door. She introduced herself as Police Constable Dall, the families' liaison officer.

'Where's Uncle Doug?' Jack asked. 'Lottie says he's away

somewhere.'

'Yes, he'll be around soon, I imagine. Have you heard from him, Gerry?'

Gerry was sitting at the kitchen table, looking out into the garden. 'Need to get something done in the garden,' he said, to no one in particular. 'Chris always loved it neat and tidy, can't let it go…'

'Dad, Auntie Mags asked you a question.'

Gerry turned round to look at Mags. 'Doug, yes, he's coming round later, can't remember when. This afternoon maybe?'

The policewoman put up her hand. 'Gerry, I think you told me your friend would be here between four and five o'clock, and it's ten to four now.'

'Oh, I'd better be going,' Mags said, starting for the door. She hugged Anna and Jack before she left. Gerry raised his hand to wave limply, but continued to stare out of the window.

PC Dall followed Mags to the front door.

'What time do you finish here today?' asked Mags.

'Very soon. Why?'

'Would you have time to call round to my house, please? Here's the address.' She fished out of her basket a card with 'Mags's Cakes' stamped on it.

'Is this something to do with Mrs Wallace?'

'Yes, maybe.'

'I'll be with you soon as I can.'

# Chapter Forty
## 2014

Lottie sat at the piano in Mags's dining room. She had just finished playing *Julia*, one of her favourite Ludovico Einaudi pieces, when she heard the front door open. She knew it would be her mum returning from seeing Gerry.

'In here, Mum!' she shouted, shutting the piano lid.

Mags came into the room, her eyes puffy, her hair greasy, wearing a crumpled long skirt. She kissed the top of her daughter's head.

'Your hair smells nice,' she said, scratching her scalp. 'I can't even be bothered washing mine. I must look like a tramp.'

Lottie gave her a hug.

'Want me to play something?'

'No, let's go and have a glass of wine.'

In the kitchen, Lottie sat down at the table while Mags brought over a bottle and two glasses.

'Mum, I've been thinking.'

Mags poured the wine and sat down. She looked at Lottie, who was anxiously biting her nails.

'It's about Auntie Chris. Well, do you wonder if, before she died, Dad told her that we had found out about everything? And do you think she might have…' Lottie swallowed. 'Well, do you think she might have killed herself?'

'Suicide?' Mags gasped. 'Oh, I don't think so. Chris would never have been brave enough. No, I really don't think she'd have contemplated suicide.'

Lottie nodded. 'Okay, just a thought. Because I still don't

see how this is possible. She was always so sensible, never reckless. So I wonder if he told her. He must have, don't you think?'

'I really don't know what he told her.'

'And where's he been all this time? Has he at least seen the three of them?'

'Gerry said he was expecting him this afternoon. I haven't spoken to him, but I know he's been at work every day, I checked with Frances at the practice.'

The doorbell rang. Mags picked up her glass and took a gulp then stood up. 'Lotts, if this is a policewoman, I need to speak to her in private.'

Lottie shrugged and swirled the wine round in her glass. 'It's fine, I'm going to phone Anna, see if she wants to come round later. I can't bear to go there, it's all too horrible.'

Mags opened the front door and ushered PC Dall into the dining room.

'So what was it you wanted to see me about, Mrs Neville?'

'Well,' said Mags, tucking her hair behind her ears, 'it's rather delicate, but Gerry told me that cannabis had been found in Chris's blood.'

'That's right. We're still waiting on some test results but it seems there was a significant amount in her system. From what I've heard, it seems very out of character for Christine.'

Mags nodded, but didn't say anything.

'Gerry told me that the two of you were best friends and, I understand, cousins as well?'

'The thing is,' Mags slid her gaze away from the policewoman and down onto the polished dining room table. 'I'd like to show you something, if that's all right. It's easier.' She looked up. 'Can you come upstairs with me, please?'

Mags led the way to the attic stairs. 'Mind your head. The ceiling's a bit low.'

The attic was bathed in summer sun from the dormer window. Doug's laptop was shut on his desk and beside it was a photo of Mags with a young Lottie, on the beach at Gairloch. They were both laughing, Mags holding Lottie's hand. Mags wore a long white cheesecloth dress and her hair was up in a loose bun; Lottie had on red dungarees and her hair was in thick plaits that rested on her shoulders. In front of them was a sandcastle, a spade sticking out of the sand beside it.

Mags pursed her lips, then the words began to rush out of her. 'Like you, I'd been wondering about the cannabis thing, because it seemed so out of character.' She opened a drawer in Doug's desk. 'But I remembered when I was tidying things out the other day and found something in the drawer. I put it back where it was, so I presume it's still here.'

She pulled the drawer fully out and lifted off the staples, pointing to the packet hidden underneath.

PC Dall drew the little plastic bag out and opened it slightly, lifting it to her nose.

'Any idea how long this has been here?'

Mags twisted some loose strands of hair round her finger. 'No. I only found it a few days ago when I was up here cleaning.'

The policeman placed the packet inside a plastic evidence bag, sealing the top. 'I'll need to take this away.' She looked at Mags. 'Is your husband a cannabis user, Mrs Neville?'

'He dabbled a bit in the past, in his student days, but he's been a bit, well, on edge over the past few weeks so perhaps he's taken it up again.'

'And is there any way he might have supplied it to Mrs Wallace?'

'They were good friends, who knows.'

PC Dall nodded and said, 'Is this his laptop?'

'Yeah, I keep mine in the kitchen.'

'We may need to take it away, but we'd need your permission.'

Mags shrugged. 'Help yourself.' She stood back as PC Dall started to unplug it. As they walked down the stairs, she asked when Doug was due home.

'I don't know,' said Mags. 'He's been away from home for a few days. But you've got his mobile number.'

'We'll need to ask him a few questions,' said PC Dall. She shook Mags's hand and left the house, Doug's laptop held firmly underneath her arm.

As the door shut, Lottie appeared at her mother's side. 'What's going on, Mum?'

'Nothing, darling.'

'She had Dad's laptop. Why did she take that? I mean, they do that kind of thing for paedos or terrorists. The whole Jack thing's nothing to do with Auntie Chris's death, Mum.'

'I know, none of this was my decision. PC Dall just wants to check a few things out.'

'You didn't tell her about Jack?'

'Of course not, darling. Why would I? Now let's get back to that wine.'

# Chapter Forty-one
October 1859

David Barrie took out the key for the cottage and pushed it into the lock. He stepped inside, pulled open the curtains and unclipped the window locks, flinging them wide open. It was an overcast day but warm for October and the cottage had not been used for a couple of weeks.

He had brought a flask of water from home and had picked some brambles in the woods. He put them on a plate in the middle of the table then pulled a slim book from his pocket. He sat down at the table and began leafing through the pages while he waited for her to come.

He was looking forward to telling her the news, but until then he tried to make sense of the words on the page in front of him. Why could he not read and write like everyone else? The dominie had told his parents that he had some strange problem with letters, it was so frustrating.

But she kept telling him that he was not stupid, that he was intelligent, even. Something in the way she said it made him believe her. He wanted to do something to better himself. And she was so patient with him, unlike the dominie who had belted him in front of the class. He felt that, after all these years, he was finally making some sort of progress.

He thought about the first day he had spoken to her, about eight months earlier. Of course he had known who she was, having admired her slim figure and lovely face smiling on Sundays in church. But it was only when he had been helping Billy with the new bench for the piano that he had spoken to her. She now played the music in church every week and had said the old bench was too low; with her height, she needed something higher.

At first she had spoken only to Billy, thanking him for the new bench. She sat down on it and dangled her feet. 'This is perfect,' she said as she pressed her feet on the pedals. 'Just the thing for my long legs.'

Both men looked down at the stone floor and shuffled their feet.

'Thank you, Mr Henderson. And, I do apologise, I have not been introduced to your assistant.' She looked at David and beamed. He had the feeling she was admiring him and he felt himself redden. What a stupid thought; how could she, an educated lady, possibly appreciate anything about him, a lowly farm labourer.

'It's David Barrie, Miss. I live along the main street in the village.'

'Like everyone else,' she said, extending her hand and smiling. He took it to shake and noticed how soft her hand was, so unlike Margaret's, calloused with hard work.

'Can you play us something, Miss?' David surprised himself by asking that, but she happily agreed. Soon Billy had to leave, but David lingered in the church, listening to her play some psalms. Once Billy had gone, she put the music book away and began to play another piece altogether. Her face beamed with pleasure as she tilted her head back and shut her eyes. He was gazing at her angelic face and her long neck when suddenly she stopped playing and opened her eyes. 'That was Chopin, but apart from the first page, I don't know it by heart.'

She looked straight at him and he noticed how silvery grey her eyes were. 'Mr Barrie, this is our little secret. The

Minister would not be pleased if he knew I was playing something written by a papist composer in the church.' She smiled at him, her face lovely, and he felt himself become hot all over. It was time to leave and he told her he must get back home.

'Before you leave, Mr Barrie, might I ask you something?'

'Yes, Miss, anything.'

'Since you are so good with your hands,' she said, rubbing one hand over the smooth wood of the bench, 'tell me, have you ever made a little tree house? I have been reading a novel that features one and it intrigues me.'

'A tree house, Miss? No, and tae be honest, it's Billy who's good at carpentry, I just lend him a wee hand. But I could gie it a try.'

'That would be wonderful, Mr Barrie, thank you.'

So he had started work on the tree house at the cottage. Margaret asked what he was making and when he told her, he added that it would of course be for her – and their bairns when in time they were blessed with them. That night she sulked the whole evening, brows knitting in silent wrath as she sat by the fire doing her darning. She never mentioned the tree house again.

Once the tree house was finished, he invited Miss Charlotte to view it, and she declared how delighted she was. He told her she could go up there whenever she wanted and she said she would do so on summer afternoons with a book to get away from the manse. It seemed strange to him that she would want to leave such a fine house to read halfway up a tree, but, well, she was a lady; what did he know.

She asked if, in return, there was anything she could help him with, as way of thanks, and he felt emboldened to ask if she could help with his reading and writing. With each lesson he enjoyed her company, and the sight of her beautiful face, more and more.

There was a tap on the door and he jumped to his feet.

There she stood, shoulders hunched, a scarf around her neck, her arms clutching a leather satchel.

'Come away in, Miss Charlotte, I've been trying to read the book frae last time but I'm still finding it difficult.'

She nodded as she sat down at the table, taking off her bonnet and laying it in front of her. She unknotted the scarf, put the satchel on the table and drew out two books, a jotter and some pencils. She sat back on her chair and sighed.

'How are you, David?'

He smiled and said, 'Well, thank you, Miss Charlotte. I was just checking on the tree house earlier, I still need to touch up the paintwork, but it's looking fine.'

'Good,' she said, looking down at the gnarled wooden table.

'Are you feeling well, Miss Charlotte?' Her skin, usually so bright and clear, had a grey pallor, and he noticed some pimples on her chin.

She looked at him, grey eyes glistening. She popped a bramble into her mouth, swallowed then said, 'I must confess, I am not, David. This is so difficult to relay as I know you and Mrs Barrie have waited such a long time to be blessed with a child and...' She looked out the windows at the sight of a couple of sparrows alighting a branch outside.

'Well, Miss Charlotte, I hae some news for ye, if I might be permitted to share it after you've finished?'

'Tell me now, David, if it's good news – for mine, sadly, is not.'

'Miss Charlotte, ye ken how Margaret and me have waited so long for a bairn, we've been married now some ten years. Well, Margaret is expecting a baby, due next spring.' He beamed and his dark eyes twinkled.

Charlotte stretched out her hand and touched his arm. 'David, I am so very pleased for you both, that must be welcome news indeed. Is your wife keeping well?'

'Aye, no bad, she didnae hae any sickness or anything. Ma says it'll be a boy.'

Charlotte withdrew her arm and clasped her hands together in front of her. 'Your child will be able to play in the tree house you built.' She glanced out the window as the sparrows flew away. 'But how coincidental to hear your news on a day such as today. I was going to tell you that I too am expecting a child. It will be born early in March.'

She glanced over at him then looked down at the table again.

David's eyes widened, then he said, slowly. 'Are you pleased, Miss Charlotte?'

'Am I pleased? David, what a question. Am I pleased that I, daughter of the manse, am to produce an illegitimate child and will soon become the talk of the parish, the shame of the village? No, I am not pleased, not at all.'

'I'm so sorry, of course you're no' pleased. What will ye dae?'

She shrugged. 'I do not yet know. I will have to leave the village for a few months, and then once the baby's here… Well, I have no idea what will transpire.'

She placed her arms out on the table in front of her and laid her head on them, turning her face away from him.

'Who else knows?'

'Only Cookie, and that is how it must be. I do not know where I shall go.'

David reached out and touched her hair. 'Maybe you could stay at Corrie. Ma's aye saying she's lonely there now my Dad's gone.'

Charlotte lifted her head up and looked at him. 'That would be too much of an imposition, surely.'

'I dinnae think so, Miss Charlotte, I was going tae see Ma on Sunday, I could ask.'

'There would need to be complete discretion, David. No one can find out.'

'Aye, of course. Ma's never been one to blether wi' other wifies, she'll no clype.'

Charlotte raised her shoulders and sat upright, rubbing her hands. 'Let me discuss this with Cookie but that might be a good option, David, thank you.'

She opened the book on top of her pile. 'And now shall we take a look at *Saint Ronan's Well*?'

'Aye, if you feel like it, Miss.'

'In truth, I do not, David. Shall we practise some writing instead?'

She took out a sheaf of papers and handed him her dip pen. 'Why do you not write something for me? Start by practising your name, then try a few words, perhaps about the joy of hearing you are to become a father.' She began to fill a little inkwell she had taken out of her bag from a bottle of ink, eyes downcast in concentration.

'I'll try, Miss.' As she screwed the lid back on the bottle, he gazed at her in adoration.

# Chapter Forty-two
## 2014

Gerry and Anna stood side by side in the kitchen, mugs of coffee in their hands. They were looking out at the garden where two crows were squawking loudly in the apple tree. Eventually Anna said, 'Remember Mum wanted our apple trees to be as big as Auntie Mags's trees, Dad, but ours never got that tall. They never even have many apples, do they?'

She turned to her father who stood, hands clasped tight round his mug, silent.

Anna continued, 'I'm going to see Grandpa today with Lottie. What is there to do?'

Gerry looked round at his daughter, as if he had only just noticed her presence. 'What?'

'Grandpa. I'm going to see him later. Is there anything you need me to do before the funeral tomorrow?'

Gerry returned his gaze to the window. 'We must do something about the garden, it was your mother's pride and joy. Can't let it get out of order, she'd not have liked that.'

Anna put down her mug. 'Dad, I'll see you later. I've got my mobile if you need anything.'

She kissed him on the cheek. 'I still can't get used to you being clean-shaven, Dad. Mum would have loved it.'

He rubbed his fingers over his chin. 'Loved the lack of beard, yes…'

'Jack's going to get out your suit and black tie and see if you need a shirt ironed when he's back from the gym.

Okay?'

But Gerry didn't reply. He was still staring out the window.

Lottie put her arm around her cousin's shoulders as they walked along the path to Charlie's house. Lottie reached for the buzzer then stopped, her hand in mid-air.

'Anna, this is going to be so difficult, both Gran and Uncle Charlie are in a terrible state, they just can't keep it together. I hate seeing old folk cry. God, you must be feeling a million times worse though.' She gave her cousin a tight hug.

Anna nodded. 'I've been crying myself to sleep every night.' She pulled out a tissue. 'Poor Grandpa. It's so wrong isn't it, to lose a child. It kind of ruins the whole natural sequence of things. I mean, remember how mum was when we had our accident.' She blew her nose then rammed the tissue into her pocket. 'Okay, let's go in.'

Lottie pressed the bell a couple of times, turned the doorknob and walked in, shouting, 'We're here!'

They walked into the hall and felt the stifling heat hit them.

'God it's boiling in here,' Anna said, opening the door to the lounge.

Charlie sat in his armchair, head bent low, bony shoulders pointing through his cashmere sweater. He turned when he saw them and tears filled his eyes.

Auntie Peggy pushed herself up off the sofa and hobbled over to hug them both, one after the other. She sighed deeply, wiped her eyes and gestured to the sofa. 'Sit down girls, I've got the coffee tray all ready.' She toddled across the room towards the kitchen and as she passed her brother, she stroked his hollow cheek. He brushed her hand away and said to the girls, 'Come and tell me your news. How are you both?'

'Fine, Grandpa,' said Anna, taking his gnarled hand. 'Well, not really but that's just what we say, don't we. How about you?' She looked into his watery eyes, the brown cornea now ringed with grey.

He squeezed her hand back and whispered, 'Not great, Anna. Love of my life, gone. It's not right, not the right order of things.' He shook his head.

Lottie began to snivel then stood up. 'I'm going to help Gran with the coffee.'

Charlie leaned in to Anna and whispered. 'It's that great-grandmother of theirs. It's her fault. She had a secret you know. I told them, your mum and Mags, not to carry on researching her history but they wanted to, your mum especially.'

'That's nothing to do with anything, Grandpa,' said Anna, stroking his hand, the skin thin as parchment.

'I think she had a curse, that's why no one could find a birth certificate or anything. It all came from her, all the bad things – your accident, and then this, I'm sure of it.' He turned to look directly into Anna's blue eyes. 'Don't you girls start looking into her past now. I want all that information they collected destroyed. In fact, you mustn't look into any of the family's past, do you hear?'

Anna frowned. 'Okay, Grandpa,' she said, as Lottie came into the room bearing a tray of mugs. She stood up and went into the kitchen where Peggy was tipping a packet of rich tea biscuits onto a plate.

'Auntie Peggy,' she whispered, 'Grandpa seems obsessed with the research thing Mum and Auntie Mags were doing on their great-grandmother. What's that all about?'

They could hear Lottie talking loudly next door. 'Here's your coffee, Uncle Charlie. I'll put it on the coaster for you.'

'He's been consumed by it, keeps telling me it was her fault, some curse. I'm worried his mind's gone even more now.' She let out a long breath then stretched out her hand to stroke Anna's curls. 'It's a terrible business, it really is.'

She looked up from the plate of biscuits in her hand. 'And where's Doug? Do you know what's happening there? I don't like to ask Lottie, and Mags wont tell me.'

'Sorry Auntie Peggy, way down my list of priorities.'

Peggy drew her great-niece to her ample chest in a hug. 'Sorry, sweetheart, of course it is.' They walked next door to join the others.

About ten minutes later, Lottie's phone rang and she plucked it from her bag and looked at the screen. It was her dad. She ignored it. A couple of minutes later a text pinged in. She picked it up and read. It was Doug, asking if he could help with transport to the funeral, and pleading with her to meet him and talk.

Lottie waited till Peggy had finished telling them about who was coming to the funeral from the extended family then interrupted. 'Sorry, Gran, that's a text from Dad. He says can he take you and Uncle Charlie to the funeral? He can pick you up at 10.15. Mum's got to help Gerry with things at the house so she can't do it, I'd take you but my car's only got two doors.'

'Well, that's a kind offer. Yes, please.' Peggy picked up her mug from the mantelpiece then said, 'Lottie, he's not living at home at the moment is he, sweetheart?'

'No, he's not.' Lottie started to tap on her phone. 'Right

I'll just reply to him just now, Auntie Peggy.'

Her text back to Doug read, 'Fine for lift. What is there to talk about?'

'Want to tell you what happened twenty-three years ago. Please?'

Anna picked up her mug and finished her coffee then typed in 'Okay. My flat, 8 o'clock.'

# Chapter Forty-three
June 1859

Charlotte tipped back her head and burst out laughing.

'David Barrie, I swear I have not laughed so much, ever.' She shook her head. 'You make teaching the written word a joy. Truly.'

David smiled back at her and gazed into her grey eyes. 'Miss Charlotte, I have to tell ye, I havenae laughed sae much in ages either.' He pointed to the book opened on the table in front of them. 'I ken ye said *As You Like It* is a comedy but it's the way they speak too, is it no'?'

'Absolutely, David, but I did not realise that until you read the words out loud to me.' She straightened her back and tried to suppress a grin. 'Methinks you are at home in the Forest of Arden, young knave!'

'No' sae young, Miss Charlotte. You could almost be my daughter!'

She frowned. 'Oh, I do not think so, David, I was eighteen years old on my birthday two weeks ago.'

'Aye, well that makes me twenty years older than you – it would be easy to be a faither at twenty!'

The smile left her face and she put her hand on the book to close it. 'You have not the character of a father. What I mean is, you have no qualities of the one I know as you are neither stern nor distant nor… bullying. And I so enjoy our time together, you make me laugh. There is no laughter in the manse.'

'To be honest, Miss Charlotte, there's few laughs in my ain home. The wife's waited so long to hae a bairn and it just disnae happen.'

Charlotte looked concerned. 'I am so sorry, David, that must cause such grief for you both.'

'Even mair since Agnes and Billy next door just got married last year and they're having twins any day now.'

Charlotte looked into his kind eyes and he looked away towards the window and the early spring sunshine.

'But in my home at Corrie, when I was a bairn, my Dad was aye one for a joke, he'd have us laughing a' the time.'

'That must have been a wonderful childhood,' Charlotte said, patting his arm.

She began to pack the books and paper into her satchel. 'Well, I must be going. I said to Cookie I would be out for an hour and would return before my father gets back from visiting the parishioners in Oathlaw.' She threaded the leather strap through the catch and put the satchel on her lap. 'It is my belief however, that he goes there primarily to partake of Lady Munro's fine claret.'

David opened his eyes wide. She noticed his shocked look and smiled. 'You are a good man, David. And one I believe to be straightforward and honest. My father is more, shall we say, complex.'

David said nothing, but pushed back his chair and jumped to his feet when she stood up from hers.

'Let us meet in another four weeks, on the last Friday of the month as usual?'

'Aye that'd be grand, Miss. I'll gie ye half an hour or so now before I gang home in case anyone sees ye coming out frae the woods.'

'From the Forest of Arden, David!' she said, laughing. She tied on her bonnet, picked up her satchel and went to the door.

'Next time we shall look at *A Midsummer Night's Dream* – now there is a truly enchanted forest!' She nodded farewell to him and stepped outside, pulling her shawl tight round her shoulders. The wind was getting up, and the branches on the hazel trees were beginning to sway gently to and fro.

She came out of the woods and crossed the road, checking there was no one around to see her, then started along the road towards Tannadice village. She walked past the little cottages, each one with smoke billowing out of its chimney. She had only been once in one of those cottages, when she went out with Cookie one day to visit an old lady, taking her some ramson soup. Cookie had said it was good for her ailment, whatever it was, but then Cookie said soup was good for all ills.

Charlotte had been shocked at how grimy and shabby the cottage was. There were no rugs on the floor, just bare stone. She shivered as she remembered how cold it had been. The pan hanging on the swee over the fire was black and the cups Cookie insisted they take tea from were chipped and filthy. How could they live in such hovels?

As she passed the Barrie cottage, she tried to imagine David living in such squalor. He was an intelligent man, humble yet bright. Was there no way to improve his lot? If she could help him with his reading and writing, could he perhaps obtain a better job? Though she had had no idea until today that he was thirty-eight, he looked much younger. Perhaps he was too old for anything new.

She had been attracted to him for some time; she used to surreptitiously watch him come through the church door, remove his cap then usher his wife into a pew. She had noticed his deep-set eyes and strong features. And his height: he towered over his dumpling wife. Though the poor thing was unable to conceive, that must be a terrible burden.

Charlotte opened the manse gate and walked up the path, praying that her father was not yet home. She pulled the door quietly behind her then crept along the corridor towards the kitchen. Cookie was sitting at the kitchen table, writing.

'Is he back?' Charlotte asked.

'No' yet,' she said looking up at the clock. 'Shouldnae be long though. I'd better get the tea tray ready.'

Charlotte ambled towards the table, removing her shawl. 'What are you writing? It does not resemble your usual lists and menus.' She peered over the older woman's shoulder.

Cookie quickly shut the book.

'It's my journal, Miss Charlotte.' She took a long ribbon and tied it round the covers of the diary. She stood up and put it in the drawer of the kitchen dresser.

'Should one not keep a journal somewhere secret?' Charlotte asked, watching her shut the dresser drawer.

'It's only there while I mak' the tea, then it'll gang back to its secret place. But to be honest, Miss Charlotte, there's nothing I need to hide frae anyone.'

'Who can tell, Cookie? Certainly not I.' She tucked a loose strand of hair into her bun then smiled. 'I too keep a journal, but mine is under lock and key! I shall be in the drawing room presently. Shall I take Mother her tincture first?'

'Aye, if you dae that please, Miss, I'll get everything ready on the tray.'

There was a loud noise from the hall as the front door opened. They both flinched and looked round. They stood still, listening to footsteps, heavy at first then fading.

Cookie walked quickly over to the coat hooks and took down her apron. 'That's him home now,' Charlotte said, shivering. She tiptoed towards the door, pulled her shawl tightly round her and sped up the stairs.

# Chapter Forty-four
2014

Lottie answered the door to find her father standing there, hair uncombed, stubble on his chin. He smiled broadly, his dimples prominent, when he saw his daughter.

He moved to hug her but she turned away. 'Go on into the lounge, Dad. Beer or red wine?'

'Whatever you're having, Lotts.'

He wandered through to the small living room and went to the piano in the corner, peering down at the sheets on the music stand. Taking his glasses from his jacket pocket, he sat down and began to play.

'Make yourself at home, why don't you!' Lottie said, bringing in a tray. He looked round, his hands hovering above the keys. 'Lotts, this is one of those Ravel pieces you did at your final concert, isn't it? It's fabulous. I'm rubbish at it though. Will you play it?'

She shook her head.

'Please, darling?'

'Later, maybe. Tell me what you're here to say.'

Doug shut the piano lid and went to sit beside Lottie on the sofa. He took a glass of red wine from the tray and lifted it up. 'Cheers!'

'I don't think there's much to be cheery about, Dad. It's Auntie Chris's funeral tomorrow.'

'I am not feeling cheerful. Believe me, the past few weeks have been a nightmare.'

Lottie took a gulp of her wine and sat back, looking at him steadily, trying not to let her emotions show. 'So, Mum says you've been staying at Bill's since you left home?'

'Sleeping on his sofa, not the most comfortable of beds, I have to say.'

Doug sighed. 'Lotts, I want to tell you what happened in 1989. She – Chris, I mean – had asked to meet up. It was only a week before her wedding to Gerry and she said she wanted to chat to me about my best man's speech. I presumed she wanted to check there was nothing dodgy in it, you've heard how her mother's side were very straight-laced, wee frees from somewhere up north. Anyway, I was up in Aberdeen helping my mum clear out the stuff from Dad's surgery – it was pretty soon after he died – and Chris had been in Forfar or Brechin or somewhere near there.'

He took a sip of his wine and glanced at Lottie, whose expression was inscrutable.

'So we decided to meet at the cottage, the place in the woods we took you to a couple of times when you were wee, just a toddler. There used to be an amazing little tree house in the garden, but that was already gone when you were there, ruined in that great storm.'

'Why did you meet there?'

'I was on my way down from Aberdeen and it's five minutes off the main road back to Edinburgh and she said she was only ten minutes away. She was the one who suggested the cottage.'

He frowned then continued, 'She was waiting for me when I arrived. We went inside and I got out my notes for the speech that I'd started to cobble together. We talked a bit about the wedding. She'd been really disappointed when Mum couldn't be her bridesmaid. You knew she had post-natal depression after having you, didn't you?'

Lottie nodded.

'Well, it was really bad and in those days they didn't have the range of medication they have nowadays. So it left Chris having to ask someone else to be bridesmaid – Lesley someone or other, an old school friend she wasn't even that friendly with. Chris was pretty pissed off that Mum pulled out at the last minute, but she just wasn't up to it.'

'Right, but where are you going with this?'

'Just listen, please. We talked about the speech. I kept telling her it was none of her business – I was the best man. But she was very... controlling.' Doug sat up straight and wiggled his neck around.

'Your neck still bad?'

He nodded then continued. 'After, I dunno, twenty minutes or so she moved the conversation onto Mum, though she didn't seem very sympathetic. I don't think she really believed in post-natal depression. I think she thought it was some wacky, selfish psychological illness, and that Mum ought to just snap out of it. She really didn't have a clue. It was as if she thought Mum was inventing an excuse not to go to the wedding.'

Doug frowned. 'Mum was really bad, you know. She could hardly get out of bed. Peggy – Granny – had to look after you while I was at work. I'd been sleeping in the spare room for about a month, with you in the cot beside me. Lotts, Mum was in a really bad place.'

He turned sideways and caught a glimpse of his daughter's face, still unreadable.

'So, back at the cottage.' Doug paused to scratch his lank hair. 'Chris began to, well, come on to me. At first I thought she was just messing around. I thought it was funny.'

He took a gulp of his wine and topped up his glass from the bottle on the tray. 'So, you know how they say any woman can seduce any man, well, I'm ashamed to say, the inevitable happened. I've regretted the whole thing ever since.'

He looked at his daughter, dark eyes imploring. 'I'm telling you the truth, Lotts. She wanted to seduce me. I reckon it was like a power thing. Of course I could have resisted, but I didn't.' He paused. 'Of course I share the blame, but I didn't instigate it.' He sighed. 'That sounds so pathetic, doesn't it?'

'But why did she want to sleep with you a week before her own wedding?'

'She said she had always loved me, fancied me – God, this is embarrassing – way before I got together with Mum. I'd chatted to her at some of the parties we all went to, but she was always in a different crowd of friends, never with Mum and her cool gang. She said she'd been wildly jealous when Mum and I got married and, though she was over that, she still wanted to sleep with me just once, because after she was married that could never happen. So, since I was, well, pretty vulnerable, what with Mum's health and…'

'And no sex for ages?' Lottie spat out the words.

Doug looked towards the ceiling. 'Yes, yes, you're right. Call me weak and feeble, but yes, that's right. I'm not trying to excuse what I did.'

'Then what happened?'

'Then she got dressed and left, without a word.' He frowned and raised a finger. 'I do remember her coming back in to open the curtains for some reason and that was when I looked up at her and she said, "See you at the wedding!" I remember she had a huge grin on her face.'

Lottie poured herself some more wine. 'So what

happened when she knew she was pregnant with Jack?'

'She told me there was a chance the baby was mine and I told her not to be ridiculous. But the older Jack got, the more he began to look like me, and it was pretty obvious. Well, to me and her anyway. Thank God not to Mum.'

Doug let out a deep breath. 'That's why I looked into the genetics of it all. We're so alike. Not that anyone questioned it, apart from you.'

Lottie looked up at the ceiling. 'Did you never think you should have told Mum? Or Jack?'

'How could I? It would have ruined our marriage, the marriage to the only woman I've ever loved. I loved her from the minute I set eyes on her. You know that, Lotts, you know I'm mad about your mum.' Doug took a deep breath. He had tears in his eyes.

Lottie took his hand. 'Dad, I do know that and, strangely, I believe you. I believe this whole horrible, sordid story. Well, what choice do I have now she's gone? I just can't believe Auntie Chris would go out of her way to do something like that.'

'Well, that was how she was about things – compulsive. You know how obsessed she was with that man who caused the accident. And she was always jealous of Mum, always.'

Lottie downed her glass and looked at her watch. 'I don't think I can talk about this any longer. It's getting late. Do you want to sleep on the sofa?'

'That'd be great. Thanks, darling. And if you don't mind nipping home for me to get my dark suit and black tie first thing tomorrow morning?'

'Okay.' She prodded his scalp with her forefinger. 'And while I'm out, wash your hair, will you?'

She went out to her bedroom, returning with a duvet

and pillow. She gestured for him to stand up then started making up the bed. Doug watched her, then said, 'Lotts, just one more thing. I want to show your mum how much I love her and how sorry I am for what happened all those years ago. There's one more thing I'm going to do for her.'

'What?' asked Lottie, picking up the tray.

Doug swallowed. 'You'll see soon enough.' He started to take off his jumper. 'Night, darling.'

# Chapter Forty-five
May 1859

She strode over the damp greenery and sniffed the air, her nose twitching like a young doe's. Of course – ramsons. It was wild garlic season. Cookie had said she was going to make some delicious soup from the young leaves soon.

Charlotte heard a noise and stood stock-still. Her immediate feeling of terror left her when she remembered her father was to be away from the village all afternoon. There was no possibility he had followed her.

David approached, hurrying over the wet leaves. He looked furtively around before he arrived at her side. His nervous expression made her smile.

'Lead on, Macduff!' She stretched out her hand as a monarch might to a lowly subject, then grinned as he pointed towards the cottage just beyond the clearing.

'In fact, David, that is a misquote,' she said as they tramped together over the squidgy leaves. '"Lay on, Macduff," were the correct words, but somehow not as dramatic.'

They walked towards the cottage where he took the heavy key out of his pocket. 'After you, Miss Charlotte,' he said.

'Thank you, David,' she replied, stepping over the threshold.

An hour or so later, she emerged, satchel in hand. That had been a good lesson; she loved how they laughed over the books and plays they read together. And she knew he was making progress, it was all about confidence and even when he had a problem with some letters, he now didn't feel so nervous or, as he had admitted at their first lesson, ashamed. He told her how the dominie had belted him, hard, when he got his spelling wrong, but he was sure it was not his fault. And so was she; he was an intelligent man, there were simply some issues with reading and spelling.

Charlotte strode through the wood and looked up through the trees at the sky. The clouds were clearing at last after days of rain and mist. Perhaps the sun would shine and May would become more spring-like. She crossed the main road and strolled towards the village where, in the distance, she could see a huddle of men in black. She slowed down and squinted at them, trying to see who they were.

She recognised the short, fat figure of Mr Lamb and realised they were a group of church elders. What on earth were they all doing in the street in the afternoon sunshine? Surely they all had extremely important matters to attend to? Her father ranted often over the lunch table to her and her mother about how crucial his kirk session were to him, and how indebted he was to those men for their sacrifice and loyalty.

'Good day, Miss Whyte,' Mr Lamb boomed.

'Good day, gentlemen. What brings you here this afternoon?'

'We have business to discuss before our kirk session meeting and we are walking to Oathlaw where Lady Munro has kindly offered to receive us. We do not like to burden you at the manse while your poor mother is indisposed.'

'And is my father not to be joining you?'

The youngest man, with a bulbous nose and thick ginger whiskers, stepped forward and she at once recognised him as the dominie's son, Dougal. 'The Minister is to join us there. He is busy discussing details for the church fair at Oathlaw House with her ladyship.'

'I see. Well, enjoy your walk, gentlemen.' Charlotte nodded then began to walk ahead towards the manse.

'Where have you been walking yourself, Miss Whyte?' Mr Lamb's resonant voice boomed.

'Oh, I have been taking a walk in the woods, looking for mushrooms. It is, however, sadly too early.'

'Indeed,' said another man, 'it is far too early, Miss Whyte.'

As she turned away, she could hear him mutter, 'I do wonder what they teach young ladies these days.'

She walked into the manse, pulled off her bonnet and flung it onto a chair. So, he was not to be home for some time; she smiled with relief and walked into the kitchen.

Cookie was nowhere to be seen but she could tell she had not been gone long: there on the table was a board covered with a tea towel. Even before she plucked off the cloth she knew what would be underneath. She had recognised the warm, homely smell: girdle scones, freshly made, ready to be devoured with butter and jam. She picked one up and raised it to her nostrils to smell. She loved that comforting, sweet aroma. Smiling, she stretched to take down a plate from the kitchen dresser then went into the larder to fetch the butter.

The back door opened and Cookie stood there, shaking her head. 'I go oot tae the garden for five minutes and half ma' scones are gone.'

'I have only taken one, Cookie.' Charlotte called out from the larder. 'Where do you keep that bramble jam?'

Cookie went to join her and reached up to a high shelf and brought down a jar of purple jam.

'Will you take tea in the parlour, Miss Charlotte? Or shall

you just sit here wi' me?'

'Since it is just me, I should be very pleased to sit here with you. Has Mother had her tea tray?'

'Aye, I'd just taken it up tae her then I went into the garden tae ask Grieve aboot the onions. I'll be needing extra this week. Have you seen the ramsons are oot?'

'Yes, I did, Cookie. Ramson soup tomorrow?'

'Aye, and that should dae your poor mother some good.'

Charlotte set the butter and jam on the table beside the scones. 'Do you know when Father is to be home?'

'Well, he said he'd be oot all afternoon as he had to be at Lady Munro's to talk aboot this fair then the kirk session were to meet there at tea time. Mr Lamb came tae see me this morning and apologise that they wouldnae be here for today's meeting. Suits me fine, I telt him!'

She fussed about the kitchen fetching cups and saucers and napkins. 'So, I believe your father willnae be home before seven, but I'm no' sure. I'll hae his supper ready for then anyway. Now, sit yerself doon, Miss Charlotte and I'll make the pot of tea.'

'Thank you, Cookie,' Charlotte smiled. 'So I can play whatever I like on the piano all afternoon! Mother loves to hear me play Chopin but of course he does not allow it. I shall go presently to see her and leave the doors wide open so she may hear.'

'That'd be grand. Now, do you want to pour the tea?'

'Yes, thank you.' Charlotte tipped her head back and laughed. 'I shall be mother!'

Charlotte put down the piano lid and swivelled round on the stool to open the little chest where she stored her music. She took all the other piano music out and replaced the

Chopin at the very bottom, then returned the other books so they were uppermost. Finally she placed the psalter on top before shutting the lid tight.

As she walked towards the stairs she felt re-energised, bursting with pleasure. It was strange the way the music imbued her with such feelings of ardour and joy, a bubble invading her body and leaving her with a feeling of elation. Playing Chopin was so much better than playing church music.

She climbed the stairs and went through the open door to her mother's bedroom. Maud Whyte lay in bed, her grey hair loose around her shoulders. She was pale and had dark circles under her eyes.

She smiled when she saw her daughter and placed her hands together to clap. 'Charlotte, I swear you are better at playing than Mr Chopin himself.'

Charlotte sat down at the end of the bed. 'I doubt that, Mother, and I could not compose such tunes – indeed any tunes – but I do so enjoy playing his pieces.'

Maud Whyte pulled out a small drawer in her bedside cabinet, lifted a piece of paper out and handed it to Charlotte, smiling.

'I know you have seen it so many times, but read it to me again, will you?'

'*Monsieur Chopin has the honour to announce that he will give a soirée musicale in the Hopetoun Rooms, this evening, Wednesday the 4th of October, where he will play the following compositions: Andante et impromptu, Etudes, Nocturnes et Berceuse, Grande Valse Brillante, Andante précédé d'un Lango, Prelude, Ballade, Mazourkas et Valses…*'

Charlotte looked up. 'Mother, I have never asked you, how did Father permit this?'

'At first he forbade it. Of course I wanted to go to Edinburgh alone, but I knew he would not allow me to travel by myself so I asked Lady Munro – the old Lady, who died last year – if her companion Mrs Shaw would accompany me. You were only about seven, but Cookie was here to take care of you.'

'And did he really not mind you going?'

'Oh, yes, of course he did. He tried to dissuade me, but with Lady Munro's approval, he had little choice.' She frowned. 'On my return, when all I wanted to do was tell him how wonderful the soirée had been, he listened for about one minute then put up his hand in his usual manner' – she thrust one hand in front of her face – 'and told me he would hear no more about this Papist Polish composer in the manse. And that was that.' Maud shook her head.

Charlotte handed her mother back the paper. 'Are you feeling any stronger today, Mother?'

'I do believe I am. I am sure I shall be able to rise from bed tomorrow, and perhaps even join you both for luncheon.'

'That would be wonderful.' Charlotte got up from the bed. 'I am going over to the church to practise Sunday's psalms but I will be back for supper.' She kissed her mother then went downstairs.

She put on her bonnet and coat and walked along the short path to the church, where she entered by the side door. She shivered in the cold of the huge, dank building and pulled her coat round her. Why had she not brought her shawl with her?

She walked past the empty pews and sat on the piano

bench. She lifted the heavy lid and looked at the old, yellowed keys. Mr Ferguson, the choir master, had told her that many of the churches around Scotland were having organs installed, and he could perhaps arrange lessons. She was hoping he would persuade the kirk session and then her father. An organ in this cold, dark building would be a thing of great beauty.

She scratched at the wax that had dripped down the piano from the many candles that had been lit either side of the music stand. A blob of wax fell off onto the keys so she lifted it to one side and blew over the keys to clean them. There was still enough daylight coming through the high lancet windows that she did not need to light any candles today. She brushed down the white then the black notes with her handkerchief, then took down the psalter from the top of the piano. She flicked through the pages until she came to the first psalm she had to practise. Straightening her back, she extended her arms and began to play.

She struck a fortissimo chord, and did not hear the church door creak open, nor see the tall, dark figure standing there, watching.

# Chapter Forty-six
2014

Mags and Lottie stood outside the crematorium with Charlie and Peggy. All four were dressed in black, watching the line of mourners at the door.

'Why on earth Gerry wanted to do that meet-and-greet thing is a mystery,' muttered Peggy. 'It's just not necessary. Look at those poor kids, having to stand and shake everyone's hands. It's a nonsense.' She turned to her brother and took his hand. She lifted it up between them as if to remind him she was there and said, 'Charlie, shall we go soon? Have you had enough, sweetheart?'

Charlie's stooped shoulders slumped even more as he nodded. He took out a large handkerchief from his pocket and blew his nose. The four of them continued to watch as Gerry shook hands with men and kissed women and Jack and Anna were hugged by strangers.

'At least Gerry's got rid of that hideous beard. Though it's sad it's taken poor Chris dying to make him do it,' Peggy sighed. 'Good turnout though, how many do you reckon, Mags. Two hundred?'

'No idea. Who cares,' Mags snapped.

'Dad said he'd take you to the do after, Gran,' said Lottie, wiping under her mascara-smudged eyes with her forefingers.

'Where is he?' asked Mags, handing Lottie a packet of tissues. She took her car keys out of her pocket and turned to Peggy. 'I can take you if you want, Mum, and Lottie can go with Doug, if he's going to the do. Is he?'

'No idea,' said Lottie. 'I'll head to the car park and see if he's there.' She looked at Uncle Charlie, whose gaunt cheeks were wet with tears. 'Mum, why don't you take Gran and Uncle Charlie anyway and if Dad's not going, I'll cadge a lift from someone else.'

Mags nodded as she watched Lottie run ahead. She reached into her pocket and took out three Murray Mints and gave them to the old folk. They took them without acknowledgement and the three of them unwrapped the sweets in unison. Mags linked her arms through her mother's and uncle's and began to wend her way with them across the road towards the car park.

Lottie had just arrived at the car park entrance when she saw the police car, blocking Doug's car in. Then she saw Doug in the back of the police vehicle. The engine started up and the car slowly began to move away. Lottie ran after it and banged on the window to stop.

The policewoman in the passenger seat opened her window. 'What is it?'

'That's my dad! What's going on?'

The policewoman got out and opened the back door. 'Okay, pop in for a minute, but we've got to be out of here soon, we're already blocking some cars.' The policeman in the driving seat kept the engine running.

Lottie got into the car, shut the door and turned to Doug, whose face was grey, his expression grim.

'What's happening, Dad?' Lottie whispered, aware the policeman and woman in front could hear everything.

'They want to take me in for some questions. I'll let you know what happens next.' He fished in his trouser pocket. 'Good job you stopped us actually, here's my car keys. Can you take my car home later?'

Lottie's mouth dropped open. She reached out her hands, palms upwards. 'Why have you been arrested, Dad?' She felt her eyes welling up and got out her tissue, wiping her eyes again.

'Supplying cannabis to Chris. It may have been the cause of her accident.' He spoke softly, in a monotone.

'But Dad, that's not true, that's just… Why are you doing this?'

'You've got to go now, darling. Tell Uncle Charlie and Gran I'm sorry I couldn't give them a lift home.' He pushed his car keys into her hand and leant over to kiss her cheek.

'I'll phone you once I know what's happening.'

As Lottie opened the door, Doug leaned along the seat and touched her arm. 'Send Mum my love, Lotts, will you?'

Lottie nodded and got out of the car. The policewoman got back into the passenger seat and Lottie stood back as the police car drove away.

Mags, Charlie and Peggy were hobbling up the hill towards her.

'Who was that in that police car, Lottie? It looked like Doug,' Peggy said.

Mags said nothing, but took out a tissue and wiped along under Lottie's eyes which were once more smudged with black.

'No idea, Gran,' said Lottie. 'I heard they sometimes let prisoners out for family funerals, he was maybe at that other funeral in the small chapel.' She took her grandmother's arm and led her towards Mags's car. Once the old people were settled inside the car and the doors shut, Mags glanced at Lottie.

'Was that Dad?'

'Yes! Mum, what's going on?'

Mags tucked her hair behind her ear, a dangly silver earring glinting in the sun. 'No idea. What did he say to you?'

'That he's been arrested for allegedly supplying Auntie Chris with cannabis.'

Mags took a sudden deep breath, and screwed her eyes shut. She said nothing.

'He sent you his love, Mum.'

Mags did not move. She heard a sound in the trees above and looked up. She saw two large black crows squawking. A single tear trickled down her cheek as she opened her door and got into the car.

# Chapter Forty-seven
May 1859

Charlotte had begun to play the final verse of Psalm 27 when she heard a noise. She glanced around but the light was beginning to fail and she could see nothing in the gloom of the church. She turned back to the piano and continued to play, far more loudly than she would on a Sunday. Her father had told her that the music was there to enhance the worship of his flock, never to overpower. She sat up straight and played the final chords with gusto, then flicked over the pages of the psalter, checking his list for the next one she needed to practise.

A voice boomed out of the gloom. 'Charlotte, where were you this afternoon?'

She flinched and swung round from the bench.

Her father stood at the front pew. As Charlotte's eyes became accustomed to the shadows, she noticed that his hands were clasped in front of him and he was twisting them round and round as he spoke.

'This afternoon, daughter. I repeat my question. Were you out?'

Charlotte gripped the edge of the bench and looked directly at him. The only parts of his body that were not black were his pale white face, thinning grey hair and those hands, turning. His black eyes glinted in the light from the window above the pulpit.

'I decided to take a walk after luncheon, Father. I am not sure if you recall my saying I might do so, as the afternoon was set fair.' She felt his eyes bore into her. 'Now of course it is somewhat chillier. Indeed, I believe I have finished practising for Sunday now, Father, and I shall return home. Mother looked so much better today and…'

'Were you in the woods with David Barrie?' He remained immobile apart from those hands.

Charlotte felt herself begin to sweat. 'No, Father, I did not walk in that direction, I…' And just as she thought to tell him that she had taken the Forfar road, not the Oathlaw road, she remembered meeting the members of the kirk session on her way home. Her knuckles were white as they tightly gripped the bench.

'You were seen emerging from the woods by Mr Lamb.' He pursed his lips. 'I had spent the early afternoon at Oathlaw House in audience with Lady Munro and then he arrived with the other members of the kirk session in the late afternoon for our meeting.'

So you had spent the entire afternoon quaffing as much claret as you cared to drink, she thought.

'Yes, Father, I am so sorry. I seem to have forgotten. I thought I had seen a young doe run into the woods so I took a short walk along there but went no further than the first clearing before returning to the main road.'

Her father began to approach, still wringing his bony hands. 'Doctor Macleod arrived late at the meeting as he had to attend to one of his patients in the village. He said he had just seen David Barrie come out of the woods. The doctor stopped to engage him in conversation but Barrie seemed to be in a hurry and sped up the road towards his cottage.' He paused and pursed his lips. 'Charlotte, did you see that man this afternoon?'

He was now near enough to her face that she could smell the reek of stale wine. He had that look often admired by the likes of Lady Munro, but feared by her: that of a zealot. It was as if there was a fire being stoked inside him. His face, previously ashen and cadaverous, was taking on a flushed, angry look. She knew that expression well and all the muscles in her body tightened. Thank God she was in the church.

'Father, I believe, now that I think of it, that I did see David Barrie near the woods – but I did not pass the time of day with him, for I was aware I had said to Mother I would be back for when she awoke after her afternoon nap.' She attempted a smile. 'It is good, is it not, that Mother is enjoying better health?' Her fists grasped the wood of the bench even tighter. She was safe in here, nothing could happen in the sanctuary.

He came even closer so that she could feel his hot, malodorous breath as he bent down towards her. 'I have warned you before of seeing any strangers, anyone of whom I do not approve. That is why we employed a governess instead of sending you to school, that is why your poor mother is often abed, her already frail constitution suffering because she worries too much about you and your insistence in attempting to be a free spirit.'

He spat out the last two words, as if spitting out a mouthful of dirt. 'You are not and never will be a free spirit. Even when you reach adulthood in three years' time, you will persist in following the rules I have set should you wish to continue to live in the manse. Commands must be obeyed.'

She looked down, silent, hoping that, since he was in a holy place, the black mood would subside soon. But he continued to shout.

'And now, you will remove yourself from that bench and come with me!' He grabbed her arm and tried to drag her up.

'No! Father, no, please!'

He was thin and gaunt but strong as an ox. She tucked her feet under the bench so that, as he pulled her, the bench came too. He saw what she was trying to do and struck her across the back of the head. Even in his most violent rages, he was always rigorous about where the blows landed, ensuring he never touched her face.

She let the bench go as the pain hit. He then dragged her up the steps towards the back of the church and out into the corridor. She began to whimper. 'Please, Father, please, no…'

He hauled her along the corridor, pausing only to kick the vestry door open. He pulled her inside and flung her onto the floor. She heard the grating turn of the key in the lock.

He stepped towards her, his face livid red, his black eyes blazing. He put his foot on her dress and began to unbuckle his belt.

# Chapter Forty-eight
2014

After the funeral, Gerry did the rounds of the guests back at the hotel, politely nodding when they said how lovely the service had been and how well he and the kids were coping. Jack and Anna sat in a corner with Lottie, each with a glass of warm white wine in their hand.

'It's times like this I wished I smoked. Any excuse to get out and away from everyone,' Anna said, taking a gulp of wine. 'This wine's disgusting, isn't it.'

Jack nodded his agreement.

Lottie's phone rang. When she saw who was calling, she grabbed it and headed for the door. 'Back in a minute!'

Once she was outside, she whispered, 'Dad? You okay?'

'Yeah, fine. Though being in a police cell's not quite as cool as it looks in the movies. I'm thinking of boring a hole in the wall with my toothbrush. Who knows, I could be out by next year.'

'Dad, it's not funny.'

'Sorry, Lotts. Anyway, they've been questioning me, but they said I could use the phone in the tea break before they start again.'

'What's the charge?' Lottie asked, brows furrowed.

'Possible manslaughter.'

Lottie gasped.

'That's why I've got to get a lawyer involved soon.'

'But Dad, this is ridiculous, I just don't get it.'

'It's something I have to do, Lotts. Right, I've got to go. How are things at the funeral tea?'

'It's all right. Dad, will you let me know what's happening?'

'When I can. Bye, darling.'

Lottie went back inside the room and over to Jack and Anna. She sat down with a thump. Anna asked if she was all right.

'Yes, fine. Want another drink? I could try and get some gin and tonics?'

Lottie nodded.

Uncle Charlie sat down beside them and turned towards Jack. 'I've been looking for that father of yours, young man. Can't see him anywhere.'

'Oh, he's over there, Grandpa. D'you want me to go and get him?'

Charlie shook his head then peered round the room, searching.

Anna took her grandfather's hand and stroked it. 'Are you tired, Grandpa?'

'Yes,' said Charlie. 'I think I am. Is it time to go home yet?'

Mags took Charlie's key from him and unlocked the front door. He followed, arm in arm with Peggy. Both their heads were bowed, stooped with sadness.

Mags went into the living room where there were piles of papers all over the table.

'What on earth's all this, Mum?'

Peggy took her brother over to his armchair and helped him take his coat off before loosening his black tie. Charlie slumped back against the cushion and shut his eyes.

Peggy joined Mags at the table. 'Last night Charlie suddenly decided to go through all of Chris's things. You know, school photos and letters from her trips, paintings and things from when she was little.' She shook her head. 'It was all just too sad.'

Mags shuffled through some of the things then pointed to an old shoebox. 'What's in that?'

'Oh, yes, take a look at that, sweetheart. He said it's for you.' Peggy looked round as if for approval from her brother but there was a gentle, whistling snore from his armchair. 'Bless him, he's done in.'

She turned back to Mags. 'He said it was from our father. I told him that was impossible – I'd been given all the things from our parents' house to sort. But he said this box had been given to our father when Granny Elizabeth Barrie died, and he'd then given it to him. He was very lucid when he told me all this last night, said he'd been determined to keep it a secret, didn't want to burden the family with whatever's in that box, but he wanted to pass it on to you before he forgot about it all.'

Mags lifted the lid off the tattered shoebox and saw inside a very old journal with faded satin ribbons tied around it. She lifted it up and saw a pouch made of black velvet underneath.

'It's a diary. Whose is it?'

'I don't know. Charlie insisted you take it away to have a good look at it. He said it was some of the few things in our granny's possession, and that she brought bad luck.'

She leant towards Mags. 'You know he's been talking every day about the fact that all the misfortune began when you girls started to research her history. You know, the kids' accident, then poor Chris. So can you just do him a favour and take it away with you?'

'Okay,' said Mags. 'Shall I stay and heat up that casserole for your tea?'

'Don't be daft, it'll give me something to do. What kind is it?'

'Beef in Guinness. I know Uncle Charlie likes that, I thought it'd keep up his strength. Just do some mashed potatoes with it, Mum.' Mags looked at her watch. 'Do you mind if I leave now? Lottie and I were going to have a quiet evening at home.'

Peggy reached across to her daughter. 'Mags, what's going on with Doug? Is everything all right?'

'Things are okay, Mum, Mags swallowed. 'We're just having a bit of time apart, but it's nothing for you to worry about.' She gave her mum a weak smile and kissed her forehead.

'I do worry, sweetheart. You look terrible, like you've not slept in days. You've got to look after yourself, Mags.'

'Don't worry, I'm fine. Anyway, give me a ring tomorrow morning with your Tesco shopping list and I'll order online for you.'

Peggy pressed the back of her hand against Mags's cheek and smiled. 'You are a treasure, my love. Such a good person.'

Mags stood up. 'Not sure I am a good person, actually, but it's too late to change anything now.' She put her hand up to wave as she headed for the front door.

# Chapter Forty-nine
26th March 1871

Cookie reached the top step with her tray and stretched out her hand to hold onto the banister. She had been up and down the stairs at least ten times a day for the past week and she was exhausted. There were those in the village who said she was foolish, looking after Miss Charlotte like this when she was so sick with the influenza. No one else, apart from Doctor Macleod, had been near her. But if she succumbed to the illness then so be it; her life would hardly be worth living if Miss Charlotte died anyway. Two women in the village had already been taken and there was a child that was bad with it too.

Of course he had been nowhere near her. His excuse to Cookie, when she served him his lone suppers, was that he could not risk infecting his parishioners. But she knew he was a coward and thought only of himself. If Lady Munro had caught the influenza, she was sure the minister would be straight over to Oathlaw House to see her. But his own daughter, well, that was a different matter.

Cookie tapped lightly on the door and went in, placing the tray on the dresser. Charlotte lay in bed, her face a flushed pink colour, sweat dripping from her brow. Her eyes opened and she attempted a smile.

'Oh, look at you, Miss Charlotte, let's put a cold towel on your broo. And I've brought up a wee bowl o' ramson soup, ye ken it's good for you.'

'Thanks, Cookie,' she whispered, as Cookie pushed back her hair and mopped her forehead.

'Can you try just a wee bit o' soup?'

Charlotte nodded. 'If you don't mind spooning it for me, Cookie. I have no strength even to hold a spoon.'

Cookie gave her a couple of spoonfuls then Charlotte raised up a hand. 'Thanks, Cookie. It's delicious, but I can't manage any more. It's my favourite soup in the world, you do know that, don't you?' She leant her head back onto the pillow and closed her eyes.

Cookie nodded and sat back in the chair. 'Aye, I ken well.'

Charlotte coughed, a deep, hacking cough that wracked her whole body. Once the coughing fit had passed, she stretched out her hand. 'Cookie, there's something I need you to do. Please.'

'Anything, Miss Charlotte,' she said, leaning forward to hear Charlotte's faint voice better.

'Over there in the bottom drawer of my dressing table is my journal. I want you to give that to Elizabeth, should I die.'

'You mustnae speak like that, you'll be just fine.'

Charlotte shook her head. 'I do not think so. I am becoming weaker by the day. Please go and see where it is, under my handkerchiefs.'

Cookie slowly got to her feet and went to the dressing table. She lifted a pile of handkerchiefs up from the drawer and saw a journal, tied with pink satin ribbons. She held it aloft. 'Is this it?'

Charlotte nodded. 'Now, please go to the drawer of the little bedside table and look in there. You will find a pouch.'

Cookie opened the drawer. There were some papers on top; one was a programme of Chopin's Edinburgh soirée in 1848. Tucked at the back was a little black pouch. She took it over to Charlotte.

'This pouch has the key inside. You must give both to

Elizabeth. But,' said Charlotte, trying to push herself up a little but collapsing back on the bed, 'only when he is dead. That is important.'

Cookie nodded. She helped Charlotte sit up, propping a pillow at her back. 'But Miss Charlotte, I am already fifty years old. He is, what, sixty-five? He may outlive me.'

Charlotte shook her head. 'I doubt it. Thank you for doing this. It is important the child understands everything that has happened.'

There was a noise downstairs and both women turned their heads towards the door. Cookie hurriedly tucked the journal and key away in their respective hiding places and went to the door. 'He is home,' she said. 'I had better go and see what he requires. There's aye something. Is there anything else I can get for you, Miss Charlotte?'

Charlotte shook her head, lay back on the pillow and shut her eyes.

Cookie descended the stairs slowly and saw him through the study door. She turned towards the kitchen and heard him call out. 'Is there any news from the sick bed, Mrs Anderson?'

She turned round and saw him lean forward from his desk. He was dressed in black, as usual. 'There is no change, sir. Will the doctor return this evening?'

'He said he might, although I do not wish to trouble him as he is visiting so many of my flock who are stricken with this illness.' He stood up straight and came towards her, towering high above. 'I shall take tea presently, Mrs Anderson.'

He blinked his ink-black eyes as if there was dust in them. He rubbed them then opened them wide as if seeing clearly once more. Eyes sharp, glinting and evil like a corbie's, thought Cookie.

# Chapter Fifty
## 2015

Mags sat at the kitchen table with Anna, Jack and Uncle Charlie. In front of them was a pot of tea, a pile of scones and dishes of butter and homemade jam. The sound of piano music floated along the corridor and through the door.

'I love that tune, it's brilliant isn't it?' Anna said, taking another scone. 'These are delicious, Auntie Mags, really light.'

Jack spread butter thickly onto his scone. 'Your food's always good.' He dolloped on some jam. 'What are you cooking for the big lunch next weekend, Auntie Mags?'

'Well, it'll be the first time we've all been together since the funeral.' She twiddled with a loose strand of hair then glanced back at Anna and Jack. 'So I thought we'd have a whole fillet of beef. You like that, don't you, Uncle Charlie?' She raised her voice. 'Imagine, you'll be ninety soon!'

'Yeah, Grandpa, we need to get you a new outfit. Not every day you reach such a milestone!' Anna took her grandfather's bony hand in hers and beamed at him.

Charlie smiled back but said nothing.

'You'll love it. I know you keep telling us you don't want a party, but that's just nonsense,' said Anna, shaking her head and looking straight at him, a cheeky grin on her face.

Charlie patted her hand then pushed his chair back and slowly stood up.

'You okay, Uncle Charlie?' asked Mags.

'Fine. Just need the toilet,' he said, shuffling towards the door.

'Granny's ring looks nice on you, Anna, the garnet suits your colouring.'

'You sure I'm meant to have it, Auntie Mags? Why don't Lottie and I share it, a few months each?'

'Nope, your mum loved it and so it's for you, only you, sweetheart.'

'Grandpa's doing a bit better now, don't you think?' said Jack.

'He's eating better,' said Mags, 'and he doesn't seem as, well, depressed as he has been for the past six months.'

'Auntie Peggy's good for him, makes him laugh,' said Jack. Charlie came back in and sat down.

'Do you want more tea, Uncle Charlie?' asked Jack.

Charlie sat down, leant over the table and cupped his hand to his ear. 'What? Speak up.'

'More tea?'

'Thank you,' he said, pushing his cup across the table.

The piano music started up again, another tune, different in style, louder.

Mags smiled. 'That's a Chopin piece now. It's like an Usher Hall concert in here today, isn't it?' She topped up everyone's tea then looked at the clock. 'Your Dad should be here soon,' she said to Jack and Anna, twiddling with an earring. 'He's doing a bit better now too. What do you both think?'

'Yeah, Dad's okay. He's working silly hours at the practice but I think that's good for him, keeps him focused.' Jack reached out towards the scones. 'Okay if I have another one, Auntie Mags?'

She laughed. 'Of course, Jack, so good to see you tuck in. I love feeding people with a good appetite.'

'I know, sickening isn't it. He eats like a horse and still manages to be the skinniest person in town.' Anna shook her head as she looked at her brother, reaching over to poke him in the ribs. He ignored her and reached for the butter.

There was a moment of silence from the dining room. Then there was the sound of a key turning in the front door lock.

'We're in here!' Mags shouted as Lottie came rushing in. She gave her cousins and Uncle Charlie hugs then sat down at the table as the piano began again.

'Why's Dad giving us a concert?' She pointed towards the dining room.

'He said he'd entertain us till Gerry arrives, then he'll stop and get the beer out.' Mags smiled at Lottie. 'He still can't play that Chopin piece anything like as well as you can, darling, but he's trying.'

Anna picked her bag up and looked at her phone. 'That's a text from Dad,' she said. 'He's running a bit late.'

Anna dumped her bag back on the floor and looked at Mags. 'He was going to tell you the latest news, but why don't we just do that before he comes, so he doesn't have to tell you himself and get all maudlin again.'

Mags leant her head to one side and swallowed. 'What news?'

'He heard from the policeman in Newcastle. That man who caused our accident eventually showed up at the court and finally pleaded guilty, so he got a fine of £180 and six points off his licence.'

'Is that all?' asked Mags, incredulous.

'I know. Not much, is it.' Jack said.

'Still,' said Mags. 'Chris would've been pleased – at least he was found guilty. Though he kept trying to claim it wasn't his fault, didn't he?'

'Yeah. There was too much evidence against him though – photos, witness statements and everything. Anyway, it's good it's all over now.' Jack leant back against his chair. 'It's a bit like when we heard the final outcome of Mum's case last week, then we all had closure.'

The piano music stopped. Jack looked over at Charlie who was staring out of the window, humming. He leant in towards Mags. 'Auntie Mags, did Dad tell you about the results of the hearing?'

Mags shook her head and looked down at her hands. Her knuckles were white, they were clamped together so tightly on her lap.

'They said Mum must have somehow forgotten the road had changed from dual to single carriageway.' Jack scratched his head. 'It was so unlike her, she was a good driver, but they blamed it on the stress she'd been suffering since our accident. We never knew she'd been on medication from the doctor for it. Did you?'

'No, I didn't.'

Jack carried on. 'So it looks like she'd taken more Prozac than she was meant to that morning and that must have affected her concentration.'

Jack looked up. 'Hi, Uncle Doug.'

Doug came into the kitchen, beaming. 'So where's the applause? Not every day you get a Chopin concerto during your tea break!'

Anna and Jack clapped politely and Charlie, after looking at them in confusion, joined in with a couple of claps.

Lottie looked up at her father. 'You need to work on the pedal more in that mazurka, Dad, makes it livelier. And watch the grace notes, you're making them too long.'

'Thanks, Miss!' Doug said, joining them at the table. Charlie stretched out his hand. 'Nice to meet you. I'm Charlie Duncan.'

Doug shook it. 'Nice to meet you too, Charlie.' He glanced at Anna and Jack, who exchanged anxious looks.

Mags said, her voice flat, 'Jack was just saying how good it is now there's closure on Chris's accident.'

Doug sat down beside Mags. Lottie glanced at her parents who were both silent. She nodded. 'The main thing is that it's over now and you can all try to move on, rebuild your lives and all that.' She looked over at Anna and Jack. 'I mean, we're six months on now and you guys are doing brilliantly.' She leant over to give Lottie a hug and reached over to squeeze Jack's shoulder.

Doug looked up at the clock. 'Five o'clock. Is it too early for a beer? Your Dad should be here soon, Jack. Want to join me?'

'Cheers, Uncle Doug,' said Jack. 'I'd love one.'

An hour later, Mags looked over the table at Uncle Charlie, whose rheumy eyes were bloodshot. He took out a large handkerchief and blew his nose.

'Hope you're not getting Mum's cold, Uncle Charlie.'

He shook his head and smiled. 'No, I never get too near her!' He pushed the handkerchief back deep into his pocket. He looked worn out.

'Doug,' said Mags. 'Are you okay to drive Uncle Charlie home?'

'Yeah, no problem,' he said, putting down his beer. 'I've only had one and a bit. Do you want me to take you home now, Charlie?' he asked, raising his voice as he always did when speaking to him.

'Thank you, I'd better get home and see how my mother is.'

Mags and Doug glanced at each other.

'You mean your sister Peggy, Uncle Charlie.' Mags smiled and looked closely at him. He seemed confused for a moment then shook his head. 'Yes, that's it, my big sister, she keeps me right.'

'I'll get your coat,' said Mags. 'Kids, come and say bye to Grandpa.'

Charlie was silent all the way to Leith as Doug chatted to him about the weather and football. The old man simply nodded now and then and looked out the window. When they arrived at Peggy's house, Charlie sat forward and stretched out his bony arm to rest his hand on Doug's forearm. He looked straight ahead and said, 'I saw you that day.'

'What day, Charlie?'

'That day in the woods, long ago. I saw you and Chris go into the cottage.'

Doug leant in towards him. 'I'm not sure what you're talking about, Charlie. Now let's get you inside.' He leaned across to release his seatbelt.

'You do know, Doug. But don't worry, I know what happened. She couldn't accept that you loved Mags from the start.' He paused, his mouth open, still staring through the windscreen. 'Chris always loved you.'

Doug sat back in his seat and looked straight ahead. He breathed out slowly then whispered, 'But how could you have possibly been in the woods that day, Charlie?'

'It was a funeral, my great Auntie Mary's in Brechin. Chris came with me, Janet wasn't well that day so had to stay at home. Chris motored up in her own car as she said she had things to do after. She thought I'd left the funeral tea before her but I didn't. I saw her car turn off the main road, the one from Aberdeen to Dundee.' He screwed up his eyes.

Doug stared at him.

'I parked my car behind hers up on the verge, at the woods. I saw the other car but had no idea whose it was till I saw you arrive at the wedding rehearsal the following week. In the same red car.'

'My Fiat 127,' Doug nodded.

Charlie got out his handkerchief and blew his nose.

'Did she know you were there?'

Charlie shook his head. 'No one knew, why would I tell anyone? The week before her wedding!' He shuffled in his seat and muttered, 'You'd do anything for your child, anything. So, my thinking was, if I told no one, I'd never have to lie.'

He settled his head back against the head rest and his body became rigid. 'A guard – that's what I've been, guarding her secret all these years.' He shut his eyes tight and grimaced as if in pain. 'Secrets are dangerous, poisonous, they should remain buried.'

'I'm sorry, Charlie. I'm so sorry.'

Charlie tucked away his handkerchief then turned to face Doug. 'What for?' Charlie looked around him, disoriented. 'Why are you sorry?'

'Never mind,' said Doug. 'Let's get you inside to see Peggy.'

'Yes, and my father will be home soon, so I mustn't be late. Mother was getting herring for the tea.'

Doug opened his door and ran round to let Charlie out.

He took his arm and walked him along the path. 'Are you all right now, Charlie?'

Charlie looked at Doug as if they had just been introduced. 'Grand. Thank you very much for the lift, young man. Give my regards to the family.'

Doug helped him over the step as Peggy opened the door and let her brother pass.

Doug gave her a kiss. 'How's your cold?'

'Oh, fine. It's my knees though, they're giving me even more grief.'

She watched her brother hang his coat on a hook then trudge along the corridor. 'How was he?'

'Okay, though he wandered a bit latterly. Seems to think he was coming back to his old home in Dundee with his mother and father.'

She shook her head and sniffed. 'He seems to be living in the past. Firmly lodged in the 1930s, with occasional outings to the forties and fifties.'

'And the eighties today too.' Doug looked at his watch. 'I'd better get back. Gerry was running late, but he'll be at the house now. Bye, Peggy.'

He looked back to the house before he got into his car. Standing at the window was Charlie, now with his dark cardigan on. His willowy, lean body was stooped. Doug waved but the old man didn't see him.

He was looking directly up at the oak tree in the garden. Doug glanced at the high branches to see some crows thrash about, wings flapping, the noise of their squawks jarring.

That evening, Mags and Doug lounged together on the sofa, feet up on the coffee table, glasses of red wine in their hands. She planted a kiss on Doug's nose. He smiled. 'I'm a lucky man.'

'No, I'm a lucky woman. I'll never forget what I did, I can't, I've ruined a family, people I love. And I can't justify anything, except that, well, she was the one who betrayed me all those years ago.' She took a deep breath. 'But the fact that you were there, Doug, willing to take the blame, to go to prison for me… I'll never forget that.'

'Thank God Gerry never told the kids about the dope in her blood. He said the conclusion from the final report was that it was all just a tragic accident caused by a serious miscalculation of the road. He thinks it was all a mistake, she'd never consider smoking dope.'

'But the whole cannabis thing was out of the equation ages ago, wasn't it?' Mags bit her lip.

'Yes, they said her recklessness was exacerbated by taking extra Prozac that morning.'

'I know, but I still don't really get how they didn't charge you for the cannabis thing?'

'Because in the end it was such a small amount in her system. And overdosing on a prescription drug like Prozac would have had a much bigger impact on her concentration. Besides, supplying someone with such a small amount of pot isn't enough to prove manslaughter. Not unless you forced them to take it and then drive or something.'

He stroked his wife's hair. 'It's all over, Mags. Gerry and the kids are doing well; they're trying to make the best of things. And you and I are getting back on track.'

'Yeah,' she said, downing her wine. 'We'll be fine.'

He lifted the bottle and topped up their glasses. 'What were you showing Lotts earlier, by the way, before she left for her lesson?'

'It was a Victorian journal I got from Uncle Charlie ages ago. I've been going through it slowly it for months now but wanted Lotts to read it too, since it was written by her great-great-great grandmother Charlotte Whyte, Elizabeth Barrie's mother. It's such a coincidence they have the same name as they were – are – both brilliant pianists.'

Mags snuggled down beside Doug. 'Now, there was someone else who had the love of a good man. And he was also willing to take the blame for something he never did.' She sighed. 'Didn't work out happily for him though.

She put down her glass and turned to Doug. 'Mum and Uncle Charlie said that Elizabeth Barrie never smiled. She was the one Uncle Charlie reckoned was cursed. He told us we should never have started researching her.' She paused and frowned.

'I don't think I would have smiled either if I'd had her life. So tragic. She must have guessed who her mother was, but it was only when she was given her mother's journal after her father, the Minister, died that it was confirmed. Elizabeth's first child, my Great-Auntie Annie, was just a baby at the time. Anyway, it was only then that Elizabeth Barrie found out her real story. It's hardly surprising she never smiled much after that.'

Lottie pushed the door of her flat shut behind her and dumped her coat on the chair. She went into the tiny kitchen and flicked on the kettle then went to the piano, opened the lid, then shut it again. No, she didn't need to practise tonight; she was going to be lazy and just read instead.

She took out the box with the old journal in it, untied the ribbons and had a quick look inside. What beautiful calligraphy; why was her own handwriting not more stylish? She flipped through a few pages then closed it and folded the faded ribbons on top. She was keen to read it, if only for her mum's sake, but not before she had finished the book she was reading; she was so near the end.

Lottie made herself a mug of green tea and settled into the armchair, propping her feet up on the coffee table.

Half an hour later, she shut the book and put it on the table. What an amazing story, she thought, everything seemed so perfect on the outside, a glittering veneer of respectability. Yet gradually the decay and poison from the past, hidden secrets, came to the surface, ending in death and murder.

Secrets are dangerous, she thought. She was so relieved that Jack knew nothing about who his real father was, and would never have to know anything; why should he? And her parents' relationship was on the mend, thank God. They were slowly getting back to where they'd been before.

The past was the past and should be forgotten. And as she mulled this over, she remembered some words she had just been reading and picked up the book. She opened it at its final page.

*'So we beat on, boats against the current, borne back ceaselessly into the past.'*

Lottie placed *The Great Gatsby* on the table, picked up her great-great-great-grandmother's journal and began to read.

# Chapter Fifty-one

The Journal of Charlotte Whyte
Addendum, written on the 26th
of March 1871

*Dearest Elizabeth,*

*I write this letter to you while ill with the influenza. I do not think I shall recover as there are others in the village who have succumbed and I have a strong sense I shall be next. So I have asked Cookie to give this to you on the death of my father, Charles Whyte. The reason I do not wish you to read it while he is still alive will be evident to you as you read my journal. I have written this diary every day since I was a girl, about the same age you are now – eleven years old.*

*Some of the early entries will be amusing, or perhaps even a little tedious, for you to read. When I helped Grieve pick the peas in the garden for example, as you used to love doing. And you also loved to pod them – indeed, I can still picture you sitting there on the high stool in the kitchen, your beautiful dark eyes intent upon each pod as you split them open. I remember your chubby little feet all grubby from the soil and Cookie swinging you up to sit on the draining board at the big stone sink as she scrubbed them clean.*

*And then there was the time when Mother made me an Easter bonnet herself, and the fresh flowers she had picked from the garden still had insects in them and they crawled down my neck during the sermon. Easter reminded me also of that first time in the church I set eyes on you again, the first time since you were a baby. You were four years old. I will never forget your deep brown eyes, little rosebud lips and mass of tight, lustrous curls.*

*But it is the entries from the age of fourteen that will perhaps shock you when you read what I had to endure, at the hands of my father. It is something that has made me so ashamed all these years. But what could I do? Mother was an invalid, and often abed, frail and sickly, and he knew I could not speak to her about it. And even if she had enjoyed good health, I am not convinced I would have wanted to trouble her with such horrors.*

*Whenever his wrath was provoked, and this was not infrequent, he would take it out on me. For the first few years it was only physical. Sometimes I was so bruised that I had to refuse my bath, for fear that Cookie saw me when she came to bring me my towel. She knew nothing, but I would entrust her with my life, which is why I know she will somehow ensure this journal will be placed in your hands some day.*

*Then, as you will read, one late afternoon in May 1859, it became more than the hits and slaps. And that was simply so awful, I cannot begin to describe to you and I shall not. I have merely alluded to it in the journal, it is impossible for me to express on paper. But throughout that terrible time, when I discovered I was expecting you, there was one constant in my life. As well as Cookie, the companionship of David Barrie was a blessing. I used to teach him in the little cottage in the woods I took you to once. Do you remember, you climbed up into the tree house that afternoon we had gone to hunt for fairy mushrooms? Well, it was he who made that little tree house up in the branches of the oak tree, with such skill and attention to detail.*

*I used to try to help him with his reading and writing at lessons every month. And we revelled in each other's company, enjoying Sir Walter Scott and Shakespeare's comedies. We* laughed a lot and this was something that was always lacking when Father was in the manse. I realise now that not only was David Barrie a good man, he was the only man I have ever loved.

When you were born, my life was filled with joy and, since I was living at Corrie with David's mother at the time, away from my father, I was blissfully content not only with you, but with life. What a beautiful baby you were. Rising every morning to tend to you was the best of times, brief though they were. You were only in your fourth month when I had to give you up.

When Mother died I was brought back to the manse and you had to live with David's wife, Margaret, who brought you up. I am forever grateful to her for that, for I simply could not have done that at the manse. I wish I had been kinder to Margaret but I found it so difficult to watch her bringing up my own child. And as you know, Elizabeth, we were very different people, both in character and in circumstance.

As you will read, there was a paternity suit, instigated by my father, whereby David was named as your father. He was such a compassionate man and so he took the blame for something for which he was not responsible. He took all the shame upon his shoulders. I perhaps ought to add that in all our time together, just the two of us, there was never any suggestion of impropriety. Just a mutual respect, friendship and understanding of each other.

It was so sad when, soon after you went to live at the Barries' cottage, he died a horrible death from eating poisonous mushrooms. I was distraught, but could not reveal my true emotions to anyone, not even to my dear Cookie, since she was on friendly terms with his wife. Father of course considered his death a welcome end to the whole dreadful affair since, to everyone else, David was the father of my baby. My precious *baby – you, dear Elizabeth.*

*Father would not permit me to attend the funeral but I used to lay flowers on his grave every week. I like to think you have some of David's kind and gentle character, certainly none of my father's overweening and haughty air. He was nothing more than a hypocrite, one whose entire life was a lie. There, I have said it. May God forgive me.*

*It is becoming dark and I must stop writing now. I can hear the clattering of dishes down in the hall which means that Cookie will soon be coming upstairs with some of her soup which I must try to eat, though I have no appetite for anything. I only feel I want to have a long, deep sleep, now I have written this letter to you.*

*Elizabeth, when you read this, remember me. I do hope you find love and joy in your life and it is also my sincere hope that your life will be filled only with good and with happiness, never sadness. I also harbour a secret longing that perhaps you might become a pianist like your mother.*

*And I like to dream that one of your children or grandchildren might perhaps take the name Charlotte so that, although you will never bear the name Whyte, there may be still something of me, your loving mother, in your own family.*

*I am convinced that in heaven I shall meet David once more and I will be able to thank him for what he did for me, and for you, my dearest child.*

*With all my love to you always,*
*Your mother,*
*Charlotte Whyte*

# Acknowledgements

Thanks for giving advice and time: Bill Boyle, Mary-An Charnley, Anne Dow, Mary Duckworth, John Evans, Faith Lawrence, Jess Lawrence, Elisabeth Hadden, Stuart Hadden, Sue Hadden, Isabel Johnson, Lauren Mackie, Ann Naismith, Sue Peebles, Isabelle Plews, Anna Reynolds, David Yates.

Thanks for their professionalism and patience to Jenny Brown and Julie Fergusson.